M000028142

THE
MEMORABLE
Mrs. Dempsey

GAIL INGIS

GAIL INGIS
THE MEMORABLE MRS. DEMPSEY
Published by

Design Ideas
Copyright © 2021 by Gail Ingis
Re-release Edition
Originally Published as Indigo Sky by Soul Mate Publishing © 2015
Cover Design: Jun Ares
Interior Book Design/Formatting: Jennipher Tripp

Published in the United States of America Published by Ingis Design Ideas
PRINT ISBN: 978-1-7373369-1-4
eBOOK ISBN: 978-1-7373369-0-7

ACKNOWLEDGMENTS

Enormous thanks to my special team for encouraging me during the rewrite of the original book.

Joanna D'Angelo, my amazing editor, publicist, friend, and confidant, for her enthusiastic support, plotting, creativity, wisdom, and guidance. She pushes me to reach higher with every word, every line, and every page. Special thanks for finding my talented cover artist.

Jean Largis, my tireless friend, proofreader, and copy editor gives my work back to me with a smile.

Jennipher Tripp, formatter, a force to reckon with, figures out the best way to display my books and turns them into works of art. She is a fabulous formatter and is always there.

Janet Rozowski for reading it first.

Barbara Gerber, my fantastic sister-in-law, never stops supporting my writing, my art and has been there through thick and thin. She reads my writing, applauds me, hugs me, and tells all her friends about my books and artwork.

Jay S. Gerber, my big brother, for his encouragement and love. We wrote his memoirs together and delighted in the brother/sister-always-there relationship.

My children, grandchildren, and granddaughters-in-law never stop giving me the greatest greetings, support, and warm hugs.

They keep me on my toes with their texts. I love each one of you!

Tom Claus, my hero hubby, crops my wild prose into something resembling a botanical garden and makes sure my books have the polish our readers appreciate.

Last, dear reader, for choosing to spend time with this book, writing to me, giving me your thoughts about my books and making me your friend.

Dear Reader,

Thank you for choosing *The Memorable Mrs. Dempsey* (formerly *Indigo Sky*) and spending time with Leila and Rork. This is a story of Leila's misguided loyalty to her husband Hank —womanizer and addict. Rork offers Leila a better life, but she resists his love to remain true to her marriage vows. But when Rork leaves town, Leila realizes her marriage to Hank will destroy her life. She takes off on a journey across the perilous plains of America to find Rork. Heartache, fear, and joy weave through this entertaining adventure.

My secondary characters are challenging, fun, and eye opening. They include my personal favorites—trapper Tom and One-Eyed Charley. Charley (Charlotte Darkey Parkhurst) was a real person. Born in 1812, she drove cross-country for Butterfield Overland Mail. But hey, is fiction less strange than the truth?

I'd love to hear from you anytime—visit my website at gailingis.com.

All the best,
Gail

DEDICATION

End-to-end thanks to my amazing husband, Thomas Harrison Claus, who acted as an editor on my behalf, tirelessly supporting me and my writing. He has shown me what happily ever after means. For that, and a million other reasons, this book is dedicated to you, Tom.

CHAPTER ONE

Catskill Mountain House, 1863

*L*eila Dempsey stepped onto the sun-dappled veranda and froze. She stared at her husband and pressed a trembling hand to her heart that all but ceased to beat.

Hank Dempsey leaned against the wall, close to a riot of red curls. His lips hovered over a lush pouty mouth. The young woman threw back her mane and laughed, a deep throaty sound —the laughter of a woman who knew what she wanted and went after it. Sissy Lanweihr wanted Hank.

The chatter stopped, and all eyes turned to Leila, not five feet away from her mother and her society friends.

Not again—blather for the ladies' morning tea time—her eyes skittered to her mother, who threw her a warning glance. The matriarch had not a wisp of gray hair out of place, not a wrinkle in her high-collared lavender gown. Her smooth face stoic, and icy blue eyes censured Leila.

Everything in Leila screamed rebellion.

1

Hank turned his head toward his wife. His bloodshot eyes fell on her, and his mouth slipped up into a sardonic smile.

Drunk again. Another piece of Leila's soul shattered. She fought humiliation and stared at the faces that swam before her blurred vision. Leila sailed down the broad steps with all the dignity she could muster. She turned and paused. The Catskill Mountain House stood proudly perched on a ledge surrounded by imposing mountain peaks. Once a cheerful place, nothing made her cheery these days. She drew a shuddering breath and immersed herself in the view of rolling forests below. A brook meandered through the lush vegetation, sparkling in the sunlight.

A sob escaped her. Hank's betrayal tore at her like talons. She lifted her voluminous skirts and ran down the slope toward the water—a breeze sighed through the long grass and set seed heads swaying in its wake.

She stopped, harsh breaths escaped her constricted chest, and tears fell. She clenched her hands, trying to combat the pain of infidelity. Her stomach churned, and bile crawled up her throat.

"He's killing my love." The breeze swallowed her whisper. Her dream marriage to a dashing author had become a nightmare. Sissy, with her brazen red hair and even more bold behavior, sabotaged our marriage. She's wanted Hank since meeting him at our betrothal. Leila would never forget the look of malice and anger on Sissy's face at her wedding.

Her knees buckled, and she sank onto the grass. Tears dripped from her lashes. Watery stains spread in uneven circles on her soft-white day dress. Leila sniffed and dashed the tears away with her fists.

"I hate her—hate that Sissy Lanweihr with her fiery red hair and-and worldly ways." Leila ripped off her fashionable bonnet and yanked the pins from her coiffured brunette hair, and sent it tumbling over her shoulders to her waist. Sweat trickled down Leila's bosom. The corset stays suffocated her.

"I want to be free." She blinked and stared at a pearl-topped pin in her hand. "Do I want to be free?" She swallowed hard. "Do I still love him?" A mirthless laugh burst from her lips, "Hank has never said he loves me—maybe he doesn't. Maybe he never did."

"Leila! Leila!"

Her head snapped around. "Mama," she whispered and scrambled in the long grass, hunting for hairpins. She fumbled with her mass of hair, trying to restore the coiffure.

"Leila, where are you? Don't make me come down there to fetch you."

Leila's mouth tightened, and her fingers clenched around five pins. One pricked her, and she gasped. She dropped the hairpins and stared at a drop of blood oozing from her thumb.

"I will not go back," she muttered. She crawled behind a tree and leaned against the massive trunk, facing the brook.

"This is most inappropriate, Leila. I shall deal with you later," her mother shouted.

A giggle bubbled up, and she put a hand over her mouth. *I won.* The high collar of the dress stifled her. She peeked around the tree to see if her mother had left and released the pearl buttons. A breathy sigh escaped her as the breeze brushed her skin exposed above the chemise. Leila looked down at the bodice. Clara and Oliva, her best friends, had rid themselves of the corset before they married. The three agreed. Her mother forbid her to honor the agreement. They'd battled about it often. "I will not wear that horrible corset!" An uneven battle, conformity always won.

Leila flopped back and lay spread-eagle, looking up at the leaves dancing in the light breeze overhead. *Has my life ever been free?* The warmth of the sun tickled her skin like a feather. She wanted to rip off her clothes, feel the sun caress her bare skin. Oh, to be free of restraints. Free of rules. Free of a philandering husband.

She closed her eyes, breathed in the fresh mountain air, and giggled again. She'd already overstepped the bounds of propriety.

Her conduct would scandalize her mother and the genteel ladies at the Mountain House.

Water gurgled around rocks. Crickets chirped, and birds flitted through the dappled shade. Nature's orchestra soothed her troubled spirit, reminding her of carefree summers where she played games on the brook's mossy rocks. She'd challenged each rock to stand steady, hopping over them until she reached the other side. Oh, to do that anew.

Why not? She jumped to her feet and surveyed the swollen brook. Water rushed over rocks in foaming eddies, leaving a few exposed as it raced to a dark green pool. *I can do this.*

She stepped onto a moss-covered rock inches from the edge of the brook. Water swirled around her skirt like champagne, soaking her hem. With each step, her exhilaration rose. I wished Hank were with me. She frowned. No, I don't! The smooth black stone sparkled, peeking above the water like an iridescent jewel between the mosses, beckoning her.

She set her foot down and stepped onto the rock, held her breath and jumped to the next one. Once stable, she put her weight on another. Buoyed by success, she planted herself. It held. Once more a child, she laughed, unburdened by the constraints of society. She held her arms out like the spars of a topsail. Halfway across the brook, confidence replaced caution. She skipped across three rocks, whooped with joy—six left to go.

Her tongue poked from the corner of her mouth as she balanced. The rock wobbled. Her foot slipped on slimy moss— she gasped, searching for a secure foothold. Arms flailing, she fought to regain her balance. Too late.

She squeezed her eyes shut and hit the rocks with a bruising impact. Icy water engulfed her, stealing her breath. She floundered and clutched at the slippery rocks, but the sodden garments hampered her efforts and the strong current carried her away. The brook, now the enemy, tumbled her faster toward the pool. A scream tore from her throat before her head slammed into a rock.

Art had been a lifelong pursuit for Rork Millburn. He hoped to paint several small works during his stay. His easel sat on a flat, grassy area above a brook. The aroma of the juicy oil paints culled fond memories of the times he'd spent in the Alps. He stepped back to examine his work. Satisfied and almost finished, he'd captured the early sun-drenched mountains lush with wispy grasses, pine trees, and fields of flowers. Just a few more touches.

Movement drew his attention. A woman crossing the brook caught his artist's eye. He took in the image of her day dress flying up as she leaped from one rock to the next like a water sprite. Something stirred in him, something not related to the warm sun, earthy forest smells, or imposing mountains. His keen eyes picked out her exquisite features. The sun danced on her hair that fell in lustrous waves to a slender waist. He set down his palette and scrambled among paints and brushes until he found his monocle. He screwed it to his eye and snatched a breath at her beauty and those luscious lips, a mouth made for kisses. A kiss he could only imagine. He shook free of fanciful imaginings. Fool, just paint.

A scream echoed across the valley and shot through him like a bullet. He scanned the brook below. "What in the world?" His breath caught in his throat.

The woman had vanished. Her bonnet still lay on the grass.

"My God!" Rork raced down the hill, the wind whipping his hair. Lungs burning, he slid down a steep drop to the brook. He searched the river, running along the bank where he last saw the woman. "Damn, where are you?" He wiped the sweat from his brow.

A mangle of hair floated to the surface, then sank again.

Rork ripped off his jacket and shoes and plunged into the frigid water. His heart pumped faster with each stroke as he swam to where he'd seen her hair. He glimpsed whitish fabric and dived. *There she is.* He grabbed her arm and kicked hard, surging to the surface. Currents had carried them to rocks farther downstream, and the weight of her soaked dress impeded progress. He fought the river's pull and dragged the woman from the water, lifting her into his arms.

She moaned, stirred, and convulsed, vomiting water.

Thank God she's alive. The uneven terrain caused him to slip and stumble.

His legs ached as he knelt, still holding her limp body in his arms. Thick black lashes contrasted with her ivory skin. The soaked dress clung to her, outlining her petite figure, making her seem helpless—fragile. The disarray of her skirt and petticoats exposed her long legs to above her knees. He shuddered.

Her head rolled to one side, she groaned, and a slender hand fluttered to her throat.

He stared at the enlarging bloodstain on his shirtsleeve. *She's injured.* He set her down with care on the grass and bent to examine the back of her head. Thick blood seeped into her hair. He parted her tresses and exposed a gash. Ripping off his shirtsleeve, he pressed it to the wound, staunching the blood. She flinched and tried to twist away. He withdrew his hand. "Can you hear me?"

Her lips moved, but her answer—a silent puff of air.

A rosy tint crept into her pale cheeks. A stab in his chest, sharp and sweet, moved through him, as though he'd witnessed da Vinci's *Mona Lisa* come alive. Icy dread cooled his thoughts of romance.

He didn't know what to do. He figured she had to be a guest

at the Catskill Mountain House as there were no other habitations in the area.

"Please, wake up. You're safe now."

No response.

Hands trembling from cold and from the emotion she invoked in him, he returned her skirt to its proper position and attempted to button her bodice. Her chest rose and fell with each breath, distracting him. His huge hands fumbled with the small pearl buttons.

"Damn ham-hands," he said. "How does anyone ever get these buttons fastened?" He struggled on. "Damn." He slipped his hand inside her bodice to get a better grip, and his fingers brushed against the soft skin of her bosom.

The woman stirred.

He withdrew his hand, wiped the water from her eyes, and smoothed the hair from her face. "Hush. It's all right. You'll be fine."

She pushed at his clumsy fingers. Her thick lashes lifted, unveiling dark blue eyes.

"Lord above, your eyes are deep sapphire." The ground beneath Rork swayed as he tumbled into the depths of her lucent gaze.

CHAPTER TWO

*W*armth enfolded Leila despite a cool breeze brushing against her. The faint smell of leather and earth tinged with musk intoxicated her. As she moved, pain shot from the back of her head to her temple. Memories of her dress dragging her under flooded back.

A rich baritone voice permeated her addled mind. "You are safe now."

She blinked and looked up at a rugged, bearded face. The stranger's intense gray eyes absorbed her. *Who is he?* Panic gripped her, and she squirmed from his arms. Nausea climbed in her throat, and she tried to breathe. Fog seeped through her mind like a mist rolling over the mountains.

The firm, masculine arms gathered her close again. His resonant voice murmured soft words. "You are safe."

This man is—is a stranger. His steady gaze—hypnotic.

"You could have drowned. Thank God I heard you scream. How are you feeling?"

"I-I'm not sure." She put a hand to her head. "My head wants to explode."

"You must have hit the back of your head on a rock."

"Oh, is that why it hurts?"

"Yes."

"Would you mind helping me up?"

He lifted her, keeping one arm around her waist.

She trembled like a newborn colt, unsure of its legs. "Thank you, sir. I'm grateful."

He inclined his head. "You're most welcome."

A breeze sighed past. She shivered and lowered her eyes. Heat invaded her face as she realized her disheveled state. She strained to button the errant pearls.

"I tried to fasten your buttons."

Leila gaped at him. "Y-you tried to button my bodice?"

"I did." He watched her with an intensity that startled her. She lifted her eyes and caught a breath. His smile refreshed her. She tried to smooth her sodden dress.

His eyes caressed her from head to toe. "You resemble a beautiful water sprite."

That one long look filled the empty spaces in her heart.

"Your boldness is offensive, sir."

"Please, I don't mean to be offensive. Forgive me."

Leila placed her hand on her flushed face.

He gazed into her eyes. "How can the truth be offensive?"

She opened her mouth to deliver a rebuke and covered her lips with her fingertips. His sheer size and latent strength bordered on intimidating. Dark, wet chestnut hair fell in waves on his forehead and curled over his collar. She took a few paces back.

The hard planes of his face contrasted with his easy, seductive smile. Those eyes pinned her in place.

She retreated, sure that he got what he wanted, she knew he wanted her. She took another step back. "I-I must go."

He held up his hands and smiled. "Please, my intentions are honorable."

Heat crept up her neck. Did I misunderstand? "I must go."

Flight. Uppermost in her mind, yet she remained rooted to the spot, staring up at him.

"I hope to see you again, m'lady." His smiling eyes teased her.

She shook her head, pressing icy hands to flaming cheeks. He'd held her and looked at her, as only a husband should. Oh, Lord, how could I forget I'm married?

Leila lifted her soaked skirts and fled.

"Wait, please wait." His heavy footsteps followed close behind as she ran through the trees and along the grassy riverbank.

She stumbled to a halt at the brook's edge, breathless, and stared at the water surging around rocks. Moments ago, this brook had tried to drown her. A wave of nausea swept over her and her knees buckled.

Strong arms whisked her up. "Wrap your arms around my neck, if I slip, I want to ensure you're attached to me—that you're safe."

She complied, her heart threatening to burst from her throat. His heart thudded hard against her chest.

He passed over the narrow section of water, stepped onto the grass, set her down, and retrieved the bonnet. He presented it to her with a flourish and a bow.

She swallowed hard and mumbled her thanks. Flushed with embarrassment, she turned and fled. No longer feeling the cold —fire burned in her veins.

Leila struggled up the steep incline until she made it to the hotel. Head down, bonnet in hand, she hurried past guests, ignoring their appalled gasps. Her dress left a wet trail down the hallway to her room. She opened the door and sagged against it, pushing it closed.

Sanctuary at last. The stranger still held her mind captive. She pressed her fingers to her temples. Don't think about the accident. Don't think about how it happened. Don't think about what happened after.

She stepped to the tall windows, wrapped her arms around her waist and stared across the wilderness. Hank's philandering crushed her, but she could never be untrue to him. She'd made vows and promised to be faithful. She couldn't forget the stranger's eyes. But oh, the way he stared at me. Shame sat in her stomach like a rock in a riverbed. "I'm a hussy!" Leila collapsed onto the settee. Her chest compressed. Sobs rose and stuck in her throat. She tugged at the bodice of her suffocating dress.

"Leila?"

She glanced up at the sound of her maid's voice and swallowed back her sobs. "I'm here, Biddy."

Biddy opened the door. "Are ya all right?" Her brows furrowed. "Lord, child, ye're soaked. What happened?"

Leila sucked in deep breaths, and tears flowed down her cheeks. Her shoulders slumped like her tattered rag doll.

Biddy's arthritic fingers wiped at the tears streaming down Leila's cheeks. "What happened, child?"

"Oh, Biddy." Leila fell into the old woman's arms, finding comfort against her ample bosom. "Frightening and dreadful." Her words tumbled out between sobs. "Remember the brook where I played in the summers? I crossed the stepping-stones and fell in. I almost drowned." She took a breath. "I hit my head hard, it hurts." She touched the back of her head.

"Let me see." Biddy tucked a loose strand of gray hair into her neat bun and examined Leila's head. "Ye have a nasty cut. I'll wash it with vinegar." She scurried out and returned with a bottle and washed the wound. "There's a nasty bump on yer head, but you'll heal well enough." Biddy set the bottle and cloth down. She put her hands on her broad hips, frowning at Leila. "How did ye escape drowning?"

"The water carried me downstream onto the rocks." Heat

filled her cheeks, and she avoided Biddy's eagle eyes. Heaven knows what Biddy would say if she knew about my encounter with that young man.

Biddy shook her head. "When will ye grow up, girl? Ye're a married woman now. Come on." Biddy motioned for her to stand. "Let's get ye out of these wet clothes." Leila stood, hands at her side as a child.

Biddy reached to unbutton her dress but stopped. "Why are yer buttons done up wrong?"

Leila blushed. "I-I think they came undone when I floundered in the water, and I shook so from the cold I couldn't fasten them properly." Biddy, her nanny, stayed on as her maid. Leila adored the Irish woman but could not bare one of her well-deserved lectures.

Biddy took Leila's face between her hands. "Child, ye can be so foolhardy."

Leila expelled a breath. "I know the talk. I shouldn't have been down by the brook. Please, Biddy, I want to forget the entire day. I need a hot bath and sleep. I'm not going down to dinner later."

"Very well, colleen." Biddy sighed and patted Leila's cheek.

Leila stared at the floor. By morning, she hoped to forget ever meeting the stranger. I must forget how attractive he is.

Biddy peeled off Leila's sopping clothes and took them to the bathing chamber. "I hope the water didn't ruin yer dress."

Leila followed her. "Please don't tell mother."

The old woman tightened her lips and sighed. "Fine, I'll not tell yer mother, but ye'll have to forget about sleepin' and join everyone for dinner."

"A small price to pay." Leila wrapped her arms around Biddy and planted a kiss on her rosy cheek.

Biddy shook her head and smiled, wagging her finger. "But ye need to promise that ye'll not go into the woods alone again."

Leila nodded. Anything to prevent her mother from finding

out. The very thought of having to listen to her mother rant would give Leila a rash.

"Leila, I am going to the kitchen for a knife."

"A knife?"

"Aye. I'll press it to the bump on yer head to keep it from more swellin'."

"My heavens, does that work?"

"Of course. Ye get into the tub. I'll be right back, and we'll get ye ready for dinner." Biddy patted Leila's back. Leila sank into the scented bathwater. She closed her eyes. The bath water soothing Leila's limbs.

CHAPTER THREE

*R*ork scanned the guests perusing the veranda and those surrounding Hank. *She has to be here.* He leaned an elbow on the back of a tall wicker chair. A polished onyx pipe hung from his mouth. Hank, a successful syndicated writer, sat in the chair opposite. He waved slim hands and talked to his audience between gulps of his fifth whiskey. Hank had a theatrical flair relating entertaining, grandiose stories.

Rork tried to focus on his new partner's ramblings, but his interest waned and he resorted to a "mmm," acknowledgment, hearing none of the inane gibberish. Once more, he searched the guest's faces. Rork's mind wandered to the view he'd spent the morning capturing on canvas when the water sprite dancing across the rocks had drawn him away.

He slid his fingers together, transported back to the smooth texture of her skin and how her fragrance had filled his senses. He wanted to touch her again. He wanted more—he wanted her. He knew, at that moment, he would move mountains to make her his. *Why not?*

"Millburn, wake up, fella. Where were you? Did you hear anything I said?"

"Of course." Rork jerked himself back to the present. "You mentioned, ah, Mormons."

"Yes. My research for our journey has brought up a group of Mormons in Utah I want to visit. I heard some thought-provoking tales about those folks. What do you think? Are you game?"

"Whatever you say, Hank. You run the show." Rork smiled, studying Hank's handsome face. The man had charm and a sharp wit, but would Hank's drinking be a problem in their new partnership? He didn't want to work with a sot—a drinking man.

"Did you have a good day?" Amber liquid swirled in Hank's tumbler, and his bloodshot eyes met Rork's gaze over the rim. Rork's heart seeped with warmth, picturing the mysterious beauty. "I met a captivating woman."

Leaning forward, Hank raised his eyebrows and grinned.

"A woman? I want to hear more."

"We had an unusual encounter." Rork took a sip of whiskey. "I saw a woman crossing the brook." His head spun. He did not usually drink strong spirits, at least not at Hank's pace. This is ridiculous. Why do I feel the need to keep up with Hank? He took another sip.

"A beauty, no doubt?"

"I'll say!"

"What's the hitch, Rork?"

"Well, I saw her from a distance. And one does not just approach a woman, however delectable." He took another sip of whiskey. "Moments later, I heard a scream. When I looked up, she had disappeared, and her bonnet lay on the grass beside the brook."

Hank's eyes bulged. "What happened?"

"I raced to the brook, dived into the water, and searched for her. The recent rains had flooded the brook. I got to her just in time and carried out an unconscious woman, concerned she may not make it, but she came round." His heart took up an erratic beat.

Hank slammed his hand down on the armchair. "Damn, fella, you're a hero. Let's have a drink—salute."

Rork raised his glass in response. He took another long drink. "I wouldn't call myself a hero. Just doing what any man would. Once she revived, the poor girl bolted."

"What made her so captivating?"

Rork shrugged. He kept her state of undress to himself and forced a grin. "I could not take my eyes off the beauty, a vision, like new leaves in spring."

Hank's laughter sent whiskey cascading from his glass. "Too brief an encounter—you're in trouble. Never let a woman captivate your mind, least of all a beauty. It leads to heartache." His mouth twisted down.

Rork cocked one eyebrow. "And you know this firsthand?"

"Yes. I've had my fair share of trouble with beautiful women. More than I want to admit. Ended up marrying one, to my eternal regret."

Hank lifted his glass to Rork. "Friend, let us toast to our meeting and upcoming journey. May we have pleasant weather and safe travels." He drained the contents of the glass.

Rork grimaced and downed his drink. "Why would you regret marrying a beautiful woman?" *Perhaps it isn't a good marriage.* Hank swayed in his chair, waving his arms as he engaged other guests. How would a drunkard satisfy any woman?

Hank poured another whiskey and stared at the amber liquid. "Humph." He looked up at Rork, rolled his eyes, and said, "All women are beautiful in their own way. My wife's beauty comes from her wealth and important family connections."

The flippant answer amused Rork. "How does your wife's beauty, in whatever form it comes, cause you trouble?"

"What wife doesn't cause her husband trouble? My wife has

17

been nothing but grief since the day we married. She is always irksome. It's because of her assets that I tolerate her."

"So, her physical beauty isn't the problem."

Hank chuckled. "You've got me there, my friend. Maybe not all beautiful women are trouble, but I wouldn't recommend letting one get in your head."

Rork rubbed his cheek. "You married for money?"

"It appears so. I run our finances and her money."

"Where is your wife?"

Hank shrugged. "Around, I guess. You're a good-looking man. You must have had your fair share of beauties."

Rork rubbed the back of his neck. "Yes, I've known beautiful women, but the relationships were brief. I prefer a solitary life. I love adventure, travel, and painting—a lifestyle not favorable to having a family. In a few days, we embark on an arduous journey that will take close to a year—most of my journeys do. I doubt any woman would wait for my return."

Hank snorted. "Oh, they'll wait. This war has left them with a shortage of men." He flapped a hand. "I don't advocate going the route of a ball and chain. Just use the women for fun."

Rork took another sip. The smooth liquor slid over his tongue. "Not my style." Erotic images filled his head, the last thing he needed. It interfered with his work.

Hank gestured to a servant for another bottle of whiskey. "Nothing wrong with a spot of dallying for a few days." He swept back a lock of brown hair that fell over one brow. "Perhaps the woman you saved is a guest here. Do you know if she is?"

"No idea. She ran before I got her name." Rork's head swam from the liquor.

"Perhaps she'll show up at dinner."

Rork nodded. Perfect, it would be perfect. His eyebrows rose as Hank downed the whiskey and poured yet another.

Hank shook his head. "They're trouble, but they can be a

good deal of fun," he said in a slurred voice. He waved the glass, spilling drops on the wood floor. His eyes slid to a redhead lounging against the railings. "We're leaving soon. Hell, why not have some fun?"

Rork followed Hank's glance. *Who is the redhead?* Clear she captured Hank's interest, too tawdry for Rork. His thoughts drifted back to the woman with the deep blue eyes. He would have a fling and based on her state of her undress she might indulge. A smile tipped his lips as an image of open buttons and a wet gown clinging to her curvy body filled his head.

Hank stumbled to his feet. "Our guests have arrived. See you in the drawing-room for cocktails." He wobbled away.

Rork finished his whiskey and contemplated Hank's suggestion of a few nights of love. Gad. How often does such a beauty fall into one's lap? He rubbed his clean-shaven chin. No, but a night or two—I'm soused to the damn gills. Fog encased his head and blurred his vision as he left the veranda. He gripped the ornate railing to steady himself and climbed the twisting, double grand staircase to the drawing-room.

Hank, there with his guests, ordered pre-dinner cocktails. He slapped Rork's back. "Have a cocktail, old boy."

Rork rubbed his clean-shaven chin. "Too foxed, need fresh air." He also needed quiet, needed to sober up before he made a spectacle of himself at dinner. The cool spring air would clear his head. He pushed aside the long curtains and stepped through French doors onto a balcony. Alive with cicada mating calls, the evening breeze sighed through the trees. He gripped the railing and savored the aromatic scent of pines.

Then he saw her.

His head cleared as he drew a sharp breath.

She rounded the outside terrace from the west wing, her emerald gown floating over the decking. She had her hair pulled back and entwined with colored jewels. Wisps framed her face and curled to her shoulders.

Dear God, she's breathtaking. Rork's mouth felt dry, and his tongue stuck to his palate. He pushed away from the railing, walked to her as one in a dream, and blocked her path. Speech eluded him as he stared, absorbing every facet of her face. He forgot everything except her. Her vanilla perfume wove its way through his senses, seducing him further.

Her eyes widened. "You!" she blurted. The color drained from her face. She fiddled with her reticule. "I-I didn't recognize you. Y-you had a beard." She pressed a hand to her stomach. "T-then."

"When I saved your life?" he blurted. "Lady, you're welcome." Rork cursed himself for his stupid response. He cleared his throat, wishing he'd said something eloquent, but the words were out.

Long lashes lifted, and her eyes flickered, catching the light of the moon. They met his gaze for a moment before darting away. She took a faltering step to the side. Almost past Rork, he realized, she would disappear again. He reached for her hand to stay her.

"Don't!" She jerked free and put distance between them. She clutched the railing, staring across the moonlit valley.

"I rescued you from death, and you won't acknowledge me?"

She turned to face him, her chest rising and falling, her mouth tightened into a thin line, her lips disappearing.

Rork smothered a laugh. Anger roused made her more desirable.

"What do you want from me, sir?" Her delicate hands slammed onto her hips. "Were my thanks not enough after the-the unfortunate event?" She stood an arm's length away, her head not reaching his shoulders.

He wanted to pull her to him and press her body against his. He smirked. "I believe at least acknowledging that I exist is in order."

Wide-eyed, she worried her lower lip. "Oh, do you? And how shall I acknowledge you for this-this bravery?"

Rork could think of several ways. Despite his alcohol-induced haze, he knew enough not to voice them. He ran a hand through his hair—he did not hide his admiration. The low bodice of her gown showed an abundance of alabaster skin. Beneath the gown were creamy, shapely legs that he'd seen. He took a step toward her.

Her hands fell to her side. She fixed her eyes on his mouth and moved up to meet his intense gaze. Her tongue moistened her lips.

He needed that invitation to close the gap. He wrapped his arms around her small waist and pulled her tight against him. A startled gasp fell from her lips. A tingle crept up the back of his neck. All sense of decency deserted him. He had to taste her. She averted her head and pushed her hands against his chest. "You're drunk." The protest registered in Rork's head. He released her as though she had slapped him.

She fell back, and her feet tangled in the hem of her gown. A cry escaped, and her backside hit the floor with a thud.

Rork unpinned his gaze from her lips and laughed. He held out his hand. "That's twice I've swept you off your feet."

She slapped her hands against the wood. A crimson flush crept from her chest to her hairline.

Rork smiled, took her gloved hands, and pulled her to her feet. "There, safe again."

She yanked her hands from his, picked up her emerald studded reticule, and took several steps back. "You arrogant, undignified blowhard!"

Rork couldn't help the laughter. "Such language. I had an incorrect assumption.."

"What assumption is that?" Her dark eyes gleamed a warning.

"That you're a lady." Rork leaned back against the railing. His eyes, wide and wild, locked on hers.

"How dare you!" Her voice rose as she continued the tirade. "You know nothing about me."

"You, madam, were rude."

"You accosted me twice, laughed at me, and insulted me."

"Do you not at least see the humor in our interactions?"

She raised her chin. "You mean, humor followed by insults."

"No, not insults, madam. I spoke the truth." Rork enjoyed crossing swords with her, and her feisty responses further piqued his interest.

"You, sir, are no gentleman. Your hypocrisy is astounding. I will not tolerate this insolence." She turned on her heel and stormed off.

"Wait! What's your name?"

She rushed down the stairs and back to the garden.

Rork shook his head, running his fingers through his hair. "Capital, Millburn. You chased her away."

CHAPTER FOUR

*W*hile running along the veranda, Leila stumbled as her slippers caught in the hem of her gown. She lifted her skirts and raced down the stairs to elude the man on the balcony. She held her breath and crept back up the stairs on her tiptoes, heading for the French Doors. If only she had been gracious and thanked him, he would be out of her life.

"Ah, there you are. Wait, don't go." He rushed toward her.

Within a few strides, he got to her as she shrank back against the wall. She put her hands up to keep him at bay. "Again, thank you for saving my life. I'm sorry. I must go." She hurried past him into a passage leading to the ladies' washroom. There! I thanked him. Hopefully, that will satisfy him.

Heart thudding, she leaned on the marble washstand beneath an ornate framed mirror and tried to catch her breath. "I'm a mess." Leila removed her gloves, splashed water on her face, tucked errant curls into place, and smoothed her gown.

"Beggin' yer pardon, ma'am."

Leila squeaked and spun to face the young woman attendant who offered her a cloth.

"Sorry, didn't mean to startle ya, ma'am."

"I feel a little indisposed." Leila laughed, her fingers covering her lips. She took the cloth and dabbed her face.

"Aye, ya look pale."

"Heavens." She turned to the mirror, pinched color into her cheeks, and pulled the gloves onto her damp hands.

She handed the young woman a coin, stepped out, and rested a moment against a paneled wall in the passage, her eyes closed. Should she tell Hank about her knight in shining armor? Her eyes snapped open. No, he's no knight, he's a rogue.

Besides, Hank would react badly. Trepidation curled through her. She had to tell her unpredictable and inpatient husband, but what if she crossed paths with her rescuer again while standing beside Hank? Despite the man's overzealous nature, he saved her life. Shoulders slumped, she pushed herself from the wall. I'd better join them for dinner. Even if Hank hadn't noticed her absence—her mother would. Leila hurried to the drawing-room. The encounter tucked away for now.

Leila paused at the entrance. Gas-lit chandeliers illuminated the gaily attired throng that milled about the drawing-room. Leila pressed a hand to her midriff and sucked in a breath. A soft laugh drew her eyes to a woman beside her.

"The décor is rather plain compared to the ballroom, don't you think?"

The woman's brown eyes sparkled, and Leila liked her right away. "Yes, it is. I suppose Mr. Herter decorated the ballroom," Leila said.

"He could well have. He designed our home in Connecticut. His work is wonderful. Oh, how rude of me, I'm Ann Louisa Lockwood." She canted her head, her blonde ringlets catching the light.

"May I ask your name?"

"Leila Ashburn Dempsey."

She clapped her gloved hands, which made a dull thud. "Oh, is your husband, the well-known writer?"

Leila nodded.

"Please call me Anna. I believe you're seated at our dinner table." She dipped into a brief curtsy. "It's been a pleasure. I promised to meet my husband. He's at the fireplace." She wrinkled her pert nose. "As usual, I'm sure he's discussing business."

Leila returned the curtsy, her eyes scanning the room for Hank. She briefly studied the prestigious art hanging from crown moldings on ribbon-wrapped wires. Her collection of landscapes by local artists flitted through her head. She lingered at her favorite, Emerald Pool by Millburn. She turned and saw Hank surrounded by a group of men at the hearth. As usual, he held court, and his audience hung on every word. She needed him alone. When Hank expounded on a subject, her intrusion frustrated him. I can't tell him at dinner and risk him losing his temper.

Leila straightened her back, her stomach in knots, and headed for the fireplace. Flames burned in the hearth, warding off the evening chill. Her cousin, Billy Ashburn, also basked in Hank's charismatic aura. Cornelius Vanderbilt stood nearby, and the man with his arm around her new friend, Anna, must be her husband. Leila prayed that stuffy old Sophia Vanderbilt didn't see her.

Anna motioned to her.

Warmth slid over Leila, she waved back.

"Well, what do you know, here comes my fair wife," Hank slurred. A grin, dripping insincerity, split his face. The orange glow from the fire flickered across the profile of a tall man with chestnut hair.

Oh, God, my rescuer. Leila's heart stopped. What do I do? I must talk to Hank, tell him about this morning. She fingered her pearl necklace, lifted her chin, and approached. She took Hank's arm and stood on tiptoe, whispering, "I need to speak with you." She slid a glance at her rescuer.

The color drained from his face, and his eyes bored into her.

Her belly fluttered. Beardless, he had a fair face, smooth and strong. Aristocratic came to her mind. He turned away from her and downed his whiskey. For some obscure reason, guilt assailed her. She averted her gaze and leaned against her husband. "Please, Hank, it's important," she whispered.

"Leila, darlin'." Hank captured one of her delicate hands, "why don't you sit with your mother and the other ladies? I'll be over in a moment." Although sounding affectionate, Hank's eyes were dismissive. He dropped her hand and waved her away. "Off you go, darlin'."

Leila stared into his cold eyes, her courage failing. She smiled at the men surrounding him. "Pardon me for the interruption, gentlemen, but I must speak with my husband."

"I said later." His eyes held a warning.

Leila twisted her hands. Her eyes darted between the men and returned to her husband. "Hank, please."

"I'm in the middle of a conversation." Hank turned his back on her and amused Vanderbilt with another tale.

She gripped his arm again and whispered, "Hank, it's important."

His jaw tightened, and he peeled off her fingers. "Leila, meet my new acquaintance, Mr. Rork Millburn."

Her mind performed somersaults. The artist Millburn? Leila kept her eyes downcast and smoothed her gown with trembling fingers. "I'm pleased to make your acquaintance, sir." She glanced at Hank. "Please give me a moment."

Hank sighed and shrugged. "Gentlemen, my wife wants my services immediately. Please excuse me while I attend to her needs."

She slid a glance at her cousin Billy. His eyes were alive with interest. Her heart sank. He gossiped, worse than his wife, Eleanor. Once more, heat flooded Leila's cheeks. She felt Millburn's eyes on her, but she didn't dare look up.

"Come along." Hank marched past her.

"Thank you," she whispered and followed him to the veranda. The moon's soft glow stroked the mountains, and a breeze added a sharp sting to the night. She wrapped her arms around her waist, forming a barrier against her husband. Her stomach swirled in a raucous mix of emotions and uncertainty.

Hank rounded on her. "Are you daft, woman?" His voice grated on the cool evening air.

"Forgive me for my rude interruption, but I'm desperate to speak with you."

Hank slammed his hand on the railing. "Good Lord, Leila. Desperate? What could be so damn important? Do you know what you interrupted?"

"What?"

"Business with Cornelius Vanderbilt. You know him, don't you? He founded the railroad."

"Important business?"

"Of course. Money is always damn important."

Leila flinched as his alcohol-laden breath assaulted her. She shook her head. Early in her marriage, she learned to shut up when Hank, in his cups, had his temper roused.

He dragged a hand through his brown hair. "The conversation you interrupted with Vanderbilt and Curtis, the editor from New York, could impact the deal," he scowled. "Have you forgotten he gave me my first opportunity to publish? You're out of place, woman." Spittle went flying. "It's thanks to him and my publications, including my articles in Harper's Weekly, that I enjoy the success I have. Which, by the way, brings in a brilliant income." He flicked the fan hovering near her mouth. "An income that buys all these expensive baubles you enjoy."

Leila kept her eyes downcast, her lips compressed behind the fan.

"Now." Hank's voice rose. "Pray tell, what could not wait?"

Her lip quivered.

"So, what is it, Leila? What do you have to tell me?" He poked her shoulder. "Well? You have my attention, so speak up."

She took a step back, desperate to take flight. This day had been a catastrophe like a herd of horses had slammed into her. *I'm a coward.* She opened her mouth to tell Hank about her rescuer, but the words clogged her throat. She took a deep breath and gathered her thoughts. In his current mood, her story would only enrage him further. He would find humor at her accident, but Leila doubted he would find it amusing to know his partner had seen her in a state of undress. Hank would call her wanton, and she couldn't bear him berating her in public again. Her thin veneer of control would never withstand the onslaught. Tales of marital strife would run rampant through the elite patrons of Mountain House.

"Well?" Hank tapped his foot, the sound assaulting her ears.

A shiver washed over Leila. *Perhaps it would be better to wait until he is sober.* She stiffened her spine and smiled. In their year of marriage, she'd discovered at least one of his soft spots. "I'm sorry, dear. I didn't realize I interrupted something so important. I feel like such a dunce." Leila caught her bottom lip between her teeth to stop it from quivering and took a tentative step closer. She looked up at him through her lashes. "Do you forgive me, Hank?"

Anger slipped from his face. He reached for her and wrapped his arms around her waist, drawing her close. "I know it's hard for you. You're only a woman and uneducated about matters of business." He dropped a kiss on her forehead.

A protest rose to her lips. *How dare Hank throw gender inferiority at me?* She knew, though, any objection at this point would provoke his anger again. Instead, Leila lifted her head and met his glazed eyes. She rose to her toes and touched her lips to his. *What happened to us, to love, to having babies? Will we ever be a family, have a home?* She recalled their first meeting when she'd fallen in love with him as a youth.

She'd been on summer vacation from the academy boarding school. They met at the Catskill Mountain House. The twinkle in his eyes had fascinated her. Bold, debonair, and quick to smile, Leila struggled to make conversation. He'd enchanted her with his charm and straightforward manner.

She studied the planes of his handsome face. Although in his mid-twenties, Hank possessed a youthful quality, despite the ravages of alcohol. His lips smashed down on hers. She closed her eyes, and for the first time, felt nothing but ice in her veins. She saw Rork Millburn's face, the way he'd looked at her, and consumed her with his desire.

She squirmed away, confused with knots in her belly. How can I kiss my husband with thoughts of another man? What kind of woman am I?

Hank pulled her tighter. She tasted whiskey on his mouth, and his hand crept up to her bosom. She pushed at his chest. They were on the veranda, a public thoroughfare. What in the world is he thinking?

A growl emanated from his throat, and he turned her, pressing her against the rail. All pretense of affection or tenderness ended—as always. Nothing more than another attempt to satisfy his primal need, enhanced by whiskey.

She fought harder, her panic rising. A sob rose in her constricted throat. To her relief, Hank's erection disappeared—nothing new.

Breathless, he retreated from her. "I don't want you—never did."

"We should get back." Leila kept her voice even.

He nodded. She sighed with relief and stiffened as he ran a finger over her breast.

"Fear not darlin'. One of my problems is that I don't find you exciting."

His words stuck like a knife. Even though her love for him had faded, his rejection still hurt.

He spun and walked away, his steps erratic.

"No, Hank, tis not I," she whispered as he disappeared through the door. "You've killed my love with your excesses." She took in a long breath, smoothed her silk dress, affected repairs to her hair, and walked to the dining room, praying for strength to make it through the evening.

CHAPTER FIVE

*H*ead held high, Leila entered the dining room wearing her brightest smile. She reached for her chair—the air stirred as Milburn rose. Her spirit fluttered to life. His hand brushed hers as he pulled out the only vacant chair between him and Hank. Her awareness of Milburn tingled every nerve in her body. Could this day get any worse—or any harder? He stood so close his body heat filled her cold, bitter places. Her senses swam with sensual sensations.

Hank's drunken chortles shattered the moment.

"You flatter me, Sissy darlin'," he slurred.

Leila swallowed and sat. The chair slid into place as though she weighed only a feather. She glanced at Hank. He had his back to her, leaning close to Sissy Lanweihr. *Is he cruel because I refused him on the veranda?* Still, she plastered a smile to her face and kept her eyes on the cutlery. "Thank you kindly, Mr. Millburn."

"My pleasure, Mrs. Dempsey."

His deep baritone ran invisible fingers up her spine. Air seemed to be in short supply as he sat, his broad shoulders almost touching her. He took a table napkin and laid it on her lap. She jerked. His soft chuckle teased the hairs at her nape.

"I merely wish to ensure you don't spoil your exquisite gown," Rork said.

She glanced up and met Sophia Vanderbilt's glittering eyes. The woman, near seventy, missed nothing.

Sophia continued to stare at Leila, unblinking—a fat frog eyeing a fly. "Well, dear, did you get everything sorted out with your husband?"

Leila wet her lips, resentment rising. What on earth does it have to do with her? Gossip said old Sophia was going batty. Leila didn't believe a word of it. Old age and a massive fortune allowed the woman to do and say whatever she pleased. "Yes, Mrs. Vanderbilt, thank you for your concern."

Sophia gestured to Millburn. "Leila, I'd like to introduce you to my new friend, Rork Millburn."

"Thank you. We have met."

"Now that you mention it, I can see you two are, ah, familiar." Sophia brayed at her own innuendo.

Heat invaded Leila's cheeks. On her return from her accident, Leila had passed Sophia and her friends. She braced herself for the inevitable revelation.

Rork laughed and took her hand, lifting it to his lips. "Once again, it's a pleasure, Mrs. Dempsey." He held her hand a fraction longer than necessary and squeezed it surreptitiously.

"You're wicked, Mrs. Vanderbilt. Beautiful, but wickedly witty. Don't you see your probing flusters Mrs. Dempsey?"

Suitably distracted, Sophia flapped her fan, giving him an arch look. "Careful, young man, or I shall believe your silky words."

He chuckled. "You had better believe my words. I can assure you, if I were the marrying kind and you were free, I would offer for you in a heartbeat."

Sophia's laugh tinkled. "The rumors have the truth, Rork. I heard you have a devastating effect on women."

"Please, Mrs. Vanderbilt. You make me sound like a rogue." He put his hands up in mock horror.

"Well, dear, you have an old hand like me believing you."

Rork's robust laughter echoed through the spacious, elegant ballroom. "I don't offer empty flattery, Mrs. Vanderbilt. I'm simply a bachelor who enjoys the company of an engaging woman like you." He had a quick and charming smile. A dimple appeared high on his cheek as humor lit his face. He looked from Leila to the matriarch.

He had a magnetic glance, and Leila could almost forget his earlier behavior.

Sophia laughed. "I think you are a flatterer." She caught Leila's eye and winked.

Despite the whirl of emotions rushing through Leila, she couldn't resist smiling.

"You have a delightful smile," Rork whispered.

Leila's cousin Billy and his wife Eleanor watched with lively interest. Sophia exchanged knowing looks with the others at the table. Billy gazed at her over wire-rimmed spectacles and rubbed his chin.

Leila forced a smile. "Thank you, Mr. Millburn, you are most kind." She kept her eyes averted for fear of blushing.

Billy chuckled. "Flattery will get you nowhere with my cousin, Mr. Millburn."

Leila did not want to be the center of attention. She feared Hank would notice and cause a scene.

Billy's eyebrows drew together. "Cousin, you're in a mood tonight. Is something amiss?"

"No, nothing is amiss."

Millburn chuckled into his wine goblet.

Leila resisted the urge to chastise him. Instead, she locked eyes with her cousin.

"The newspaper said the draft is only for the poor and riffraff. If you have enough money, you can escape the draft." Her mouth set in a hard line, she glanced at Hank. "My husband paid three hundred dollars."

Hank turned and glared at her. "I'm reporting on the War, my dear. Hard to fight and write."

Sophia snorted. "My goodness, what is the world coming to?" Leila fiddled with the cutlery. "War is dreadful. So many are dying. *Harper's Weekly* had news about the death of General Stonewall Jackson, killed in action." She leaned her arms on the fine linen tablecloth. "President Lincoln only wants what is best for our country. Is not freedom for all?"

Leila took a sip of wine. "Perhaps we should have avoided War and turned to dialogue first. At least until the South accepts our constitution, frees their slaves and gives them back their dignity." Taking courage in both hands, she looked at Rork. "Do you agree, Mr. Millburn? Do you think we should support the War?"

"Of course. Why not hire and pay your workers? A man, no matter the color of his skin, may make choices and receive fair pay."

Leila nodded and turned to her husband. "Hank, what is your opinion about sending men to a senseless War?"

He raised one eyebrow. "It would be better not to have War. If we fight amongst ourselves, what does that say about our unity?" He took his hand out from under the table and waved it. "Besides, we could suffer the indignity of losing. The South has a powerful incentive—money."

Rork held up his hands. "Europe holds the South is going to lose."

"I believe that as well," Leila said. "And based on what I've read, the Europeans don't like the Confederacy's support of slavery."

"That doesn't mean they intend to help us if that's what

you're thinking." Hank touched Leila's cheek. "You shouldn't bother your pretty little head with politics, darlin'. It doesn't become you."

"I think your wife's assumption is valid." Rork leaned in to meet Hank's eyes. "But they don't intend to get involved."

"Exactly." Hank turned back to his source of entertainment—Sissy Lanweihr.

Leila shifted in her seat with her eyes fixed ahead. Her husband's hand once again disappeared under the table. Subtlety and restraint were not traits he possessed—drinking and blatant flirting were. Leila seethed, her eyes drifting to the exotic Sissy. The woman's low cut, scarlet evening gown hung off her shoulders. She had swept up her curly red hair in a mass of tousled twirls. Leila ate each successive course of dishes, tasting nothing.

Sissy giggled in response to something Hank said, and her hand flittered under the table.

The subtler innuendos escaped Leila. She pushed aside a strawberry dessert. Is Hank still furious about the interruptions?

She worried he would express his anger when they were in private, then leave and indulge in his dreadful activities.

A quartet on a dais switched from soft background music and played the first waltz.

Rork took a drink from his goblet. "Mrs. Dempsey, may I have a place on your dance card?"

"I'm sorry, Mr. Millburn. Please excuse me. I feel indisposed." She caught a disparaging glance from Hank. He staggered to his feet and took her arm. "Bedtime, I suppose. Come, I shall escort you."

She narrowed her eyes. "I can manage, Hank, thank you."

"Very well." He sat again, giving Sissy his full attention.

Billy rose and followed her. "Wait up a moment, Cousin."

She turned slowly. "What, Billy? I'm exhausted."

Despite his flaws, Leila adored her decade older, tall, lanky cousin. His wife, Eleanor, snickered--as tall as her husband—and the suffocating corset lacing squeezed Eleanor's breath away. Eleanor looked like an overstuffed teddy bear. Billy leaned close to Leila's ear. "Do you know Hank is planning a trip west with Millburn? They leave on Monday." His eyes slid to Sissy. "Supposedly, he invited certain, ah, *friends* to join them later. I arranged their train passage to St. Louis."

Leila swallowed. "Thank you." She moved down the passage, her belly in turmoil, and walked into the empty bedroom, thinking about her empty life. But worse, she couldn't stop thinking about Millburn. How could the man who scooped me from death possibly be Hank's friend? She shrugged. Why should that make a difference? Somehow it did.

Leila milled about, then stopped and pulled the lace curtains aside, allowing a sliver of moonlight to spill over the oriental rug. She stared blindly at the moonlit mountains before sagging into an armchair in the corner and contemplating her miserable existence. Why can't I confront Hank—challenge him?

Disturbed sleep claimed her.

The handle rattled, the door creaked, and Leila's eyes snapped open.

Hank slinked through the door. The sun peeked over the mountains. Filtered rays of orange and yellow shafted through the lace curtains, casting willowy shapes on the walls. A rooster crowed in the distance.

Leila watched him cross the room. Determined to confront Hank, she figured it would be pointless. There would be no conversation with him. He'd be too drunk.

Her mouth twisted. Hank hated it when she waited up. I must talk to him. Not only did she need to tell him about her encounter with Millburn, but Billy's distressing news at dinner warranted immediate discussion.

A giggle gurgled from Hank's lips as he tripped over an

ottoman. "Hello?" he slurred. "How d'you get there, Mr. Otto Man?" Shaking with mirth, he clapped a hand to his mouth.

Leila clenched the chair arms. His laughter made her want to vomit, scream, throw a vase at his head, hurt him the way he hurt her. Instead, she crossed her arms and waited.

Hank stumbled again. He pulled the undone pale gray silk ascot from his neck. It floated to the floor, followed by his evening jacket and waistcoat. He unbuttoned his linen shirt. "Leila? You're awake." He peered at the corner where she sat. "What're you doing? I told you never to wait up for me. You know I like to work at night." His voice still held a hint of laughter. "Well, most nights." The light from the window illuminated his face. His lips tipped in a crooked smile. Still suave, despite his swollen eyes, underscored with dark shadows and unruly hair. His smile grew wider. "But since you are awake." Hank's tone dropped, thick with desire.

"I heard distressful news."

Hank cocked an eyebrow. "Distressful news? What now, Leila?" He stopped, the humor and desire gone from his voice. "What's so important you had to wait up?"

Leila's heart skipped a beat, and she rose, her knees threatening to buckle. "Billy gave me some peculiar information at dinner."

"Out with it, woman. You know it irritates me when you dither."

Leila's throat went dry, as though a strong wind had passed through the bedroom and dried all in its path. She dug her nails into her palms to keep from trembling. "Billy said you're going on a trip west and leaving on Monday. Is this true?"

Hank's nose scrunched up, followed by a laugh and a loud burp. Leila's ire rose. "What is so funny? Is it true?"

"Yes, I have a nine-month job out west. What of it?"

"Just when did you plan on telling me?" The words seethed from her lips.

"Good Lord, woman, you're making a fuss about nothing." His hand sliced the air as though brushing away a fly. "We were working on the plans and would let you know when done."

"Monday seems rather definite." Suspicion clawed at her stomach. "Perhaps you weren't planning to tell me at all. Imagine my shock hearing about your trip from Billy?"

"I would have told you." He turned his back on her and crossed the room to change into his nightshirt. "Now, if you don't mind, I'm tired."

"Billy said he arranged train passages for you and your party to St. Louis." He would never admit Sissy coming along.

Hank glared at her. "You want the whole thing?"

"Of course. What route are you taking? And who, exactly, are you traveling with?"

"St. Louis by train, stop to pick up supplies, and the train to St. Joseph. There we're taking a ferry to Atchison to catch the Overland Mail Coach to San Francisco. Satisfied?" He turned down the bedcovers and blew out a heavy breath. "We'll discuss the specifics later. I'm going to sleep."

Leila straightened her back and swallowed hard. "What if I told you not to go?" She stared at him.

He lifted the covers, one knee on the bed. He stopped and turned slowly to face her. Light reflected in his eyes, giving them a demonic aspect.

Leila focused on each breath she drew, her fingers clenching and unclenching. I can't force his fidelity, but I can make it difficult for him.

"I am sorry, Leila, did you just say I couldn't go?"

Her stomach churned, and her words leaked out in a squeak. "No, I asked what you would do if I said don't go?"

"What you did is fan my temper. And, you know, my temper is short. Cut the damn inquisition. I am going to sleep."

Leila stared at her husband. He settled among plush pillows and pulled the duvet over himself. She knew better than to push him, especially after a night of carousing. But she couldn't shake the ominous stab in her gut. *I'll accompany him if plans are all set or not.* Tears welled in her eyes and rolled down her cheeks. Wrestling with her conflicted emotions, she sat beside him on the bed and held his angry gaze, hoping his heart would soften. She ran her fingers through his hair. "I'm sorry. I didn't mean to upset you."

"I forgive you this time." He pulled the top of her gown off her shoulders and gave her his hungry look.

She shuddered, and he let her go. "Now, let me get some shuteye."

"Perhaps I could assist with your writing."

He yawned and turned his back to her. "Tomorrow, darlin'."

Pricilla Ashburn paced the floor, ranting. Leila felt an automatic tightening in her stomach. "Is something wrong, Mother?"

"Have you taken leave of your senses, Leila?" She spun, glaring at her daughter. "How can you demand to go on this bachelor trip with your husband? For heaven's sake, what do you think people will say? The railway doesn't run to California. You must travel the vast distance by wagon, hardly suitable transport for a lady. Not to mention the threat of Indian attacks and robbers."

"Why should I tolerate my husband taking Sissy Lanweihr with him?"

Pricilla waved her hand. "That is what men do. Our job is to maintain the moral high ground. Ignore the woman. Acting like this is undignified."

Leila almost choked. "*I* am undignified?"

She backed away and held up her hand to stop her mother's protest. "What do you mean, Mother? I am undignified? That's degrading. Why am I undignified?"

"Yes, my dear," she said, sounding somewhat dictatorially.

"You must rise above the situation and keep your poise." She straightened her already ramrod back and pinned Leila down with her look of reprimand. "At least his mistress saves you the onerous duty of, ah, submitting to your husband's baser demands."

Leila almost laughed. If Mother only knew, Hank couldn't carry out his base demands. She rose from the bed and rang for Biddy. "Well, like it or not, I am going."

"I despair of trying to save your reputation. I shan't be able to hold up my head in society again."

"I'm sure you'll manage, Mother." She expelled a sharp breath as her mother stormed from the bedchamber.

Biddy walked in. "So, yer goin' to chase after yer husband?"

"Hardly chasing."

"I need to tell ya something, child."

Leila cast her eyes down and rearranged her jewelry in a velvet box. "It sounds serious."

"I want to go back to Ireland for a bit. My youngest daughter is havin' her first babe."

Leila dropped a pearl necklace and hugged her. "Of course, you must go. I'll miss you, though."

"Aye, I'll miss ya, too, colleen. But I'll return one day."

Leila held her at arm's length. "Retire, my dearest, and enjoy your life."

Biddy blinked as tears welled. "Ya mean that?"

Tears slid down Leila's cheeks. "I do. I'd hoped you'd be nursemaid to my babies one day, but I'll probably never know the joy of holding a baby of my own."

"Ya will, colleen. Ya will."

CHAPTER SIX

*R*ork choked, his lungs filling with the smelly soot-laden air. He pinched his nose and checked his pocket watch for the tenth time—thick smoke billowed from the steam engine. It wrapped around the people milling about the platform. Porters stored the luggage, sidestepping their owners.

Jostled by the chaos, he searched the crowd for Hank. They'd agreed to meet at noon. Rork got to the station early.

He journeyed west four years ago. He planned to collect rare images to paint to further his artistic reputation. A smile tugged at his lips.

A beauty in a vibrant yellow dress, matching ribbon in her hair, crossed the platform. Leila Dempsey. Damn. Now there is no hope for peace of mind. Servants trailed behind, laden with her luggage.

Leila's eyes met Rork's, then flickered away. She stopped in front of him, her eyes lowered. "Good day, Mr. Millburn." Her voice held as much warmth as an icy mountain brook.

"Mrs. Dempsey, what a pleasant surprise." He took her hand and brought it to his lips for a moment too long.

She yanked her hand away. Her toes beat a tattoo on the

wooden planks, drowning in the sounds of the crowd weaving around them.

Hank emerged from a nearby bar. He strode to them, wriggling his nose. "Why do women douse themselves with that smelly French stuff? Damn expensive too."

Rork raised one eyebrow. Leila's perfume invoked a longing in him. "You never mentioned your wife is coming. What a wonderful surprise."

Hank glared at Leila. "It sure as hell isn't *wonderful*, and I didn't know either—until now."

Leila's mouth tightened. "I told you I intended to come."

She stalked off, her back stiff.

"Must have slipped my mind, darlin'," Hank called after her. "That damn, willful woman."

Rork followed her retreat. Lord, if she were mine, I wouldn't let her out of my sight. He glanced at Hank. "Correct me if I am wrong. Is Miss Lanweihr joining us in Philadelphia?" He cocked an eyebrow. "Could make things a little awkward."

"Damn awkward." Hank's mouth pulled down. "I had the situation under control. Unfortunately, Leila got wind of our trip. You're not married. You 're lucky." He blew out his cheeks and released a long breath.

"Women can be a bloody curse. Leila thinks Sissy is tedious and flighty—pure jealousy." "And Sissy says Leila joyless and prissy." Hank smothered a laugh. "Think I'm inclined to agree with Sissy." He pulled a hip flask from his pocket.

"Now that Leila has taken it into her head to join me, having time alone with Sissy will be tricky. Keeping them apart is a must." He took a swig of whiskey from the flask. "I don't suppose you'd consider keeping my wife entertained?"

Rork slid a glance at Leila, mounting the step into a railway carriage. "I can't make any promises. Your wife is not partial to me. And don't ask me to keep Sissy occupied."

"Well, that's counterproductive. Sissy is the one I want to roll."

"That woman grates on my nerves. I don't know what the hell you see in her. She seems useless."

Hank snorted. He rocked forward on his toes and raised his voice, shouting above the station noise. "Useless? Nope, the opposite."

Rork hid his distaste. "Why not forget the marriage? You have what you want."

"Told you, money, dear boy." Hank took another swig and put his flask back in his pocket. He picked up his valise. "Women, my life's scourge."

Rork grinned. "How did you wangle this mess?"

"At first, Sissy agreed to meet me later. She harped to start sooner after she heard I would hop the train to St. Louis. I refused, but she turned up luggage and all." He rubbed his cheek. "Luckily, before Leila showed."

Rork hoisted his valise. "No romance. No complications," Rork said, swiping his hand in the air. "One woman is enough here on the train, but two?"

He put his arm around Rork's shoulders. "You're a wise man, my friend. No getting out of my sweet situation. Leila's damn father doles out a sum every year for his daughter. I manage it and keep any spillover. I don't need it, but a little extra doesn't hurt."

"I'm impressed."

"Not a word about this foul-up." Hank held up his hand, mimicking a pistol to his head.

Rork chuckled. "You're a scoundrel. I won't say a word." He groaned—quite a bachelor trip.

Hank grinned. "It'll provide entertainment. You occupy my wife while I dally with Sissy."

Rork's belly lurched. *God, the man is serious.*

CHAPTER SEVEN

A swirl of voices echoed in the dining car. Gaslights cast a sickly yellow glow on the passengers. Somewhere a child cried, followed by a sharp reprimand.

Leila sat alone on a plush red velvet bench and sipped her tea, grimacing as the brew scalded her mouth. She stared past the burgundy silk curtains—the blurring landscape draped in the warm afternoon sun. Muted conversations coiled around her bruised ego. Hank had accepted the invitation to join her for tea.

"Hello, darlin'." Hank, reeking of whiskey, bent and pecked her cheek.

"Can't stay. I'll return shortly—need to attend to business." He slipped into the adjacent bar.

Leila's unease beset her belly. Traveling with her husband across the continent to ensure his fidelity, while he dallied with Sissy in public.

Her mother worrying about a breach of etiquette by joining her husband on a bachelor spree didn't matter. Rumors surrounding Hank's excesses and philandering had plagued her marriage from the outset.

She poured more tea and took a sip of the hot brew. She contemplated returning to her compartment.

"Leila?"

She looked up. A tall woman with blond curls pinned high on her head stood beside the booth. A smile touched the woman's alabaster face. "Leila Dempsey? Is that you?"

"Cornelia?" Leila gaped at her friend. She and Cornelia Hancock had attended boarding school together for eight years. "I haven't seen you in ages," she bubbled, taking Leila's arm. "Oh, give me a hug."

Leila rose, and Cornelia enveloped her. "How wonderful to see you."

"Yes, it is good." Cornelia dropped into the opposite seat, smiling. "Where are you going? Last I heard, you were in Florida."

"Yes, well, we were back in New York, now we're on our way west with my husband and a colleague." Cornelia would have heard the latest from her social circle. Leila furrowed her brow. She suspected Cornelia still corresponded with everyone from their class.

"I'm stopping in New York City to volunteer with Doctor Smith, who works with orphans. Afterwards, I will go to St. Louis to pursue a nursing career."

Leila smiled. "I'm delighted you are here—we can catch up. I want to hear more of your exciting plans."

Hank's disrespect for his wife gave Rork heartache. He unclenched his jaw and left the bar, leaving Hank pawing Sissy and stepped into the crowded dining car. Leila's laughter curled around Rork's heart. Her smile lit her face while she chatted.

She looked up, and their eyes met. Her smile faded.

"Is everyone ready for dinner?" Rork hoped no one noticed the slur that slid off his thick tongue.

Hank stumbled into the dining car and plopped down next to Cornelia.

"Why, hello, darlin'. I didn't realize you were on the train. What a surprise." He took her hand and kissed it, his eyes flirting with her. "Haven't seen you since our wedding—where have you been?"

A flush crept into Cornelia's cheeks. She glanced at Leila.

Rork hesitated. He had no choice but to sit with Leila.

Hank gestured to Rork. "Cornelia, this is my traveling friend, Rork Millburn. Rork, this lovely lady is my wife's friend, Miss Hancock. Watch out for him, darlin'." Hank winked. "He's an artist, and you know what they say about artists."

Cornelia held out her hand. "Pleased, Mr. Millburn."

Rork nodded and raised her hand to his lips. "Charmed, Miss Hancock."

"Cornelia is going to St. Louis to pursue a nursing career," Leila said, her eyes alight with admiration.

Hank took a swig from his hip flask. "Seems a waste of a beautiful woman."

Rork's eyebrows rose. "I admire your courage, Miss Hancock."

"Thank you, Mr. Millburn." Cornelia canted her head. "I hope you don't mind me asking—are you not inclined to join our brave soldiers in the fight?"

He shrugged. "I expect to portray the War on canvas." His eyes shifted to Leila. "I'm sure Mrs. Dempsey will enjoy having a friend on the trip."

"Yes, I will."

Hank waved his hand. "Sit, Rork. My wife won't bite."

Rork met Leila's eyes. Rork slid onto the narrow bench and only had to shift his knee a fraction to touch. He cleared his throat. "I gather you and Miss Hancock are close friends?"

Leila nodded. "We were schoolmates."

"Ah, before you met Hank. How *did* you and Hank meet?"

"We met in the mountains while on holiday. The summer before I turned eighteen, my family went to the Catskills to take the waters, baths for anything that ailed you. We met there." Sadness washed over her face. Rork's heart went out to her. Leila plucked at her reticule. "Anyway, on a walk in the woods, I passed Hank surrounded by children telling them stories. I wanted to listen, but he said no grown-ups. So debonaire calling me a grown-up." A smile crept across her face telling the story of their meeting.

"Darlin', Rork doesn't want to hear that tired old tale." Hank turned his attention back to Cornelia. "What have you been up to?"

Cornelia glanced at Leila. "Oh, not a great deal. Hank, I'd like to hear the rest of Leila's story."

"Well, the children were so adorable, they hollered at him, so he relented and allowed me into his story group."

Cornelia reached across the table and patted Leila's hand. "She returned to Philadelphia after that summer completely smitten. Within months she married."

Hank yawned. "Yes, we had a rather peculiar courtship. Her fastidious father procrastinated and withheld permission for weeks. The reason evades me still. I didn't press him, but we wed after he agreed to the marriage." Hank brushed a speck of dust off his lapel. "Her father and I don't hide our dislike of each other."

Leila's mouth drew into a tight line. "Father can be a little mistrustful." She looked at her husband. "Hank's book, *The Hasheesh Ride*, published three years before we married, got glowing reports in *Graham's*. The reviews said the descriptions in the book sounded frightening. I never read it, but the book gave my father cause for concern."

Cornelia nodded and looked at Hank. "Yes, Leila mentioned

it to me. The book is about your experiences with hasheesh, a substance of question, is it not?"

Hank scowled. "Yes, about my experiments and the strange journeys from the effects." Hank downed his whiskey. "Frankly, her father's disapproval shocked me. I had many followers. Newspapers published my writing." Hank tilted his head back and laughed out loud. His sinister laugh dampened his words. "I got paid plenty. Isn't that what every father wants for his daughter?" He flicked one hand. "Enough of that. I want to hear what Cornelia has been doing."

A faint smile graced Cornelia's face. "Where can I buy your book? Say the name again?"

"*The Hasheesh Ride*. I'm sure it's in the bookshops."

"Does it still sell well?"

"Absolutely. Sales are brisk. It's made it through to a fourth edition." Hank sat back as a server set a plate of hors d'oeuvres on the table.

Cornelia helped herself to oysters. "Tell us one of your experiences. What is it made from? How did you find it?" She popped an oyster into her mouth. "What possessed you to ingest it?"

"It's a long story."

Cornelia dabbed her lips with a table napkin. "We have time, please."

"If you insist." Hank stretched his arm along the back of the chair. "I got sick, runny nose, fever, cough when working at a pharmacy as a young student at Princeton. The druggist gave me a new drug and said it would make me feel better. The bottle had skull and crossbones on the label. He told me the dosage and not to take more than prescribed."

As Rork piled caviar onto a slice of toast, he stopped and stared at him. "Don't tell me you played the fool and took more than you should?"

Cornelia raised her eyebrows. "It made you better?"

49

"It intrigued me, so I read about it and found that it helped a variety of ailments. Quite vogue at the time." Hank summoned the server and ordered a whiskey. "I tried it and sneaked ten grains. Nothing happened. Cautiously, I waited several days more. This time I took fifteen grains. Still nothing. It seemed ineffective. I thought I would give it one more try and snitched thirty grains. I went to visit a friend, and after several hours of conversation and music, I prepared to desert the experiment, when at last—pow!"

Cornelia gaped at him, wide-eyed. "But here you are to tell all. Did it hurt your stomach?"

"Hurt my stomach? Hardly. Although it would have been wiser if I'd never swallowed the damn things. That did not stop me, though. I continued to enjoy the mind-altering rides described in my book—for example, intense colors blinded me, and my friends and I floated in the air on heavenly clouds. The strange trips varied each time I imbibed the grains."

"This is the first time I've heard this story. No wonder my father had reservations. He refused to let me read your book. I should read it."

Hank's eyes flickered. "Don't be ridiculous. You don't need the book. You have me." He returned his attention to Cornelia. "I'll get a book for you in New York."

Rork raised a brow. "I'd like a copy of the book as well. Sounds fascinating. Is there a character description in there? You sound complicated. What have I gotten myself into?"

Hank laughed. "No worries, Rork. I'll be happy to share my grains with you."

Cornelia cast a sympathetic look at her friend and glanced at Hank. "I look forward to reading it." Hank touched Cornelia's golden curls. "Enough of my damn book. Tell me what you've been doing."

"There isn't much to talk about. After school, I stayed with my family in Buffalo. My brother, passionate about fighting for the North, joined the war." She pushed an empty oyster shell with her fork. "Not long after, he died from wounds." She took a breathy sigh. "After that, I volunteered to nurse. Florence Nightingale, the British woman who became a nurse, inspired me."

Leila touched her friend's hand gently. "I know you'll succeed."

"You never married, Cornelia?" Hank ran a finger down her arm.

Leila took a sip of water. "I heard you and Michael are betrothed."

"True." The light in Cornelia's eyes dimmed, and her voice dropped. "He-he died at Bull Run."

Leila gasped, and tears welled in her eyes. "Oh, my dear, I'm sorry."

"Did he die early in the battle?" Hank slurred. "At Bull Run —they realized the war wouldn't end in a hurry."

Leila stared at her husband and compressed her lips.

Rork glowered, aghast at Hank's lack of sensitivity. He had an urge to kick him under the table. The awkward silence broke as a server stopped at their booth with a tray of food.

"Ah, food, our feast has arrived," Hank drawled.

Rork's eyes narrowed as Hank's hand disappeared. Cornelia scowled and shifted away from him. Hank's hand reappeared, but Rork didn't miss the challenge in his eyes. Rork glanced at Leila. She stared at the table—her face crimson.

Rork rose. "The ladies might like to converse, while we discuss our trip, Hank. Do you mind changing places, Miss Hancock?"

Cornelia cast a grateful look at him and sat beside Leila. They finished their meals in silence while the men discussed the trip.

Cornelia rose. "Please excuse me. I'm rather tired."

Hank lurched to his feet. "Let me escort you. The hour is

late, and I'd be remiss if I didn't see you safely to your compartment."

Cornelia shook her head. "That's kind of you, Hank. I can manage. Perhaps you should rather accompany your wife."

Rork stood and smothered a smile. She seemed to have the measure of Hank.

Hank swayed stretching his hand out to Leila. "Yes, of course. My dear, shall we go?"

Leila rose, her cheeks flaming.

Hank gave a bob to Cornelia. "We can all walk together."

Leila lowered her eyes, but Rork noticed the flash of irritation. He offered her his arm.

CHAPTER EIGHT

While dining alone on freshly baked scones and green tea, Leila viewed the open fields, wet from the heavy rains. She gasped, stunned at the double rainbow appearing in the clouds.

Leila leaned her face in her hands. So much for my presence curtailing his philandering. After Hank had escorted Cornelia to her compartment, he left and crawled into bed at dawn, wrapped in the stench of smoke.

A deep voice caressed her senses and tempered her mood. "Mind if I join you?" Rork slid into the seat beside her.

Leila forced a smile. "Strange, you are up early. Given the time my husband returned, I assumed you would also sleep until nightfall." She bit her lip to control a tremble and turned back to the window. Millburn, the last person she wanted to speak with —kept her back to him, gaze transfixed on the scenery. Despite the snub, he stayed. Warmth crept into her face as his arm brushed against her.

Seconds ticked by.

Leila, sure she'd snap, peeked at Rork over her shoulder, and her soul fluttered to life.

He stared at her.

The silence stretched between them like mist. A strange calm filled empty spaces in Leila's heart as Rork continued his scrutiny. She jerked back to reality. Leila glared at him. "I beg your pardon, sir. Is there a reason you study me so?"

"Forgive me for staring, but you seem agitated. Is there anything I can do?"

"Oh, you've done quite enough."

Rork's eyebrow rose, his face turned white. "I'm sorry, have I said something to offend you?"

A sharp laugh burst from Leila's throat. "Spare me your innocence, sir. From the moment we met, you've done nothing but offend." She held up a finger. "One, you took inappropriate liberties with my body." The next finger came up. "Two, you spoke to me as if I were no better than a whore." She raised a third finger. "You laughed at me, mocked me, and to add insult, you took my husband on this pointless bachelor venture. Yes, Mr. Millburn, you've deeply offended me. Now, if you do not mind, I would prefer to spend my morning in solitude enjoying my breakfast."

Rork's brow furrowed. His robust laughter filled the dining carriage.

Leila rounded on him. "You're infuriating, Mr. Millburn," she snarled, heat invading her cheeks. Hands trembled, and her bosom rose and fell. She wanted to hit something, anything—Rork perhaps.

"I apologize, Mrs. Dempsey." His voice still held a hint of laughter. "I regret offending you. Can you forgive me?"

She stared at dancing eyes, and her heart melted. "For which indiscretion do you seek forgiveness?"

"All of them. All except the last. I cannot apologize for this. Ah, what did you call it? Pointless bachelor venture."

Leila opened her mouth, but the words stuck in her throat.

He pressed a finger to her lips. "Believe what you will, but this trip serves a greater purpose than satisfying my voyeuristic curiosity."

Part of Leila connected with his vision. She brushed it aside. "That's romantic, but I cannot see how my husband can serve you on this mission."

"My brushstrokes will give life to the canvas, and Hank's words will expand on what I depict." He spread his arms. "Imagine showing the world the beauty of America's wild, seldom-seen landscapes."

Despite herself, his vision drew her in, intriguing her.

"With my last trip to the west, I didn't have anyone to journal my progress. I divided my time between sketching, painting, and recording what I experienced. As a result, I didn't accomplish what I'd hoped. Chronicling took time from painting. Hank will chronicle our progress on this trip, and I'll be free to sketch and paint. Not only will the world get to see the sights, but they can live it through Hank's articulate writing."

"That's a wonderful goal," she conceded with hesitation. "I understand your need for a companion, but I wish my husband weren't your choice." Leila turned to the window. The flora and foothills became a blur as her eyes pooled.

"I apologize for offending you. And I'm sorry that my association with your husband distresses you. He's a brilliant writer and the best man to do the journaling." He took her hand, and she jumped. "Will it help if I assure you, I'll endeavor to make sure no harm comes to him?"

Her eyes widened. "It isn't Hank's safety I'm concerned about." Leila shifted in her seat and faced Rork.

"I-I'm not . . ." She twisted her hands. Her concern did not include the dangers inherent to wagon rides across the continent. Hank's dissolute reputation and his ability to snag women like rainbow trout concerned Leila. His safety hadn't crossed her mind. She dabbed her tears with a lacy handkerchief. "Thank you for your apology, Mr. Millburn."

He cast his eyes down for a moment. "Now I've made you cry. I always seem to say the wrong thing." Rork apologized again. "Each time I open my mouth, I sound like a fool. If I were smart, I'd clam up and be on my way."

Her hand fluttered to her throat, and she stared at him. Honesty, a rare gem in her life, married to Hank.

He leaned forward and drew a breath. "Will you accept my apology for my poor behavior on the Mountain House veranda?"

Leila's mouth opened, but nothing came out.

"What is it, Leila?" He had an uneven edge to his voice, concern maybe, almost pleading.

Her mouth closed. She stared at Rork and spoke with a hint of exasperation in her voice. "We seem to have misunderstanding in our words and our actions."

Rork's eyes held her captive, and every part of her tingled with longing for that elusive quality in a relationship, the union of two souls. Rork moved an empty cup back and forth. Her eyes fixed on his long fingers. What would it be like to feel them on her body? Her innate sense of right and wrong rejected the licentious thought.

"I drank too much. Still, that doesn't excuse my inappropriate behavior. I'm sorry I offended you. Could you put this behind us?"

"Why is my forgiveness important to you?"

"Why? I don't know." He rubbed his chin. "I want your acceptance, I suppose. Besides, we'll be traveling companions for several weeks. Meals will be tedious if you refuse to forgive me." He smoothed a sharp crease in the tablecloth. "The tension of misunderstanding between us doesn't help one's digestion."

Pity welled up in her for his obvious discomfort. "It's not exactly a misunderstanding."

"No, absolutely not, but I hate that my reprehensible behavior is a source of discomfort between us." He glanced at her. "I don't know you—yet." His eyes twinkled. "There's a great release in forgiveness."

She laughed. "I'm not unhappy to accept your offer of apologies and move on."

"We agree?" He flashed a smile and held out his hand. "Truce?"

"Truce." His smile did strange things to her stomach. She placed her hand in his and there went her belly butterflies. He gave her hand a light squeeze. She'd let go of her sensitivity, at least for the rest of the trip.

Rork chuckled, running his fingers through his hair. "I cannot describe my relief." He sat back and gazed at her, caressing her profile. A delicate flush crept into her cheeks. His eyes moved to the landscape, smoke billowing from the engine and wafting between tall oaks and maples. Black ash speckled the windows.

"I should go," she said in a whisper.

He all but drowned in the liquid depths of her eyes. *Lord, that I could change the sadness in her eyes to happiness.*

"I need you to move, Mr. Millburn."

Her smile alone had the power to throw his mind into disarray. He stared at a small dimple playing next to her lips—such a kissable mouth.

"Mr. Millburn."

He forced his addled senses to obey. "My apologies." He moved and stood, offering his hand. Her gloved hand seemed fragile, engulfed in his. An overwhelming desire to protect her swept through him as he helped her up. "I'll see you to your compartment."

"Thank you."

He followed her from the dining car, admiring her slender

waist and the gentle sway of her hips as she negotiated the narrow passage.

Outside her compartment, she turned and smiled up at him. "I'm glad we reached a truce."

Truce? He clamped his lips to avoid saying something that could sabotage their tenuous friendship. Still, he would rather have a truce than her anger.

The train lurched as it swept around a bend, throwing her against his chest, and his arms enfolded her. Their eyes met. He closed his eyes, savoring the fragrance of her perfume. He savored the sensation of her body pressed hard against his. The train lurched again. He tightened his hold, and she gasped. He opened his eyes. She ran her tongue across her lips.

"Why do you let Hank mistreat you?"

"I-I don't know. I don't think it's your place to pass judgment." She shoved his chest—he opened his arms and she wriggled from his embrace.

"You're quite right. I'm sorry." He bowed and spun on his heel and walked away. He glanced over his shoulder, and his belly contracted. Had she watched him? Her eyes said something to him. Longing?

CHAPTER NINE

*N*ew York crackled with tension—cloying smoke stifled the hot air. Leila stepped onto the train depot's wooden platform—her hair pulled back with a white ribbon matching her day dress. The tied leather boots reached her ankles. She held a handkerchief over her nose to block out the stink.

"Ugh, what is that stench? Cornelia asked, screwing up her nose. "Is New York always like this?"

Leila shook her head, scanning the low buildings surrounding the depot. "Something is wrong."

Rork joined them. "What's that noise in the distance."

Hank took a long swig from his hipflask. "This war has New York divided."

"They're protesting the draft." Rork pointed to a plume of black smoke mingling with dark storm clouds. "Look at that."

Cornelia shook her head. "Let's not go to Tiffany's."

Hank took Cornelia's arm. "Well, darlin', we are checking into St. Nicholas Hotel. You girls need to occupy yourselves. We'll meet up later." He flicked one of her golden curls. "Can't let a little unrest bother your pretty head."

Cornelia glared, pulled her arm from his grasp, and moved closer to Leila. "We should be wise."

"Tiffany's is on Lower Broadway, far from that smoke," Leila said, noting her friend's rejection of Hank. "We'll hire a buggy."

"You can't go alone." Rork snapped up a four-wheeled buggy to take them to Tiffany's. "Let's go, ladies."

Leila put her hand on Hank's chest. "Come with us. We can check into the hotel later."

Hank pushed her away. "I'll meet you at the hotel later."

Leila's mouth tightened. "Shall we go?" Leila smiled. She avoided the sympathy in Cornelia's eyes. Leila slid a glance at Rork. He handed her into the open four-seater carriage, his face grim. Settling back, she fanned her face. "This heat is oppressive." The billowing smoke curled around the humidity and made the air smell like burning manure.

The carriage took off toward Broadway. Rork sat opposite, next to Cornelia, who leaned forward. "Where are you going from here, Leila?"

"St. Louis to St. Joseph is the farthest west the train travels. We need to get from St. Joseph for Atchison. There we can hire a wagon to California, the only means of travel that far west." Leila pouted. "Hank doesn't want me to join him." She swiped her hand in the air. "He thinks I can't handle the rigors of a wagon trail."

Cornelia expelled a breath. "I know the sentiment." She half-smiled. "My father has a similar philosophy. He insists women are unable to help in the war effort. I could not persuade him. I've taken it upon myself to learn nursing and go where needed."

Leila glanced at Rork, who seemed preoccupied with the buildings. She leaned toward Cornelia. "I had to convince Hank to allow me to come on this trip. He expressed disappointment in my desire to travel with him and insisted I remain in the Catskills."

"How did you convince him?"

"I simply arrived at the station." Leila fiddled with her hair, smoothing down loose ends. "Cornelia, you've been to New York several times. Why haven't you shopped Tiffany's? It's popular."

"I don't see why the fuss. It's just a shop."

"It's not just any shop. It is an emporium famed for its stationery, fancy goods, watches, and more. You'll see, the merchandise is unusual. You will want to buy a trinket or two. Once we get there, you'll understand why it's magical." She smiled. "Wait and see. You will love Tiffany's."

"I'm not sure about that. I'm not fond of shopping, but I'm looking forward to the experience. If you love it, I probably will too. After Tiffany's, can we make a stop on the way back?"

Leila nodded. "Where?"

"I promised to meet Dr. Smith at the Colored Orphan Asylum on Fifth Avenue."

"Of course." Leila took Cornelia's hand. "You are caring and noble."

The driver turned to them. "Sorry, folks, but the traffic stopped, so I cain't get ya any closer. Tiffany's ain't more than a block from here. I'll get close to the entrance when the traffic clears a bit and wait for ya."

Leila jumped from the buggy and yanked Cornelia's hand. "Let's go."

Rork laughed and followed. "I can't believe how excited you are about visiting the shops."

Leila tittered. "Men don't understand." She pulled Cornelia, who struggled to keep up.

"You can keep pulling my arm, Leila, but I can't walk any faster."

Leila glanced at her friend. "We have little time to get our fill of Tiffany's."

"What do you want to buy?"

"Nothing. I want you to see it. And perhaps I'll buy Hank a gift."

"You're a thoughtful wife." She squeezed Leila's hand.

A stone settled in Leila's heart. Would Hank like a gift? He never gave *her* gifts, not since they married. He'd probably ignore anything from her. "Besides," Leila said, trying to brush away doubt, "it gives me an excuse to spend for myself."

"Let's hurry."

Rork chuckled. "Tiffany's isn't going anywhere."

Leila squeaked and sidestepped dung. "The streets reek of horse droppings. We'll be a mess by the time we get there." They beheld the elaborate portals of Tiffany's. "At last." Out of breath, Leila pushed through the turnstile doors of the brick building.

Cornelia gasped. "Oh my, you're right. This shop is divine."

A short, balding man wearing a dark suit approached.

"Ladies, sir, welcome to Tiffany's." He smiled. "I'm delighted you're visiting our emporium. How may I help you?"

Glass jewel cases glittered, sending shafts of color dancing across the walls. Leila scanned the exquisite diamond jewelry, gold watches, and sterling server sets on display.

"I'm interested in purchasing a gift for my husband."

"Madam, I'm Claude Christi, and I'm here to help you." He bowed. "And you are . . ."

"Mrs. Dempsey."

"Dempsey? Like the writer?"

Leila giggled. "Yes. I'm his wife. Do you know him?"

"Not personally, but I've read his work in *Harper's*. He's very imaginative. Perhaps you would like a timepiece that suits his personality?"

"I had something more, shall we say, *frivolous* in mind." Leila clasped her hands at her chest. "Is this place not a dream, Cornelia?"

"My, yes."

"I have the perfect gift in mind for Mr. Dempsey. Right this way, ladies." He placed a hand on Leila's elbow and steered her toward the back of the shop. Rork and Cornelia followed. Leila glanced over her shoulder. "Aren't you glad we came, Cornelia?"

"It's perfect." Cornelia leaned over a showcase displaying necklaces. "This locket is beautiful and delicate."

Leila spied a gold jewel box. "Oh, Mr. Christi, my husband, would love that for his cufflinks. And I'd like that locket over there for my friend."

Cornelia put four fingers of her gloved hand to her mouth. "Thank you, but you really shouldn't."

"I want to. I'll take both items, Mr. Christi."

"We really ought to go, ladies."

"We have one more place Cornelia wants to visit."

Leila put her hand on Rork's arm. "Please, Mr. Millburn." He laughed and shook his head. "How can I resist? One smile from you, and I melt. But we have to meet Hank at the hotel." Leila paid for her purchases.

"Here, let me put the locket on for you." Cornelia turned, and Leila put the simple gold chain with a small heart locket around Cornelia's neck. "There." She stepped in front of her. "That looks lovely."

Cornelia's eyes gleamed with tears, reflecting the myriad of surrounding colors. "I shall treasure it. I'll insert my miniature of Michael."

Leila's mouth quivered. "Oh, my dear friend, I cannot imagine the pain of losing the one you love."

Cornelia hugged her and whispered, "You deserve better than Hank, my sweet friend." She leaned into Leila and glanced at Rork before whispering, "This man likes you a great deal."

Leila's eyes widened. "Don't be silly, Cornelia. How can you even suggest it?" But she couldn't help her heart racing. Cornelia chuckled and patted her arm. "There is such a thing as divorce."

Leila shook her head. "I-I can't afford to think like that."

Cornelia tossed her head. "Oh, tish, this is the nineteenth century, and women are becoming emancipated."

"Not me." Leila stared at her hands.

Rork joined them, smiling. "Ladies, I hate to interrupt your tête-à-tête, but we must go." He urged them from Tiffany's. "Miss Hancock, did I hear you have an appointment? Where to?"

"The Colored Orphan Asylum."

Leila's stomach fluttered as Rork held her arm. "It's on Fifth Avenue and Forty-Third Street. Cornelia wants to visit Dr. Smith to do volunteer work there."

Admiration gleamed in his eyes. "I applaud your humanitarian sentiments, Miss Hancock."

She blushed. "I enjoy serving the less fortunate. My goal is in nursing. Working with Dr. Smith offers experience."

"Very well, the orphanage it is." He hustled the girls to the buggy, thankfully parked outside, and issued directions to the driver.

Leila canted her head with her handkerchief held to her nose. "You seem tense, Mr. Millburn."

"The smoke has increased," he said, looking north at a cloud of black smoke. He took out his pocket watch and flipped it open. "It's almost one o'clock. We need to hurry if we're to reach our hotel."

Leila's lips turned down. "The noise is growing louder."

"I agree. Driver, hurry," Rork yelled.

"Goin' fast as I can, sir." He flicked a whip across the two bays, and they picked up the pace, cutting a path through the crowded streets.

Rork pulled his hat off and raked his fingers through his hair. Unease swelled through him, and his eyes darted from left to right. They neared Twenty-First Street. Instinct set his nerves on edge.

They picked up speed on Fifth Avenue. Without warning, the buggy jigged, and the driver swore. Men milled around them, brandishing sticks, guns, and knives while screaming abuse. "Get the rich bastards, lads."

They surged toward the buggy, spooking the horses. "Aye, strip 'em o' their fine clothes."

"Move, dammit," Rork shouted at the driver.

The driver sawed at the horse's mouths. "I cain't keep 'em nags under control."

"Damn!" Rork clambered onto the driver's seat, shoved him aside, and grabbed the reins and whip. He flicked the reins and sent the whip singing over the horses' ears, galvanizing them into action. He glanced over his shoulder at the girls.

Cornelia clung to the buggy.

Leila swung her lace parasol like a sword, fighting off men who tried to rip her from the buggy. "Get your hands off me, you miserable knave."

Rioters snatched at the horses.

"Hang on." Rork cracked the whip from left to right. The tip sliced open faces and arms. Neighing, the horses broke free under Rork's firm command and took off. The smoke grew denser, choking them.

"There's the orphanage," Leila shouted.

Leila kneeled on the seat--her head against Rork's shoulder. Held on by ribbons, the bonnet bounced on her back. Her hair unraveled and fell to her waist. He tore his eyes away and concentrated on getting the team through the gates to the orphanage.

He leaped down and ran to the horses, grabbing the halters and calming the animals with a soft voice. "Easy does it." They trembled, foam coating their mouths. Their red-brown coats gleamed with sweat. Rork leaned his forehead against one horse's soft nose. "Damn, thank God for these horses. How the hell do I get everyone out of here?" Rork hurried to Leila. She flopped back against the squabs, panting, and looked at Rork. "Lord, I thought we would never escape."

His belly jolted as her eyes settled on him. "I don't think it's over." He reached out and put his hands around her tiny waist, lifting her from the buggy.

Leila stared up at him, her hands on his forearms. "Once again, you saved my life. Thank you."

"It's a pleasure, but we're not out of trouble yet. I can hear a crowd approaching. Maybe we'll luck out, and the troublemakers will pass the orphanage." He released her and turned to Cornelia, holding out his hand. "Are you all right, Miss Hancock?"

She took his hand and stepped down, leaning against the buggy, her eyes wide as she tried to tuck blond curls into place. "I-I'm shaken. Thank you for leading us to safety, Mr. Millburn."

Rork gave a nod. He nudged the driver trembling in his seat. "Take the buggy behind the building in case the rioters attack this place."

"Yes, sir. Sorry, I lost it back there."

"Don't beat yourself up. Come into the orphanage after you've hidden the horses and buggy, but don't unhitch them. We may need to leave in a hurry."

"Yes, sir."

"Lord above, folks, get inside." A tall man ran to them, waving his arms frantically. His white hair and full mustache contrasted with his ebony skin.

CHAPTER TEN

*R*ork guided Leila toward the orphanage steps, stumbling on the uneven surface.

Men in work clothes lounged against the fence surrounding the building, their hard stares filled with resentment.

Leila pulled free from Rork's grasp. "I can manage, thank you, Mr. Millburn."

Cornelia kept up with them, casting glances at the workmen. "Those men's stares cut through us as though slicing us up for dinner."

Leila straightened her shoulders. "Let's ignore them." Her spine tingled, and fear coursed through her. She glanced up at the four-story brick building. The afternoon sun struggled through smoke and clouds, reflecting on small-paned windows the staff had not yet shuttered.

Rork took Leila's and Cornelia's arms and hurried them into the building. Sweat ran down his face. He loosened his stained ascot. He put out his hand. "I'm Rork Millburn." He turned to the women. "These are my companions, Mrs. Dempsey and Miss Hancock."

The man grasped his hand. "I'm Dr. James Smith." He bowed to the women. "Ladies."

Cornelia smiled. "I'm happy to meet you, Dr. Smith, albeit under dreadful circumstances."

His brown eyes twinkled. "Ah, Miss Hancock. I received your letter volunteering your time to work with us. Come, we'll go to the sitting room." He shut and bolted the door behind him and walked down the hall with his visitors.

Cornelia pushed her hair back. "Delighted Dr. Smith, if I may say, those workmen outside the building are threatening."

"Those poor men are working class and are suffering the consequences of the draft. I'm sure your well-dressed appearance upset them. You represent the rich. When President Lincoln declared the abolition of slavery, it shook the South's economic foundations and started this senseless war. Now the Union needs soldiers. The Union requires the working class to join the fight. They have no choice. The problem is anyone could buy exemptions from the draft for $300 or find a substitute draftee."

Rork snapped open his handkerchief and mopped his face. "So, that's what the placards represented."

Dr. Smith brushed soot off his sleeve. "I don't blame them for protesting. Initially, the draftees targeted government institutions, but I fear they are now out of control. The mobs burned the *New York Tribune*. The owner, Horace Greeley, is an avid abolitionist. He disapproves of rich men buying their way out of the war, but that's happening in great numbers." He blew out his cheeks. "There's concern about the antagonism toward colored people."

Children's laughter filtered down the passage. Cornelia stared at the doctor, a hand to her throat. "The orphanage is vulnerable for an attack."

Deep creases furrowed his brow and bracketed his mouth. "True. I'm careful not to cause panic." He shook his head. "I've been the physician of this orphanage for almost twenty years, and I've never seen this level of violence. Excuse me. I need to see if the children in the yard are safe."

Rork followed the doctor. Leila and Cornelia quickened their pace to keep up. They stepped aside as staff herded children into the orphanage.

A plump woman calmly called out orders. "Hurry along, children." She caught the doctor's eye and jerked her head toward the back door.

He nodded and lifted his chin to Rork. "It isn't safe out there. We must get all the children inside."

Leila stared at the chaos. "Surely it's safe in the yard with that six-foot brick wall?" She looked at Rork. "Where are the driver and buggy?"

He rubbed his cheek. "Hopefully, safe in the yard." He waded into the crush of small bodies and scooped up children, carrying them inside.

"Ladies, please account for everyone," the doctor shouted above the excited chatter.

Bile rose in Leila's throat. She swallowed her fear and ran to assist a motherly woman as she ushered children through the doorway.

Glancing at Leila and Cornelia, the nurse smiled as she spoke. "I'm Gertrude Adams, the director of nursing. It's good you're here."

"What do you want us to do?"

"Go to the hall on the second floor, seat the children for lunch, and count heads."

Leila nodded and hurried off with Cornelia.

An hour later, they'd rounded up the children, counted heads, and fed them. The children chattered happily, unaware of the danger.

Cornelia and Leila sank into a threadbare couch. Rork joined them and sat on the arm. "I believe we gathered all the children." He glanced at them. "Thank God they don't understand the dangers." He chuckled. "They complained about not playing in the yard."

Leila looked up at him. "I don't blame them for wanting to be outside. The heat is oppressive in here."

Rork nodded and smiled. "Still keen on volunteering, Miss Hancock?"

"More than ever. I think Dr. Smith and his staff offer an invaluable service to the public, and I want to be a part of it."

Leila sighed. "He said there had been attacks on many folks of color. I don't understand such hatred."

"I know it's terrible. Dr. Smith has seen his fair share of hatred." Cornelia glanced at the doctor feeding a young boy.

Leila fanned her face with the sweat-soaked handkerchief. Exhaustion got the better of her. She gazed at the children with longing. When she first married Hank, she'd dreamed of having children, but Hank crushed that dream.

A hand rested on her shoulder, jolting her from her sad thoughts.

"Are you all right, Mrs. Dempsey?" Dr. Smith asked, sinking into the chair opposite. He looked at Cornelia. "You also look pale, my dear."

Cornelia smiled. "I'm quite fine. Thank you."

Leila lay back on the couch. "We're just tired."

"You look rather flushed, Mrs. Dempsey." Dr. Smith patted her hands, clasped in her lap.

"No need to worry about me. Are we safe here, Dr. Smith?" Leila asked.

"I don't know. I heard reports of riots all over the city. I pray we don't become a target."

"Why would anyone do such a thing?"

"I suppose they see this war as the fault of colored folk. Other than that, not much is clear to me. I don't know why people do the things they do." Dr. Smith shook his head, his lips pressed into a hard line. "Come, we have work to do."

The sound of breaking glass echoed through the hallway. A scream followed.

Rork grabbed Leila's arm as a rock sailed through the window, hitting the wall near her head. He dropped to the floor, taking her with him. She fell to her knees, shielded by his massive frame.

Dr. Smith pulled Cornelia down and crawled to the broken window and peered out. "My God!"

They all scrambled to the window on their knees and peered over the sill. Leila suppressed a cry.

A mob surrounded the orphanage. People crawled over the high wall, shouting, wielding torches, and throwing rocks as they stormed the building.

"What do we do?" Leila trembled.

"Gather the children. We must get them out," Dr. Smith yelled. Hunched over, he ran to them. Cornelia followed.

Leila, hand clasped to her mouth, watched more people crawl over the wall.

Rork shook her. "They mean to set the building on fire. We must get the children out."

"Yes, of course." She jumped to her feet. "Oh God, there are too few of us. We'll never get them all out," she sobbed.

"Leila," Rork said. "Look at me." She met his steady eyes. "Breathe, calm down. You don't want to instill fear in the children."

Rork's deep, calm voice steadied her. Acrid smoke filled the hall.

"They've set fire to the building."

"Leila, let's go. Get the children out."

Shards from shattered windows lay on the floor. Thick smoke billowed around them.

Rork got down. "Crawl, follow me."

She crawled. *Keep calm.* Chills ran up her back.

She held her head down with the children close behind. Smoke filled her view, and tears ran from her eyes.

The crackle of paint pierced her ears.

"Keep down. Keep moving," Rork shouted. "Head for the stairs." A child clung to his neck, two under each arm. "Hold tight."

The glass fell from broken windows as Leila clasped crying children. Flames blocked their way. "Rork, look," she croaked, smoke clawing at her throat.

"Damn. This way."

Crawling, she pushed ahead. Children followed.

A child emerged with a bloodied forehead.

Leila said, "Child, here, now!" She turned to Rork's ghostly figure.

"Leila, move!"

A boy ran past, screaming. Rork reached out and grabbed his tattered shirt. He held onto the wriggling child. "Hang on," Rork hollered.

The boy nodded, his mouth quivering.

"Hurry!"

The boy wet his lips. "I'm scared."

"We'll be safe!" Leila shouted.

"Stay together," Rork ordered.

They stood and raced downstairs. They reached ground level with three more children.

"Keep together. Crawl."

The smoke grew thicker.

Children's fearful faces wet with tears. They coughed and gasped for air.

Rork hollered above the roar, "Get to that door!"

The injured girl wound her arms around Leila's neck, weeping. Rork turned to Leila, who crouched low beside him. "When we get near the door, run like hell."

She nodded.

Rork coughed. "Run when you hear three."

"Yes," Leila said in a muffled voice.

"One, two, three!" Rork jumped up.

Leila followed with her charges and raced through the smoke. She hoped freedom and fresh air were close.

"Keep together!" Rork yelled. Children stumbled. He opened a wooden door, and smoke billowed in. "Drop to the ground!" he growled.

Leila crouched, her heart thundering in her ears. She moved forward, cursing the long skirt.

"Get down, move," Leila said, her throat burning.

An eternity passed. They reached the end of the narrow hallway. Leila looked back to ensure they were all together and silently prayed they would make it out.

Fire crackled and hissed.

Something slammed onto the floor behind them. Leila and the children screamed. A burning beam had fallen and sent sparks flying, missing them by inches.

"Go!" Rork roared. "For God's sake, hurry! The entire roof is about to cave in!"

Rork scooped up children.

Leila did the same with strength she didn't know she had. "Hurry, we're close," she said, her throat sore and tight. She stumbled through the burning debris, heading for the open door. Leila fought for air, her throat and eyes afire.

The doctor and his staff appeared from the murky surroundings and took the children from them. "We need to get out of here. Take cover behind the shrubbery. We don't want them to see us."

Once outside, Rork ran to the bushes and dropped to one knee. Leila followed him, brushing tangled hair from her face. He laughed. "You look like a chimney sweep."

"So do you." They laughed out loud.

She looked around and stared at Rork. "Where is Cornelia?"

CHAPTER ELEVEN

"*C*ornelia's with the children, behind Dr. Smith."

Rork ignored the churning in his stomach and kept to the shrubbery's shadows, scanning the chaotic scene, backlit by orange and blue flames. Rain-filled clouds hovered high in the sky over the burning building.

"Listen, Rork. The fire trucks—Oh God, I pray they save the building."

Rork held Leila's arm. "Can you make it to the gate?"

"Yes. How can these men be so cruel?" Leila cried.

Rork stayed low, avoiding the crowd. "Mobs turn into vicious beasts, losing direction and control."

A short distance away, Dr. Smith, Cornelia, and the staff urged frightened children away from the conflict.

Rork and Leila hurried to them. He looked back. Flames leaped high, seeming to touch the underbelly of the roiling storm clouds, like a scene from hell.

"We need to get the children further away before the crowd attacks us," Dr. Smith said, running a hand over his soot-stained face.

Rork narrowed his eyes as the mob surged toward them. "We'd better make it quick, wherever we take the children."

The mob closed in—the children screamed—an Irish bloke stepped out, and faced the angry crowd, his arms spread. His voice rang out above the uproar. "If there's a man among you with a heart, help these poor children."

"Ya damn turncoat!" a rioter yelled and brought a stick down on the brave man's shoulders. The mob fell on him.

"Bastards!" Rork roared and moved to help.

Dr. Smith grabbed his arm. "Don't do it. We must get the children away," he shouted above the noise.

"They'll beat him to death. I can't stand by and watch."

Dr. Smith took Rork's shoulders. "They will kill you and us and the children."

Rork's mouth tightened. "Fine, let's get the hell out of here!" Hurrying, they herded the children away from the orphanage. "Where will you take them?"

"Thirty-Fifth Street police station for now. I'll move them to the almshouse, their first home, on Blackwell's Island."

Except for the children's whimpers, they made a hasty retreat in silence. Rork kept his arm around Leila. The panicked whinnies and screams of distressed horses ripped into his head. The mob had surrounded the buggy and beat the horses. "Dear God, they have gone mad." The driver broke free and disappeared down the street.

At the station, they heard reports of atrocities committed around the city. A constable shook his head. "The mobs are killing colored folks. They're beating and burning the abolitionists and their homes. God knows where it will end." He shut the doors and guided them to the back of the station. "How many children do you have, Dr. Smith?" the officer asked.

He sank onto a bench. "Two hundred and thirty-three. We got them all, thanks to these good people." He glanced at Rork, Leila, and Cornelia. "I'll be ever grateful for your help. If not for your assistance, we would not have them all." He stood and took Cornelia's hand. "You were courageous, Miss Hancock. I know you'll be an asset to our orphanage if we rebuild."

Cornelia stared at the doctor. "We will rebuild. I have contacts. I'll ensure they donate to your cause."

Leila coughed and rubbed her eyebrows. "I will donate."

Rork patted her back. "We need to get to the hotel. News of the riots must have reached Hank by now. He'll be anxious."

Leila shook her head and mumbled, "I doubt it."

Rork turned to Cornelia. "Are you coming with us?"

"I need to fetch my luggage." She put her hand on Dr. Smith's arm. "I'll return after I've bathed and changed."

He hugged her. "Stay at the hotel. It isn't safe for you anywhere else. I'll get a message to you when we're at the almshouse."

"You need me."

"Thank you. I will reach out. The almshouse has limited accommodations."

"Very well."

"How can we get to our hotel?" Rork asked the officer.

He grinned. "If you don't mind riding in a prison carriage, I can get you there."

"All right, let's go."

Guests stared at the filthy, bedraggled trio disembarking from the police carriage.

They walked into the hotel foyer where Hank reached out, his eyes widened. "God's truth, Leila, what the hell have you been up to?"

Rork released her waist. "We got caught up in a riot. Leila braved the fear. She assisted in evacuating orphans from a burning building."

"Everyone assisted," Leila said, beyond exhausted and in no mood for a battle of words.

"Lord, Le-le, you're a mess."

Leila's head snapped around at the familiar voice. She balked at the useless nickname. Gritting her teeth, she shuddered and struggled to plaster a smile on her face. "Sissy, I thought you got off earlier?" My God, Leila hoped she would never have to see that sorceress again.

Sissy's eyes glittered with malice. She leaned against Hank. "This is not a private hotel."

Leila shrugged. "I thought you'd gone on to visit your cousin."

Sissy smirked. "I changed my mind. Has that upset you, honey?" She burst out laughing.

The high-pitched braying grated on Leila's shattered nerves. "I couldn't care less what you decide."

Sissy gazed up at Hank. "When I heard about the excursion west, I couldn't resist Hank's sweet offer to join. It will be such fun."

Hank blinked. "I also thought you were stopping in St. Louis to visit your cousin."

Sissy tapped his chin playfully with her fan. "It will be more fun going west."

Dear God, will I have to endure this woman the whole way west? Leila scowled at Hank, then Sissy. "Is trip out west your idea of fun? I doubt there will be any of the luxuries you enjoy."

"So, what, it's an opportunity for adventure." The words came out as if there were too many teeth crammed in her small mouth. She tossed her fiery red curls and pulled a lock of hair over her shoulder, enhancing her seductive pose.

Leila clasped her hands together, fighting the temptation to slap the smile from Sissy's face. Rork's gentle nudge drew her from the brink of violent action.

"I am equally surprised to see *you* embarking on this trip, Leila." Sissy leaned her head on Hank's shoulder. "You're also a creature of comfort." Her eyes swept a filthy and mussed Leila from head to toe. "Until now, I suppose." She brushed an imaginary speck from her green muslin dress. "Can't imagine why you would embroil yourself in a mission to rescue a bunch of wretched orphans. Colored ones, I suppose."

"Yes," Leila ground out.

"Lord above, gal, why bother?"

Cornelia gasped.

Leila clenched her teeth. "You never were particularly sympathetic to the plight of those less fortunate."

"No, but nor were you—or so I thought," Sissy sneered.

Leila's back stiffened. "You don't know me. And I don't care to continue this conversation."

Hank sliced the air with one hand. "Enough, both of you." He glared at Leila. "I can't abide catfights. I suggest you take yourself off to bathe and change."

A chill slid over Leila. She swallowed, her hand at her throat. Hank had invited Sissy. Can our marriage be salvaged?

Rork took her elbow. "I'll escort you to your suite." He stopped. "What number are you in, Hank?"

"Suite twenty-three. I booked you and Miss Hancock into suites flanking ours."

"I'll show you to yours, Mr. Millburn." Sissy caroled, malice dripping from her lips, slanting her eyes at Leila.

"Thank you, Miss Lanweihr. I can find my suite." He steered Leila and Cornelia from the foyer. Cornelia glanced at Leila. "Lord, I don't know how you keep your composure around that creature."

"With a great deal of difficulty," Leila said between clenched teeth.

Rork squeezed her arm against his side. "You were the perfect lady in the face of that strumpet's venom."

Cornelia shook her head. "You don't have to put up with Hank's flagrant affairs. Those two are alike."

Leila held up a grubby hand. "Please don't go there again, my dear friend."

"Here is your suite, Leila." Rork opened the door.

"Thank you, Mr. Millburn."

His smile lit his whole face. "Are we back to formalities?"

She nodded, escaped into her suite and closed the door. Pressing her back to it, she released a long breath. Tears fell. Leila brushed at them. "That damn Sissy nearly pushed me over the edge—to hell with her."

Rork leaned against a column close to Leila's suite.

She emerged, tugging at long cream gloves and smoothing her cream lace gown that fell in layers over her hoopless petticoat.

His eyes drifted to the low neckline of her dress and her bare shoulders, and his pulse rate soared. The overblown Sissy sailed into view. "That bitch is doubtless spoiling for another fight."

"Le-Le," she sang. "You look, ah, virginal, to say the least." She arched her eyebrows. "Where is your beau?"

Leila paled. "My what?"

Sissy flapped her fan. "Oh, my dear, no need to be coy. You're quite besotted with him."

Rork pushed away from the column. Time to intervene. He strode to Leila and bowed. "Good evening, Mrs. Dempsey. I must say you look lovely." He ignored Leila's tormentor.

Sissy tapped his arm with her fan and fluttered her lashes. "My, Mr. Millburn, you do look handsome and dashing in your dress suit." Her eyes swept him hungrily.

"Miss Lanweihr," Rork said. "I didn't notice you. Will you excuse us? Hank gave me a message for his wife. I am afraid it's private."

Sissy sniffed and lifted her chin, all but stamping her foot. "Certainly, Mr. Millburn." She glared at Leila and walked off.

Rork chuckled.

"What's so funny?"

"Seeing that woman's nasty remarks crushed."

Leila giggled. "Yes, rather satisfying."

He held Leila's gaze. "Why do you put up with Hank's philandering and that woman's insufferable insults?"

Her eyes skittered. She drew herself up to her full height. "Enough."

Rork moved closer. Heat radiated from her body, stirring desire in him. She turned her head aside, cheeks glowing. He longed to run his fingers down her neck to her bare shoulders. He fought his urge for her as his eyes caressed the soft swell of her bosom. "I would cherish you," he whispered.

"Please don't."

He smiled. "I can't help my growing feelings for you." She lifted her eyes—he lost himself in the deep blue depths framed by thick black lashes. "You are so beautiful. I want to replace that tragic look with laughter."

She turned to go.

He put a hand on her shoulder's smooth skin. He wanted to pull her into his arms and kiss her until she grew breathless with desire. "Please don't go. I promise to behave."

"Thank you."

He offered his arm. "Shall we join the others in the sitting room?"

"I suppose." She slipped a small gloved hand into the crook of his arm.

"Why does she call you Le-Le?"

"I hate it when she calls me that."

"It's not the most flattering nickname. But I'm curious, why does she call you that?"

"I suppose because she knows I hate it." Leila shrugged. "She's called me that since school. A prig then, she is a prig now. Nothing has changed."

Rork cocked an eyebrow. "And that causes what Hank called a catfight?"

Leila's mouth quirked into a smile. "It might well have if she'd carried on. Sissy and I never got along. Even when we were children, I couldn't stand her. And the feeling is mutual."

"I didn't realize you've known each other from childhood. Why tolerate her flirting with Hank?" Pain flittered across her face, and he instantly regretted asking.

"Sissy flirts with every man. Even at school, she enjoyed the challenge of stealing beaus from other girls." She laughed with disdain in her voice. "I don't know if she would stoop to stealing husbands, but she's working on mine."

His mouth tightened. Is Leila that naive and unaware that Hank's association with Sissy has gone beyond a mere flirtation? "Has she always been a coquette?"

"Cornelia will tell you how appalling Sissy is. She has always been a spoiled, selfish brat." Leila smoothed invisible creases from her skirt and glanced up. "Please don't look at me like that. I don't need your pity."

"Sissy hasn't changed one whit since her youth."

He scowled. "I don't understand why anyone tolerates her— including Hank. The woman has fewer brains than a peahen."

Leila blushed. "There are many reasons men tolerate Sissy Lanweihr."

He laughed. "I'll wager it has nothing to do with intelligence or personality and everything to do with her overblown assets and loose morals."

Leila shrugged. "Men can't seem to resist her, ah, charms."

Rork snorted. "That's certainly one way to put it."

Leila's blush deepened, and she cleared her throat. "Was my husband honestly looking for me?"

"Would it make you happy if he were?"

"Of course, it would, but please stop taunting me, Mr. Millburn." She stared at the floor.

"I'm not taunting you. I want to know how you feel. It must be difficult to endure your husband's rudeness and his mistress' mockery."

Her eyes flew up, and she stared at him, her mouth trembling. "M-mistress?"

Rork bit the inside of his cheek. Damn, have I gone too far? But he wasn't going to back down. She deserves better. "I'm sorry to be so blunt, but can't you see what's going on?" He stopped and took her shoulders. "Why, Leila? Why put up with this?"

She shook her head. "No, what you say isn't true. I went into my marriage, thinking it would be forever. You say, a message from Hank?"

"No. You looked like you distressed."

Leila fiddled with the pearls around her neck. "Was I that obvious?"

"Yes. I can't blame you though. I'd be uncomfortable with Sissy's spiteful comments."

"I'm obliged. Losing my temper at Sissy is the worst. She's like a wild animal when she smells weakness. Why do *you* dislike her?"

Rork shrugged. "She reminds me of a vulture."

Laughter bubbled from Leila's lips. 'Vulture' that's her."

He grinned and touched her cheek. His heart tripped. "At least I made you smile."

"Yes, you did." Their eyes locked.

CHAPTER TWELVE

*R*ork reeled from alcohol and fatigue. He skirted his way past the tables set for breakfast in the deserted dining room. Hank had droned on about their trip west for hours in the hotel bar, while Sissy clung to Hank like a limpet. *What made me think I could stop Hank from cheating? Why the hell am I stopping him?*

Rork staggered against a hallway wall. He needed time to think. The quiet boomed in his ears. *I only have to sniff in Sissy's direction, and she'd open her legs for me, too. Damn, those two are poor excuses for human beings.*

A door creaked. Rork squinted in the dim light of lanterns on the passage wall—he'd recognize Leila's scent anywhere. He stopped and waited for her approach. *Why is she out and about? No doubt searching for her carousing husband.* He couldn't let her find Hank with Sissy. *The knowledge of an unfaithful husband is one thing, but quite a different matter catching him with his pants down. He had to stop her.*

"Leila."

She drew a sharp breath. "Good heavens, Mr. Millburn, you startled me." She sidestepped him.

Rork moved in front of her. "You shouldn't be wandering about at this time of night."

Leila took another step sideways, and again Rork blocked her.

"Mr. Millburn, I don't know what your problem is. Since you're here, have you seen my husband?"

"I saw him earlier. Perhaps you should go back to your suite and wait for him. Allow me to accompany you."

"No, thank you, he could be in the smoking room." Leila's forehead furrowed. She tried to squeeze past him.

"I cannot allow you to walk alone," Rork pointed his index finger at her and spoke in a sharp tone.

"*Allow* me?" Leila's voice rose an octave. "Thank you for your concern. I'm sure the hotel is secure."

"People will talk if they see you alone."

"What others say about me is irrelevant." A smile tweaked her lips. "Besides, wouldn't that raise questions about you and me together at this hour?"

He gripped her elbow as she tried again to pass him. He groaned as desire burgeoned.

Leila's eyes flared with passion. For an instant, she leaned into him, her body making solid contact.

Her scent consumed him. He bent, her face inches from his, her lips, plump and inviting. How would she taste? The question flooded his mind for the thousandth time since he'd met her.

Leila took a step back and stared at him for several moments. "Fine, if you insist, escort me to my suite."

Taking her elbow, he guided her to her door. He opened it, and Leila gave a brief nod, stepping inside. The door closed with a rebellious click. Rork interlaced his fingers and leaned against the opposite wall. Within moments, the door opened again.

"Why are you still here?" Leila planted her hands on her hips. A flush crept up her slender throat, turning her face the color of sunset before a storm.

"Making sure you don't wander about alone again." He didn't bother to suppress a grin.

"Are you my guardian now?" Her voice rose. "You have no right. If I want to be out at this time of night, it's none of your business."

"Hush." Rork slid his hands around her waist and pulled her body against his. He dipped his head and took her mouth hungrily. Her body went rigid, and her lips sealed shut. He gently ran his tongue over her lips. They parted and let him in, her body sinking into his. A groan resonated in Rork's throat. Leila's hands crept up, flattening against his chest. His hands fisted in her loose hair, gently pulling her head back, giving him greater access.

Abruptly, she pushed him away. "What are you doing?"

"This is what we both want, Leila," Rork whispered in a hoarse voice, pulling her back.

"No, Rork. This is wrong."

Rork. She called him by his first name. It sounded sweet. He longed to hear it again. "You cannot deny what's between us. It's been there since the brook incident."

"Oh, Rork." The words purred from her lips.

His heart swelled, and his breath caught in his throat. He pushed Leila back into her suite, not caring about anything except the woman in his arms. Kicking the door shut, he turned, pressing her against it. "God, I want you so." He crushed her to him and sought her lips again.

Leila jerked her head aside and delivered a stinging slap to his cheek. "I'm married, Mr. Millburn. Take your hands off me."

"Leila, please."

"Go."

His elation vanished. "If this is what you want, Leila . . ." He released her.

She backed away until a chaise longue stopped her. She

scooted around it, creating a shield between them. "Leave now, Mr. Millburn."

Rork studied her. Her lips still swollen from his kiss and her chest heaving with agitation stirred something new in his heart. Disappointment curdled in the pit of his stomach, crawling upward through his body. *How could I have been so stupid to think she would want me?* Turning on his heel, he headed for the door. *If she wanted him to leave, he'd leave. Don't go—don't leave her.* He stopped, arms slack at his side. "Don't deny yourself, Leila. He isn't worth it. He doesn't deny himself."

She drew a sharp breath. "What do you mean?"

Rork didn't want to face her and risk seeing her tears. But he did. Their eyes connected. "I'm talking about Hank."

"I know you are. What are you accusing him of?" Her voice shook.

"He doesn't honor your marriage vows."

"Hank might not, but I do. He may not deserve my loyalty, but I pledged it to him. I will not break that vow." Her words rang with conviction.

Rork's shoulders sagged. "It won't happen again." He opened the door and stepped into the dark hall. *If she wants to find Hank with Sissy, so be it.* He strode away.

Hank stared at Sissy through a hasheesh and alcohol-induced haze. He blinked rapidly to clear the vision of red hair and redder lips.

Her hand came up to stroke his face.

He squeaked and stumbled back onto a barstool, hands up to ward off the threat.

"What're you doing, woman?" Panic gripped him. The walls closed in, the roof came down like an iron claw, and lamps flickered like satanic tongues. "I have to get out."

"God, Hank, what's the matter with you?" She tossed her hair and pouted. "Too much of your so-called substance?"

"Don't you start on me," he growled. "I need to write—got an idea." He staggered from the bar.

Sissy hurried after him and grabbed his arm. "Better come to my suite, Hank. That prissy wife of yours will throw a tantrum."

Nodding, he allowed her to lead him to her suite. He wove his way unsteadily into the sitting room and flopped onto a chaise longue, holding his head. He pulled a velvet box from his pocket, and tipped a few grains into his palm, and threw them on his tongue. "Whiskey—I need a drink," he mumbled.

Sissy filled a tumbler with a generous jigger of whiskey and handed it to him. Giggling, she sat on his lap and wrapped her arms around his neck. "I feel neglected. You haven't made love to me for days." She turned and straddled his lap. Her mouth tensed at his lack of response. "What's wrong with you? I'll arouse you." She slipped off his lap and knelt, fumbling with his fly.

"Stop!" He thrust her away and sent her tumbling onto her back. Jerking to his feet, he threw the glass across the room. "What is it with you damn women? You bitch, keep your miserly mouth off me." He ranged the room, plucking at his messy hair, eyes darting about. The curtains moved, and he screamed. "What the hell was that?"

Sissy ran to him and threw her arms around him. "Lordy, must you take that remedy? It gives you daytime nightmares. The window is open, that's all."

"Get away from me!" His arms flailed, and his signet ring glanced off her temple, leaving a bloody streak. She cried out, fell to the ground, and scrambled away from him.

"Hank, stop!"

Sweat beaded his face, and he trembled, staggered to a writing desk, and ripped open a drawer. "Paper, I need paper— need to write." He clutched his chest to still his racing heart.

Shaking uncontrollably, he poured another whiskey and took a vial from his pocket. He tipped a few grains into the amber liquid, swallowed it in one gulp, and sagged into a chair. He dropped his head onto the writing desk. Slowly, calm washed through him. He breathed a sigh of relief and drew a pen from his pocket. He ran one finger reverently over the carved bone handle and touched the metal nib.

Sissy stood slowly. "Are you feeling better now?"

He nodded and dipped his pen into a bottle of ink. Pressing his palm to the warm, comforting paper, he sighed again. He wrote rapidly, the brilliant hallucinations of his mind flowing from the tip in a flowery script.

Sissy stood behind him, pressing her pelvis against him and massaging his shoulders.

Oblivious to her overtures, Hank pulled out a second sheet and wrote with frantic haste. Sissy's exotic perfume invaded his heightened sense. He stopped—pen poised. A drop of ink fell and spread on the paper. Slamming the pen down and spattering ink across the paper, he jumped up and pulled Sissy roughly into his arms. "Now—I need you now!"

She giggled as he dragged her to the chaise longue, tearing at her dress to gain access to her voluptuous curves.

As quickly as his lust ignited, it disappeared, and his fury erupted. With a growl, he struck Sissy across the face.

With a yelp, she brought a hand up to her reddened cheek.

"You bitch, you're responsible for my lack. This-this failure to-to perform." A cry from across the room brought his head around. He tried to focus through a veil of anger and substance.

"Leila?"

Sissy giggled and pulled his head back to face her. "Let the prissy bitch watch. Maybe she'll learn something."

Uncontrolled rage erupted in Hank. He jumped up and thrust Sissy aside roughly. She squealed, landing on the floor in a flurry of crimson silk and lace.

Hank fumbled with his fly. The buttons finally united. He turned to reprimand Leila, but he stopped, trapped in the innocence of her wide eyes.

Leila pressed a fist to her middle. Her other hand fluttered to her chest, and her mouth opened and shut. "I came to find out if Sissy knew where you were. I-I went to the bar and couldn't find you. I worried you might have gone out for a walk and met up with the rioters or-or something."

Her stricken eyes went to Sissy. I thought I heard Hank yelling, and you did not hear my knock. She turned to Hank. "How could you, Hank? How could you betray me? How could you defile our marriage?" A sob caught in her throat.

Sissy scrambled to her feet and burst into peals of laughter. "And how dare you barge into my room? You stupid bitch. What makes you think Hank would want an ineffectual milksop like you?"

The veins in his head were fit to burst. He brought his arm up, slamming the back of his hand across her cheek. Her head snapped to one side. He shoved at her chest and sent her plummeting to the floor again. "Shut up. Shut the hell up, Sissy!"

With a sob, Leila spun in a flurry of Chantilly lace, the peignoir swirling around her legs, seeking her escape.

"Leila, wait. I can explain!" He stumbled after her, stomach cramping and heart pounding. His world spun, and his legs refused to move cohesively. He reached their suite and tore the door open.

Leila stood with her back to him, head bowed, and shoulders jerking as she sobbed.

He approached slowly, shaking his head to clear the buzzing in his ears. "I'm sorry, but I can explain."

"How could you, Hank?"

Again, fury invaded his brain. "What do you expect? You're bloody frigid. You aren't even a damn wife!"

She turned, and the truth in her eyes mocked him.

Somewhere in his soul, a glimmer of humanity and reason remained. The fault lay with him. "Stop looking at me like that."

"Shocking words from Mr. Millburn, Sissy is your mistress. Intolerable."

A chill of betrayal settled on him. "Millburn said that?"

"I refused to believe him. I'm such a fool."

"That sneaky son of a bitch!" Hank slammed his fist on the table, shattering the legs. Hands clenched, he advanced on her, emotion clogging his throat and pain shooting through his temples. "So, has he had the pleasure of taking your precious maidenhead?"

"How dare you!" Her hand shot up, and her palm connected with his cheek.

He lifted his lip in a sneer. "Hit a nerve, have I? Traitorous bitch." He lifted his arm. "I'll kill you." A large hand clamped around his wrist, holding it in a vise grip. Rork's deep voice burned into his brain, fanning the flames of his wrath.

"Enough, Hank!"

He turned, still in the iron grip. "You bastard, you violated my wife!"

Rork's nostrils flared. "I've done nothing of the sort. You need to calm down and go to bed."

Cramps beset Hank's gut, and he wanted to vomit. "You betrayed me!"

"You betrayed yourself." He lifted Hank by his lapels and hustled him into the bedchamber, throwing him onto the tester bed. "Sleep it off." Spinning on his heel, he strode out.

Hank shot up and raced after him. The door to the suite slammed shut, and Hank turned his head, glaring at Leila. "Your lover is too much of a coward to stand and fight."

"I want a divorce."

Hank gaped. Her father hadn't yet released all of her finances. Could the old bastard legally withhold the money if she insists on divorce? "You want what?"

"You heard me," she said in a voice somewhere outside herself.

He stared at her. Indifference and determination had supplanted her tender love. This can't be happening. He ran his tongue over parched lips. "I won't give you a divorce."

She squared her shoulders and stared into his empty eyes. "Why ever not? You don't love me. I've had enough of your philandering and drinking—not to mention all the remedies."

"Those were for the pain and this incessant cough I suffer." He had to stop her from filing for divorce. "Please, Leila, I don't want to lose you."

She sagged into a chair and waved her hand at him, her eyes half-closed. "Go back to your mistress."

Hank pressed his palms against his temples. His head throbbed. "I'm going to kill Millburn!"

Her eyes flew open. "Do nothing stupid, Hank. He has nothing to do with my decision. I decided weeks ago our marriage is over."

"I need to sleep." He turned and stumbled to the bedchamber. His last thought before passing out—Millburn would pay for his betrayal.

CHAPTER THIRTEEN

*L*eila stared at the door through tear-filled eyes, one hand pressed to her lips, the other to her stomach. A sliver of moonlight crossed the floor, creating shadow shapes of wolves. The night chills crawled up Leila's legs. She pulled her nightgown tighter around her body and leaned on the wall.

Hank's snores came from his bedchamber and hung in the air. The image of Sissy's legs wrapped around Hank burned into her mind. *He betrayed me in the vilest way. But I kissed Rork.* A door opened and closed down the hall, snapping Leila out of her stupor. Her stomach churned.

Footsteps echoed in the passage.

Her breath caught in her throat. She counted the steps, matching her breaths to the heavy tread drawing closer. She could still smell Rork on her skin—a combination of earthy pine, cigar smoke, and something male that sent shivers between her thighs.

Hank always reeked of alcohol and the sickly-sweet odor of hasheesh. She closed her eyes. *How many times has he come* tainted with the perfume of his women? How many times have I ignored the truth?

I had honor—honor that dissolved the moment Rork's lips touched mine. She wanted to wrap her arms around Rork, press her body to his.

The footsteps stopped. If it is Rork, what will I do? Dear God, I don't have the strength to refuse him again. She yearned for the heat that penetrated her with the brush of his hand. She knew she wouldn't be able to deny him. Wide-eyed, she stared at the door and held her breath. Seconds ticked by, a gasp trapped in her throat, her heart squeezed in a vise. Tempted to open the door, she waited—she listened.

Nothing.

The footsteps retreated.

She slid down the wall in a crumpled heap. Alone. So alone.

Late afternoon, Hank, still in his pants and shirt, woke from a troubled sleep and looked around. He dropped his head as though it were too heavy to hold up and groaned. "God, I feel like crap." He struggled through a quagmire of images of the night before and slipped from the bed. "I need a drink." He stumbled through to an empty sitting room and poured a tumbler of whiskey, tipped a few grains into the amber liquid, and swallowed the contents in one gulp. He shivered.

Sagging into an armchair, he pinched the bridge of his nose. "Damn, Leila caught me with Sissy." Throwing back his head, he glared at dancing prisms of light from the gas-lit chandelier. "Rork. It's that bastard's fault. He poisoned Leila's mind. If she divorces me, that miserable father of hers will withhold the money."

He slammed his fist on the arm of the chair and lurched to his feet. He walked with uneven steps to the bedchamber, rummaged around in his valise, and withdrew a pistol. "I'll kill Rork, that traitorous son of a bitch!"

Hank staggered to Rork's suite. Empty. The smoking-room, the bar. "Where is the bastard?"

He searched the street and spied Rork in the distance, walking up Broadway. Hank picked up the pace and grabbed Rork's shoulder from behind. "Got you."

Rork turned, his pistol drawn. His eyes narrowed in the fading light. "Hank, what are you doing? I could have killed you." He shook the gun in Hank's face. "Never do that again." He slipped the weapon into his pocket. "What ails you, Hank?"

"Like you don't know," Hank snarled. "You betrayed me and turned my wife against me. Now she wants a damn divorce."

"Let's talk."

"I don't fraternize with my enemies."

"What is with you, Hank? Be realistic. You play around and expect your wife to ignore it. It doesn't work like that."

Hank buckled, coughing uncontrollably. He recovered and glared at Rork. "You're responsible."

"Responsible for what?"

"Divorce, she wants a divorce. You had no damn right interfering in our marriage."

Rork brushed dust off his lightweight coat. "I don't know what you're talking about."

Revulsion welled up in Hank's soul, and he laughed, choking from the bile in his throat. "You want her for yourself. I'm not blind, nor am I a fool. I've seen the way you moon after her."

"You don't know what you're talking about–Leila isn't stupid. You blatantly flirt with other women and speak to Leila like she's dirt."

"I had a happy wife before you showed up."

"You cannot seriously believe she had no awareness of your philandering. And she sure as hell wasn't happy. Did you forget your obnoxious behavior at the Mountain House? Why couldn't you give her a minute to talk? You demean and insult her in front of anyone and everyone. Not to mention the alcohol and substance you consume."

"My medication is none of your business."

Rork sighed and shook his head. "Are you stupid? Your alcohol and hasheesh habits are the root of your problems."

"Crap. And my wife's happiness or the way I deal with her is not your goddamn business. Why the hell did you have to complicate things?"

"You're delusional. And you're a fool, Hank. Haven't you noticed your wife's misery?"

"Leila miserable? What the hell are you talking about?"

God, did she tell him we didn't consummate our marriage?

"She has no idea how to cope with what you do, and it frustrates her. Your flaunting Sissy in her face and not giving a damn how she feels is the ultimate insult. You've mistreated her over and over."

Hank stared at the sun sinking behind buildings and the dark cumulus clouds. *Nobody takes me, the great Hank Dempsey, to task.* He blew out his cheeks and rolled his eyes. He had to tilt his head up to look at Rork, and that enraged him even more. Drawing himself up to his full height, he stood inches from Rork. "I treat her just fine. She has everything she ever wanted."

"You forget she's even your wife. You're blinded by your own desires, a blustering idiot with no concept of how to value a fine woman."

Hank stared at the angry, sneering face before him. All reason fled, and blood pounded in his head. He pulled a pistol from his pocket and stepped back, firing blindly.

Rork groaned, blood blooming on his white shirt.

A woman screamed, and people ran down the street, away from the scene.

Hank couldn't breathe. He dropped the pistol, clutched his

chest, and dropped to his knees. *Oh, God. What now?* He glanced up at the people surrounding them.

"Has someone fetched an ambulance . . . the police?" screamed a bystander.

"Yes," said another.

Head hanging, Hank covered his ears to drown out the clanging bells of the ambulance. Rork was right. I am a blustering idiot. I better get the hell out of here. A dull ache throbbed in his head—an ache that would soon turn to blind pain.

He picked up his pistol, stumbled to his feet, and ran without looking back until he found a familiar place. He ducked into the doorway and leaned against the wall, panting. Screw Rork. I hope the bastard dies. Sweat slid down his face, back, and between his legs. His tongue felt as thick as a water-filled sponge. He gripped the railing and dragged himself up the stairs and doubled over as nausea climbed up his throat. His stomach heaved, and he retched on his shoes. The thick vomit puddled at his feet in the narrow stairwell. He gagged at the reek of vomit, slipping on it as he stumbled up the stairs, and banged on the first door. He gritted his teeth at the sound of giggles piercing his ears. He rattled the handle. "Come on, bitches, it's Hank. Open the damn door."

The door flew open, and two girls grabbed Hank's arms, pulling him into the perfumed boudoir draped in red velvet. They released him and sent him stumbling, pinching their noses. "My God, Hank, what in the world ya been up to?"

He fell and rolled onto his backside and stared at them. "I-I'm in trouble."

A redhead put her hands-on voluptuous hips. "Didn't know anythin' could touch the mighty Hank Dempsey." She giggled and glanced at her equally curvaceous blonde friend.

The blonde wrinkled her nose. "Ya stink, me fine cockerel." Without waiting for a response, they ripped off his shoes and tossed them in a corner. Amid squeals of glee, they stripped him of his clothes and any dignity he had left.

"Back off, you stupid tarts!"

"Hank, where ya been, and what trouble ya in?" The blonde picked up his clothes using two fingers and held them out—her face screwed up in disgust.

Clutching his genitals and trembling with cold, he choked on his breath. "Bath, I need a bath. I don't feel so good."

The redhead brought buckets of water and prepared his bath in a tin tub. "C'mon, darlin', get ya ass in here."

The blonde tugged his arm. "It's a real smart idea to sit. Ya look like ya is goin' to have a heart attack."

Hank tested the water. "It's hot," he whined.

"Ah, don't be a damn milksop. Get in there." The redhead gave him a shove.

Too weak to argue, he stepped into the tub and lowered himself gingerly. He hung his feet over the edge, dunked his head, and closed his eyes. The blonde sponged his chest. "There, ya feelin' better now?" Nausea left him, but what he'd done stuck in his throat, as though he had swallowed shattered glass chips.

Hank gave them his brightest smile. "You've both been gems. I need to leave the city, but I can't go without Sissy. Think you can help me out with fetching her? She's at the St. Nicholas Hotel."

The redhead twisted her mouth. "You still messin' with that tart disguised as a lady?"

"Watch your damn mouth."

She threw up her hands. "Fine, I'll fetch the bitch."

"And tell her to pack our clothes." Hank pinched the bridge of his nose. *Crap, I hope she doesn't run into Leila.*

The whore slid into the hotel foyer and smoothed her mauve satin dress with nicotine-stained fingers. She scanned the opulent surroundings.

Light from the chandeliers gleamed on the manager's black patent-leather hair as he glided to her, mouth pinched and eyes steely. Blocking her advance, he clasped bony fingers behind his back and looked down his long nose. "How may I assist you, ah, madam?"

She tucked a red curl behind her ear, eyes darting. "What room is Sissy Lanweihr occupyin'?" she rasped.

He sniffed and flicked a speck of imaginary dust off his perfect jacket. "We do not reveal our guests' room numbers. Wait here." He eyed her imperiously, daring her to take another step on his pristine marble floor. "I will locate Miss Lanweihr. Can't imagine she knows you." He spun on his heel and sailed up the ornate stairway.

She pouted scarlet lips and flipped up her hand, making an obscene gesture. "Make it snappy."

Eyebrows raised, guests gave her a wide berth, husbands shielding their wives and children.

She snorted and tossed her tangle of red curls. "Straightlaced pricks." She flipped her tongue at an elderly gentleman steering his wife away from contamination. "Want me to help ya get it up for the old lady, gramps?"

They gasped and hurried out of sight.

Sissy appeared, chin held high as she sashayed down the stairs, the train of her dress elegantly brushing the steps behind. The manager followed close on her heels. He hovered as Sissy stopped in front of the whore. "What could you possibly wish to discuss with me, woman?"

"Hank Dempsey be in trouble and askin' for ya."

Sissy gasped, and her eyes widened. "What's wrong?" The whore glanced at the manager. Her painted eyebrows dipping. "Tell the watchdog to get his ass out of here."

Sissy sighed and nodded at the manager.

"Are you sure, Miss Lanweihr?"

The whore flapped a hand at him. "Just piss off like the lady says, ya little prick."

Sissy gave him a sweet smile. "I'm sure I'll be fine. Thank you."

He bowed and walked off.

The whore sniggered. "Gawd strike me blind. Ya could freeze burnin' coal on his ass." She ran the back of her hand under a pert nose and sniffed. "Hank said to tell ya to pack up yer things an' his and come with me. He ain't far from here."

"Why all the mystery?"

"I ain't no mind reader. I'm sure he'll tell ya. Just move yer ass. How long will it take ya to pack? I ain't got all day, ya know. I'm a-workin' gal."

"I'll only take a few moments. Wait outside." She turned to a porter. "Please come to my suite in fifteen minutes."

"Yes, ma'am."

Leila took a last look in the mirror and adjusted her coiffure—she glanced at the rumpled bedding through the open the door to his bedchamber. Hank had disappeared again. She would see Rork at dinner. Her belly fluttered, and she stepped out of her room, running into Sissy. "If you're looking for Hank, he isn't here," Leila hissed.

Sissy's eyes narrowed to slits. "Not surprising, after your little display of hysterics this morning." She tossed her head. "However, I am not looking for him."

"Where is he?"

"Wouldn't you like to know?" Sissy's lips lifted in a feral sneer.

"I would not." Leila clenched her hands and gritted her teeth. Her fingers itched to slap Sissy's smug face. "I couldn't care less what he's up to." She tilted up her nose. "Or you." Disdain dripped from her words. "I have never met such vulgar individuals as you and Hank."

"I'm warning you, shut the hell up!"

Leila kept her smile plastered to her face. "Or what?"

"Or I'll slap you."

Leila laughed. "Your veneer of gentility is thin." Her blood boiled, but she kept her poise. "You're a liar and no better than a common whore. You've always been a liar, sleeping with my husband while pretending to be my friend. I never liked you, Sissy, but I didn't think even you would stoop that low."

Sissy snarled, and a slap reverberated in the empty passageway.

Leila's head snapped to the side. Lights exploded in her head, and her cheek burned. Don't react. Keep calm.

Sissy shoved past her. "You're a damn cold fish. No wonder Hank doesn't want to screw you."

Leila walked back into her suite. She splashed cold water on her reddened cheek and patted her face dry. She smoothed her blue brocade off-the-shoulder gown. They deserve each other. A knock sounded on the door, and she jumped. "W-who is it?"

"The manager, Partridge. Might I have a word, Mrs. Dempsey? It's about Mr. Millburn."

Dread crept over Leila. Premonition chilled her heart.

CHAPTER FOURTEEN

*C*omposing herself, Leila opened the door and stared at Partridge.

"Somebody shot Mr. Millburn. He is in the Hospital for the Ruptured and Crippled."

She took in a deep breath and placed a hand on her chest. "Oh, my heavens, is he going to be all right?" She quickly wiped away the tear that crept from her eye. He peered past her. "Is your husband here?"

"No."

"I looked for him in the, ah, saloon, but they haven't seen him."

Leila scowled. "I'm sure I can deal with the problem. They need what?"

"I don't have any details, but they cannot keep Mr. Millburn at the infirmary. The facilities are inadequate. They asked if someone could fetch him."

Leila furrowed her brow. "How bad is he?"

"I couldn't tell you."

"I shall go to him at once." Leila's heart pounded, and her

knees turned to butter. "Please arrange for a doctor to attend him when we return."

"Madam." He bowed and backed away. "A woman of questionable character visited asking for Miss Lanweihr." He flushed and smoothed his jacket.

"How is that relevant to me?"

He coughed lightly. "I overheard the woman tell Miss Lanweihr to pack your husband's clothes and meet him."

Heat crept into Leila's cheeks. "What my husband does is his affair." She avoided the compassion in his eyes.

"Of course, but I'll be discreet. I shall also arrange for a carriage to meet you at the door." He bowed again and slipped from the room.

She studied her face in the mirror. The beginnings of a bruise marred her cheek. She opened an armoire and chose a black hat with a veil. Throwing a cape over her shoulders, she donned the hat, drew the veil over her face, and walked out, her heels echoing in the passage. Candle flames wavered in brass wall sconces as she headed for the stairs.

She swept through the crowded lobby and stepped into the carriage waiting in the porte-cochère. *I wish Cornelia were here.* The carriage rumbled over rough cobblestones, jolting Leila against the side. *Please, God, let him live.* She pressed trembling fingers to her temples to stop the buzzing in her head.

The carriage drew to a jarring halt at the infirmary. Leila adjusted the veil, ensuring it covered her face, opened the door, and stepped out. She stared at the imposing four-story building and slowly mounted the stairs to an open door. The odors of ether, blood, and unwashed bodies assailed her senses. She pressed a scented handkerchief to her nose and looked around the emergency room.

Depressing green walls closed in on her. Ragged children sat huddled on benches. A toddler with a bloodied rag tied around her head wept. Temperatures soared outside, but a small boy sat on a bench, his teeth chattering. Gasoliers offered a soft, warm light to the atmosphere.

Leila's footsteps echoed on the wooden floor as she approached the nurses' station.

"Excuse me." A nurse looked up with a glary, haughty stare, and Leila tightened the hold on her reticule. "Where will I find Mr. Millburn?"

"I cannot give out that information, madam. May I ask who you are?"

"I'm a close friend."

She consulted a sheet of paper. "I see admissions called a Mr. Dempsey."

"He isn't available." Leila lifted her chin.

"We don't take adults. We cannot keep Mr. Millburn overnight."

The nurse reminded Leila of her youth and the academy's teachers—cold, callous, and uncaring. *My heavens, a pathetic nurse, indeed. I must get Rork out of here.*

"I'm aware of that. Is he able to come back to the hotel?"

"Does he not have a relative we could contact?"

Nerves stretched to the limit, and losing patience, Leila leaned on the desk.

"I would not be here if he did. Now, may I please see him?"

The woman's mouth tightened. "Please take a seat. The doctor is tending to him."

Leila's mind raced. *What in the world happened to him? A street fight? Robbery? Hank?*

The nurse glared at Leila. "Wait over there." She waved at the crammed benches.

I'll get nowhere being high-handed. Leila smiled and her insides quivered. "Why aren't adults permitted in the infirmary?"

"It's a children's hospital. Dr. Knight is the chief surgeon. He donated his home for poor children in need of medical care."

"The hours must be taxing. I admire such dedication."

"Yes, they are."

"I have a friend who will train as a nurse."

The woman gave her a skeptical look.

"We helped Dr. Smith save the children from the burning orphanage. Draft rioters set it alight."

"You did?" The woman shook her head. "Nasty business, that. Why in the world attack defenseless children?"

"Terrifying." She waved a gloved hand in the general direction of the passageway.

"My friend, Rork Millburn, rescued the children and me."

"My, such bravery." The nurse lumbered to her feet.

"Let me see how things are going with him."

"Thank you." Leila released a breath. Within minutes, the woman returned.

"Follow me, dear."

"What's the prognosis?"

"I'm not sure, but I don't think the bullet hit any vital organs." She glanced at Leila. "Is he your beau?"

"Ah, yes."

"Don't get a fright when you see him."

Her heart jolted. Dear God, how bad is he?

A matron approached. "Your name, please, madam?" Leila bit her lip and fiddled with the wedding ring under her glove.

"Ah, Miss Ashburn."

The nurse chuckled. "He's her beau."

The matron nodded. "Nurse will take you to him." Walking along the endless corridor, the pounding in her ears grew louder and louder. A chill invaded her, as though she'd walked barefoot in the snow. She scrabbled in her reticule for a handkerchief and dabbed her eyes. The nurse ushered her into a room with four beds, and the hospital odors intensified.

"I'll leave you with him."

"Thank you." A single lamp cast a pool of yellow light. Hesitating at the door, Leila stared at an iron bed containing a figure covered in bloodstained sheets.

The nurse touched her arm. "Take courage, dear. He's alive." She turned and left.

Leila tripped on her skirt and stumbled to the bed. She leaned over Rork. Her heart ached to see his skin pale and the dark rings under his eyes. The doctor had swathed his right shoulder in bandages. With her trembling hands, she touched his rugged cheek.

"Leila?"

"You're alive."

"You're here. Now I am."

She nodded and shook her head.

He chuckled. "Yes or no? You look exhausted and frightened. Don't worry, I'm tough. I won't die."

"I am here to take you back to the hotel. They don't hospitalize adults here."

"Suits me." He tried to sit up.

"Please don't move. I'll see if I can find the doctor who treated you." The door opened, and she turned—relief flooded through her.

A tall, whiskered man in a white coat entered the room. "I see our patient is awake." He looked at Leila, his brown eyes twinkling. "Your husband had a lucky escape."

Leila opened her mouth to protest, but Rork chuckled and took her hand.

"I'm Dr. Knight. Luckily, the bullet passed through and through. The attacker shot him at close range."

"W-where is his attacker?"

"A passerby who ran to the hospital for help said the swine fled the scene."

"Did anyone identify him?" Leila asked in a raised tone.

"Not really. Witnesses said that his clothes were of fine quality, but he seemed intoxicated."

Rork squeezed her hand. "It doesn't matter, Leila."

She glanced at him. "Of course, it mat . . ." A warning look from Rork shut her up. "I suppose not. You are alive."

"The swine should be behind bars," Knight said, taking Rork's wrist. "His pulse is strong." He grinned. "I suspect a certain little lady has something to do with that."

Heat rose in Leila's cheeks. "Is it safe to take him to the hotel?"

"I'll send him in the ambulance. With care, he will recover well." He winked at her.

"Thank you for treating him, Dr. Knight. Can I offer a donation for your hospital?"

He beamed. "Most kind of you, my dear. We can use the money." He patted her arm. "Excuse me. I must tend to the children." He bowed and left.

Rork grinned. "So my betrothed, do I at least get a kiss?"

She laughed and sagged onto the bed. "You're incorrigible." He settled his hand on her hip. She jumped up. "Please, Rork, stop that." She felt the heat of his touch through the voluminous skirt and petticoats. Her belly flipped. "What happened, Rork? Did Hank shoot you?"

"Yes, but liquor controlled him and his actions. I doubt he knew what he was doing."

"Which is why you didn't press charges?"

He nodded.

Her admiration for Rork blossomed. "It makes you the better man."

He laughed. "I only did that because I didn't want you to live with the shame."

"Thank you."

Propped up on cushions at the hotel, Rork kept his eyes on the dark clouds moving apart for a speckle of sunlight into his room.

He enjoyed the challenge of painting skies where scenes vary from minute to minute, and skies have fifty shades of pink. The door opened. He feigned sleep, watching Leila through half-closed eyes. She came in with a tray of food. The light caught the metallic bronze highlights in her hair and outlined her exquisite profile. Desire for her consumed him.

She set down the tray as her eyes skittered from Rork's body, outlined under the blanket, to his face. Her cheek colored like a sunset. "You cad, you aren't asleep at all, and there's no question that you are feeling much better."

He laughed and grabbed her hand. "I'm in a great deal of pain here and need tender loving care." He pulled her down onto the bed. "Kiss me, Leila," he whispered, drawing her close. He opened his mouth and captured hers, teasing her lips apart with his tongue. "I want you. It's a constant ache." She clasped her hands around his neck. Heat coursed through his veins. "I need you." Ignoring the pain in his shoulder, he flipped the loops off the buttons running down the front of her dress.

Her breath caught. She did not pull away.

"God, you are beautiful." His mouth moved to her ears. He nibbled her lobe until she trembled. "Let me make love to you." With a tortured cry, she pushed against his chest. "I can't, Rork. I want to, but I can't."

He lifted one eyebrow. "Why not? Hank has disappeared with Sissy, and you're filing for divorce."

She sat with her hip against his and fumbled with a button, doing it up. "I-I haven't told you everything."

His heart seized. "What haven't you told me?"

She lurched to her feet and paced, wringing her hands. "We never consummated the marriage."

He blinked. That's the last thing he had expected. "How is that possible?" A primal thrill ran through him. She was his and his alone.

She shrugged. "Hank hallucinated from his medicine—I

thought." She turned and stared through the window. "It offended and shocked me to find him entwined with Sissy."

"Come here, Leila. Let's entwine." He held out his good arm.

She laughed and turned to face him. "There is another thing. I sent a message to my father a week ago. Despite his initial opposition to our marriage, he's insisting

I attempt to mend the rift. He said it isn't uncommon for husbands to take a mistress."

"I would never do that to you. Divorce him and marry me."

"You don't need the stigma of marrying a divorced woman. It would ruin your career and standing in society."

He laughed. "Do you think I care about that?" He canted his head. "So—will you do as your father commands?"

"No, but th-this thing between us won't work. Not while I'm married."

He reached out and grasped her hand. "It can, and it will."

She shook her head and ran from the room. "I have to get away from New York."

"Leila, wait!" The door closed with a click of finality, and his head sagged. "I'll follow you wherever you go," he whispered.

CHAPTER FIFTEEN

*C*onfident of her course, Leila wrote Hank the required letter to inform him of her decision to divorce him. Hesitating, she wrote another letter informing her parents of her intention. She dripped wax on both missives, sealing them.

"I'm not sure that father will accept this news," she sighed, picking up her pelisse and reticule on her way out. She stopped first at the letter carrier station. Hands trembling, she handed the postmaster the letter to her parents.

He slipped it into a pigeonhole. "Should arrive in about a week."

Leila walked out, her hard thudding and her mouth dry. "Well, that's it." The carriage ride to her next stop was too short. She alighted, tried to compose herself, and walked into Allan Pinkerton's office.

A scrawny youth at a desk greeted her. "Good Day, Madam, may I have your name, please?"

"Mrs. Dempsey. I'm here to see Mr. Pinkerton."

"Thank you. Please have a seat. I'll inform Mr. Pinkerton you are here." He rose and hurried off on spindly legs.

Sitting stiffly on a black leather couch, she twisted the reticule cord in her hands.

Before long, the young man ushered her into a simply furnished office.

A small, bearded man bowed. "Please sit, Mrs. Dempsey." He sat and folded his hands on the neat desk. "How may Pinkerton help you?"

She put an envelope on his desk. "I wish to have this letter of divorce delivered to my husband, Hank Dempsey. All I gleaned is that he caught a train to St. Louis and then St. Joseph. From there, he intended to take a ferry to Atchison. He's ultimately heading west."

"We'll find him and deliver the letter."

She waited for incriminations or an admonition on the scandalous act of a woman filing for divorce, but he said, "You have submitted your required divorce request to *Harper's Weekly*, have you not?"

"Yes, sir, I have. I'd like you to ensure he signs the document, and you must deliver it to the high court here in New York."

He inclined his head. "Of course."

She pushed another envelope across the desk. "Your fee, as requested."

He took the envelope without opening it and slipped it into a drawer. "It's a pleasure doing business with you, madam."

Leila stood, dropped a brief curtsey and walked out of the building—*I've done it.* Entering her hired hack, she said, "New York Station, please." Leila hoped Cornelia got to the station. She rummaged in her reticule and pulled out a crumpled letter. *You cannot escape me, my love. I will find you. Yours for all eternity, R.* She pressed the letter to her heart and stared out the small window, not noticing the tall buildings and the people out and about.

Descending from the hack, she hurried along the train platform, clutching her pelisse. Drizzle driven by a gusty wind collected on her bonnet and dripped down the back of her neck. She caught sight of a tall woman with blond hair. "There she is, thank goodness." Leila took the woman's arm. "Cornelia, I thought you . . ." She put a gloved hand to her mouth. "I apologize, madam. I mistook you for my friend."

Leila turned and wiped the moisture from her face. She scanned the crowd milling on the platform. "I must go without her. I can't afford to miss this train. The next one is a week away." Disappointment assailed her. Shoulders slumped, she switched the valise to her other hand and shuffled to the passenger carriages.

"Leila!"

Leila spun and smiled. "Cornelia, thank goodness."

Cornelia waved, picked up her skirts, and ran to Leila, embracing her. Breathless, she held her at arm's length. "I've been here for an age and thought you weren't coming."

"And I thought you weren't coming." Leila looked around. "This place is such a crush. It's good to see you. I have so much to tell you."

"I can imagine. We got word at the orphanage that someone shot Rork."

"Yes, but the bullet went through his shoulder without too much damage. He's recuperating at the hotel."

"What about?" She waved her hand. "Oh, never mind, let's talk on the train."

Leila pulled the pelisse tighter to her. "Hurry, let's get out of this smoke and soot. We'll have tea in the dining carriage. I have much to tell you." Cornelia followed her onto the train.

Leila slid into a seat and ordered. "Two teas, please."

She studied the menu. "Also, crumpets with fruit. And you, too, Cornelia?"

She nodded. "Rork can go to his Tenth Street studio rather than the hotel, can't he?"

Leila fiddled with the cutlery. "He needs looking after. He is not well enough yet to cope on his own."

"Oh, of course." She slanted her head and reached out to Leila with her opened palm. "There's more to it, isn't there?"

Leila nodded.

A piercing train whistle sounded. Iron grated on iron as the wheels turned. The train jerked with groans of wood and metal and picked up speed, finding its rhythm. They headed for the open country.

Leila stared at the passing buildings as the train gained momentum. Smoke billowed past the window and dissipated into space. "You must be excited about nursing, Cornelia."

"I would love to travel west with you, but first I must train and work with our soldiers." Tea arrived, and Cornelia poured two cups of the dark brew. "Why did you leave Rork to fend for himself?"

"I hardly left him to fend for himself. The hotel staff and a physician will see to him." Leila sighed. She felt a hollowness in her stomach as she explained what happened. She spread her hands. "After Hank betrayed me, he shot Rork. That's when I filed for divorce."

"My God, Hank shot Rork? For heaven's sake, why?"

"I don't know why. We must ask either of them."

Where is Hank?"

Leila shrugged. "Going west, I guess."

"Why did you leave Rork without waiting until he recuperated?"

"I had to get away."

Cornelia put cream in their teas and pushed a cup to Leila. "I think you have feelings for Rork and don't know how to deal with them."

Leila laughed and stirred her tea. "You know me too well. But I don't know if I can ever trust a man again. Even Sophia Vanderbilt accused him of being a charmer."

116

"Don't assume all men are the same, and charming doesn't mean 'philanderer.' "You were so in love with him at school. Apart from the flaws Hank flaunts, why didn't your marriage work?"

Leila glanced at Cornelia and took a long, lingering breath. "I have a secret—about our marriage."

"Do you want to tell me? It might unburden you."

"You are a good friend." A tear rolled down Leila's cheek. She pulled a handkerchief from her reticule and dabbed at her cheek.

"Hank and I have not been intimate." Cornelia blinked with the teacup halfway to her lips. "What?" She shook her head. The cup landed on the saucer with a clatter. "How is that possible, or rather, why?"

Leila shrugged. "I suppose I didn't appeal to his tastes the way Sissy does."

Cornelia blew a raspberry. "Hogwash, it's those nasty habits of his he claims are medicinal that inhibit his ability to, ah, perform."

Leila giggled. "How is it you know so much about intimacy?"

"I have learned a great deal from medical books."

"Anyway, he is capable. I saw him with Sissy."

Cornelia waved her hand flippantly. "Just because you saw them in a compromising position doesn't mean he achieved anything."

"Goodness, you are knowledgeable."

Cornelia sighed. "I would love to be a doctor, but few women can aspire to that."

"Why shouldn't you do just that? Clemence Lozier became a doctor against all odds." Leila leaned forward. "Why, last November, she opened a college for female doctors in New York. We should have gone there to find out what you need to do to enroll."

"Lozier had the support of her husband and family. Without my family, I don't have the money for medical education."

Leila's mouth tightened. "This notion that women are idiots and incapable of the things men do infuriate me. It's about time we stood up for our rights."

Cornelia smiled. "I agree, but I'm happy to embark on a career as a nurse. If I were ever to marry and have daughters, I'd teach them to be independent." Her eyes clouded, and she stared at her hands.

"You still miss Michael, don't you?" She leaned over and clasped Cornelia's hand.

"Yes, and part of the reason I want to nurse our troops is to honor his memory. Hopefully, I can save a few husbands, sons, and fathers."

"My dear friend, your concern is admirable."

Cornelia squeezed Leila's hand. "Leila, go back to Rork. When he's well enough, go out west with him. You could help him by recording all the events around his paintings. Do what Hank was going to do."

Leila's eyes widened. "Lord, Cornelia, I'm not good enough to write like Hank."

She tossed her golden curls. "Oh, rubbish. Of course, you are. You write beautifully." She tugged Leila's hand. "Why did you run away from Rork?"

"I-I told you. Anyway, I can't think about being with him while I'm still married to Hank."

Cornelia rolled her eyes. "You've already pushed the boundaries of society by filing for divorce. Why not go all the way and take Rork as your lover?"

"You say the most outrageous things." Heat burned Leila's cheeks, and a giggle escaped. A tap on Leila's shoulder brought her around. "Billy. What are you doing here?"

Grinning, he slid into the seat and ordered coffee from the

hovering server. "The same as you, dear cousin. Going to St. Louis." He smiled. "Greetings, Cornelia."

"Hello, Billy."

Leila pecked his cheek. "How did you get away from Eleanor? I thought she had a stranglehold on you."

"It wasn't easy, I assure you, but that wife of mine loves her creature comforts. Roughing it in the wild is not her idea of fun. Is Hank around?"

"Ah, no." She wet her lips. "I've filed for divorce."

He raised his pale eyebrows and looked at her over his wire-rimmed spectacles. "Good for you. Care to tell me what finally provoked such a radical step?" He held up one finger. "No, don't tell. I'll guess. He ran off with that tart, Sissy?"

"That about sums it up."

"Say nothing to that wife of mine. You know what a damn gossip she is. Not that you could, with her still at the Catskills." He chuckled and sipped his coffee. "Where is Rork Millburn?"

Leila shrugged. It didn't do to tell Billy too much either. "In New York."

"I heard somebody shot him."

Eager to steer Billy in another direction, Leila stared intently at her cousin. She smiled a smile that reached her eyes. "Can you believe Cornelia is embarking on a career as a nurse?"

"Well, I'll be. Good for you. How are you, gal? I haven't seen you since Leila and Hanks' wedding." He leaned forward. "When did you two meet up again?"

Cornelia sipped her tea. "We met on the train to New York and had quite an adventure in the city. Did you hear about the draft riots?"

"I read about it in the newspaper. Did you get caught up in it?"

Leila sighed. "It's a long story. We have a couple of days to talk before we arrive in St. Louis. How about we meet for lunch?"

"I'm with a crew going west to Tis-a-ack. I need to check in with them, so that won't work for me. Maybe supper or something." He rose briskly. "I must be off." He landed a peck on Leila's cheek and blew Cornelia a kiss.

Leila followed his uneven departure as he negotiated the passage between tables on the swaying train. "Now, my impending divorce will be common knowledge."

"It couldn't stay secret forever. Promise me you'll at least consider having Rork in your life. You deserve to be happy."

Leila arched one eyebrow. "And you don't? How many years has it been since you lost Michael?"

"Almost three."

"You need someone in your life, too."

"No, I want to nurse, and that won't leave much time for men."

"I suppose." They both stared out the window.

Leila gaped at the man in the booking office in St. Louis. "The pier burned down?"

"Yes, ma'am, and it damaged the ferry. It will be at least three weeks before they finish repairs."

"Is there any other way to Atchison?"

"Horseback, I guess, but ya cain't go alone, mighty dangerous out there. Ya could fall foul of Rebs, an' no tellin' what them slavers will do to a fine lady like yerself."

Cornelia touched Leila's arm.as they walked away. "Volunteer to nurse with me. It will keep you occupied."

Leila shuddered. "I'm not equipped to treat injured or dying men."

"It could be useful out west. Just do it for a few weeks."

"I suppose you're right. It could be useful. And at least I'll feel as if I'm doing something for the war effort." Cornelia grinned. "Exactly." She took Leila's arm. "I'm off to Benton Barracks now. They have a hospital there. Come with me."

"Very well." Leila's thoughts settled on Rork as they climbed into their hired carriage and headed for the fort.

Cornelia took off her bonnet as they stepped through the doors of the hospital. She took a deep breath. "I love the smell of medicine and ether."

"Offensive to me," Leila whispered.

"You'll get used to it." With long-legged strides, Cornelia walked up to a man in a blood-stained white coat leaning over a patient. She cleared her throat. "I'm looking for Dr. Russell. I believe he's the surgeon here."

He glanced up—a creviced face drooped with fatigue and despair. He wiped his hands on his coat, adding more blood-stains. "I'm Dr. McBride. I'm afraid Dr. Russell is in New York. What can I do for you, madam?"

"Do you know if he got the letter from Dr. Smith saying I wanted to volunteer as a nurse?"

Life surfaced in his brown eyes, and he smiled, smoothing his gray walrus mustache and smearing blood on it. "Bless you, lass. God knows we could use the extra hands. I don't know if he got the letter, though." He took her arm and guided her to a small desk in one corner of the massive hall. He released her, leaving a bloodied handprint on her arm, and shuffled through a mountain of papers. "I suppose the letter could be here. Been so damn busy I don't have time to fart, let alone read mail."

Cornelia smiled at Leila's shocked expression and leaned closer. "Not much in the way of social graces in hospitals." She pushed Leila into the only chair around. "You look a bit pale."

"I'm fine. I'm just not used to so much blood."

Cornelia stared across the expanse of pallets lined up on the floor between iron bedsteads. The stench of vomit, feces, and ether permeated the hospital. Groans and cries of pain echoed off the high ceilings. Nurses moved between them, ministering to the injured soldiers' needs.

Despite the din, there was a cry, like an echo in a cave. A familiar name resounded in the hospital corridor. "Cornelia!" Leila glanced at Cornelia, and their eyes locked. "Oh my God, Cornelia!" Cornelia's mouth worked, but no sound came out.

Dr. McBride looked up. "That poor man has been calling that girl's name since he arrived a week ago. He lived through the Bull Run battle and found his way back despite losing an eye and being injured. The poor bastard took a cannonball that damaged his left leg so badly I had to amputate immediately after they got him here. It looks like his left arm might have to go as well." He peered at Cornelia over wire-rimmed spectacles splattered with blood. "You all right, young lady? You look mighty pale. I hope all this blood and gore isn't too much for you. I could use those extra hands."

Cornelia turned toward the man writhing on a pallet and shouting her name.

CHAPTER SIXTEEN

$\mathcal{C}$ornelia's footsteps pounded on the floor as she approached the pallet. She stopped and stared down at an emaciated man covered in a filthy blanket. She sank to her knees, skirt billowing around her. "Michael." She reached out and touched his gaunt, bearded face. "Oh, my God." Tears fell. She ran her fingers over the bandage covering his eye. He ran a tongue over cracked, bloodied lips. "Thirsty."

"I'll fetch the water."

Leila put a hand on her shoulder. "Stay with him. I'll get water."

"Thank you, Leila." The doctor had set his damaged arm in a splint. Cornelia took his free hand and brought it up to her cheek and kissed each torn finger. "I cannot imagine the hell you went through to get here. We'll get through this together."

Leila returned and handed her a mug of water.

"Thank you." Cornelia slipped her arm behind Michael's shoulders and leaned his head against her chest. He gulped the water. Cornelia stripped the blanket off him. "Leila, please fetch a basin of warm water to wash Michael."

Leila gasped. "Perhaps Dr. McBride should wash him."

Cornelia scowled at her friend's shocked face. "There's no room in war for delicate sensibilities. Never you mind. I'll find a basin and water." She surged to her feet.

Leila grabbed her arm. "Stay with him. I'll get it." She returned moments later with a sponge and a basin of water.

Cornelia hung her head. "Leila, please forgive me. I didn't mean to snap at you. Michael is the love of my life from childhood. The day I heard he died in battle was the day my heart withered and died."

Leila hugged her. "I'm sorry."

"I'll ask Dr. McBride what I can do to help."

Cornelia set about undressing Michael, working methodically, gently sponging his wasted body. With only a filthy blanket to cover him, she rose, clutching his torn and stained breeches and shirt. She strode to McBride. "Are there clean clothes and blankets?"

He stared at her. "Ye gads, gal, we don't even have enough to go around, let alone spare."

Her mouth set in a hard line.

"Leila, find a supply store. I'll give you money."

Leila waved her away. "I don't need money. I'll return as soon as possible."

McBride stared at a cartload of blankets, sheets, and nightshirts. "You are more than resourceful and generous, Mrs. Dempsey. I thank you sincerely. How did you do it?"

"I smiled and asked the nice man in the supply store." Leila grinned. "I'm happy to help. Let me know what supplies you need, and I'll find them. Can you give me a list?"

McBride scribbled on a scrap of paper. "Thank you."

Leila studied the list. "It's meager, Doctor."

"I don't set my hopes high. Thank you." The doctor set off to a new wave of injured soldiers.

Leila climbed up beside the driver of her hired cart. Traveling along potholed streets, she noticed Negroes mingling with the crowd. A white woman walked ahead of a Negress, who carried the woman's child. Will they ever have freedom? Leila shook her head. Change would be slow. The cart halted, and she jumped down at the boarding house where she and Cornelia rented rooms. Leila smiled at the taciturn driver. "I won't take long."

Running to her room, she swapped her pelisse for a hooded cape and stuffed money into a leather bag. She ran to the cart and scrambled up onto the driver's seat. "Please hurry. I must get supplies before dark. Can we find a riverboat trader?"

The driver raised one eyebrow. "It ain't safe, lady."

"Nothing is safe. Just take me to one." Dismay beset her as they left the town and neared a wooded area. The carriage stopped among some trees, and she stepped out, stomach-churning. The afternoon shadows seemed menacing.

"I ain't goin' no closer. No tellin' if them bushwhackers are skulking around."

Leila expelled an exasperated breath. "Fine. Will you wait for me?"

"I'll give ya an hour."

"Might I remind you I hired your services for the day?"

He ejected a stream of brown tobacco. Leila rubbed her arms to ward off the early chill. Her fine kidskin boots squelched in mud, walking toward the river where she reached a narrow road leading to a rickety wooden jetty. Leila faltered and glanced at a group of rough looking men sprawled against the trees. They followed her progress to the jetty. Leila's spine tingled, and her mouth dried. Her boots echoed dully on the boards as she hurried to sailors boarding a longboat.

A rotund man stopped and stared at her. "How can I help ya, li'l lady?"

"I need supplies for Dr. McBride. I have money." She pulled a pouch from under her cape.

He grabbed her arm. "Lordy, gal, put that away. The place is crawling with vermin. Hell, ya shouldn't even be here."

Leila's mouth tightened. She allowed a tear to fall. "Please, sir, our brave soldiers are dying for want of medication."

He watched her and stroked his pepper-gray beard. "Well, the government hasn't paid up. I guess I can let ya have some."

She smiled and dabbed her eyes. "I shall be grateful." She handed him a scrap of paper. "Do you have what's on this list?"

He squinted. "Not all. It ain't safe for ya here. I'll bring the stuff to the hospital soon as I've collected what ya need."

"Thank you, but I have a carriage waiting."

"Lady, like I said, it ain't safe. Ya go on ahead, an' I'll get the supplies to ya."

Leila jutted her chin. "I'll wait at the carriage."

He shrugged. "Suit yourself." Handing the list to a man in the longboat, he held his hand out. "I need payment upfront."

"How much?"

"Hundred an' fifty dollars."

"That seems high."

"Ya want the stuff or not?"

She nodded and handed him the money. He yelled garbled instructions and stepped into the boat. They took off, rowing to a paddle steamer anchored mid-river.

Her breath escaped in puffs of condensation in the chilly air. She shivered, not sure if it was from cold or fear. Drawing a deep, steadying breath, she gazed across the water that reflected autumn colors. She turned and walked along the jetty. Heavy footfalls sounded on the rotting planks, and her head snapped up.

Three men swaggered toward her.

She swallowed and considered her chances of hurrying past them.

One man hitched his trousers and leered, exposing a row of

rotting teeth. "Ya need an escort, li'l lady?"

"No, thank you." Lifting her chin, she forged ahead, intent on passing them.

A hand grabbed her arm. "No need to be uppity." They surrounded her.

Heart pounding against her ribcage, she stopped and glared at them. "Unhand me." She brought up her parasol and wacked one against the head.

With a growl, he snatched it from her and grabbed the back of her head. "Let's see if ye're as feisty on ya back." He snatched the reticule from her wrist and tossed it to one of his buddies. "See if this filly has anythin' of value while I sample her." He fingered her cheek and snickered. "Ye're a pretty li'l thing."

Paralyzed with fear, she struggled as hairy arms wrapped around her.

"I'd leave the lady be if I were you."

Leila stared at the biggest man she'd ever seen. The setting sun gleamed on his ebony face.

"Piss off, darkie!"

"Not going to happen, you damn peckerwood!" A massive fist came up and slammed into the attacker's face, leaving a bloody mess of crushed bone and cartilage.

The man screamed and collapsed, clutching his shattered face. Snarling, his mates made a dive for the man.

Effortlessly, he grabbed their ears and slammed their heads together. He kicked them into the water and dusted his palms together. "That sorted them out." He grinned and bowed. "I trust you are unharmed, madam."

"Y-yes, thank you, I'm fine and indebted to you." Her knees threatened to give way, and she clutched his forearm.

"You aren't fine at all." He held out his arms. Threads hung from the sleeves of his tattered black jacket. "May I?" She nodded, and he lifted her into his arms. "Where were you going?"

"I have a carriage waiting for me at the top of the road."

An explosion ripped through the air.

The force propelled the man forward. He dropped to his knees, still clutching Leila and shielding her with his immense body. Splinters of wood and chunks of metal hurtled through the air. He grunted and crouched over her—his mouth pulled into a grimace of pain.

"You're hurt," Leila whispered and tried to wriggle free.

"No, just a scratch. Stay where you are."

Once quiet descended, Leila peered under his arm. She watched the paddle steamer burning in a ball of flames. "H-how did that happen?" She hid her face against his chest. "Oh, my soul, those poor men who went to fetch my supplies."

He looked around and set her down next to him. "Look!"

She stared at the brown river. Crates bobbed on the surface. Some had lost their contents, others still intact. She stumbled up and staggered to the end of the jetty. A cry escaped, and she clapped a hand to her mouth.

The men in the longboat had almost made it. Their bodies, stripped of clothes and flesh, hung like carcasses over the edge of the boat.

"Oh, my God!" Bile burned in her throat. She vomited, sank to her knees, and pressed her hand to her chest. Her heart beat erratically. Her rescuer's shadow fell across her, and she looked up. "I-I'm to blame."

He smiled and shook his head. "No, they were about to board, anyway. Your money is still there."

Leila gaped at him and shuddered. "Are you suggesting I take it from a dead man?"

He shrugged. "It could buy more supplies, and he sure as hell doesn't need it."

"I suppose you have a point."

He thrust out his hand. "I'm Joshua Manning. I worked on the Manning family's plantation."

"I'm Leila Dempsey." Her hand swallowed in his." Pity welled in Leila's heart. "You speak well."

He smiled. "The only good person in that family was Manning's eldest daughter, Kate." He gazed across the now calm water. "She taught me to read and write."

"She's a good person indeed."

"Yes, the education is valuable. I will retrieve those boxes for you." He stripped off his jacket.

Leila stared at a red bloodstain on his shirt. "You are hurt."

"It's nothing." He dived in, cleaving the water and surfacing among the debris. "I'll push the boxes to shore. Fetch your driver to help me carry them."

Leila lifted her skirt and raced along the jetty, barely sparing a glance at the men who'd attacked her. Their bodies were in shreds. She couldn't believe Joshua hadn't suffered the same fate while saving her life.

Thank God the carriage is still here. Gasping for air, Leila looked around. "Hello?"

The driver's head popped up from behind bushes. "What the hell was that explosion?"

"The paddle steamer blew up."

"How?"

"I have no idea. Come with me. My friend needs help to get the supplies into the carriage."

He followed her to the river. "How come yer supplies didn't go up with the boat?"

"Come."

"Yes, ma'am." As they arrived, the driver rocked back on his heels and stared at the wreckage and bodies floating on the water. "Holy mother of God!"

Joshua waded to the edge, dragging the fourth crate to shore. He tapped one. "All these are medical supplies. The explosion busted the other crates."

The driver helped him drag the box out. "You speak fancy

English for a darkie."

Leila's head shot up, and she glared at him, preparing a sharp rebuke.

Joshua stopped and settled cold eyes on the driver and held out his hand. "Name's Joshua Manning."

"Alf Johnston." He shook Joshua's hand.

Leila hid a smile and tried to help drag the boxes. Joshua pushed her aside gently. "Leave them." He hoisted one on his shoulder and staggered up the incline to the carriage.

Alf stared at him, open-mouthed. "Lawdy, ye're mighty strong."

Joshua dumped the box and came back, grinning. "They chose the best stock from Africa."

"I see another box," Alf said, and waded in to fetch it.

Before long, they had six boxes loaded. Leila placed her hand on a box. "I don't think we can carry more. I'm sure Dr. McBride will be pleased."

Leila put her foot on a wheel-spoke and turned to Joshua. "Were you going somewhere? Why were you here?"

"My master is trying to catch up to me. I must leave the area to avoid him."

"Come with us. You'll be safe at the barracks." He followed her and Alf up onto the cart.

The loaded wagon wobbled its way to Benton Barracks. People turned to stare as the wet, mucky trio made their way through town. Leila was beyond exhausted, but she couldn't weaken now. "Joshua, you must stay at the boarding house with my friend and me."

Laughter rumbled deep in his barrel chest. "That might be harder to accomplish than you think, Mrs. Dempsey."

"Please call me Leila."

He shook his head. "We don't want to draw more fire than necessary."

She scowled. "Why? Because you're a colored man, and I'm

a white woman?"

"Yes. The North might fight for emancipation, but that doesn't mean equality."

She caught her breath and looked at him. "I am not worried about others' opinions." Alf glanced at her. "He's right, ma'am. This town has a foot in both camps. Plenty o' folk won't see it yer way."

"You think so?"

They finally trundled through the gates to the hospital. Joshua jumped down and lifted Leila off.

"Here, I took this." Joshua thrust a bag into her hands. "It's the money you gave the trader."

She smiled, her eyes flashed, and she handed the bag back. "I want you to have the money." Leila glowered as he opened his mouth to protest. "It's offensive to refuse my gift."

He stuffed it into his pocket. "Thank you. I will repay you one day."

"Joshua, please, you owe me nothing. I owe you my life." She took his arm, and they walked into the hospital.

McBride turned from his duties. "Lord alive, gal, what happened to you?"

Leila gulped and glanced down at her soiled dress and cape —her heart skipped a beat. "The trader's paddle steamer exploded."

"That would be the Confederates. Not the first time." He washed his hands in a bowl and covered his patient with a blanket.

Leila shook her tight shoulders. There are six crates of medicines and supplies."

A smile creased his exhausted face. "You *are* resourceful." He looked past her and blinked. "Who's the big fellow?"

Leila glanced over her shoulder. "Joshua Manning. He saved my life, not once, but twice."

"Manning, you say? Oh, Lord, that is not good."

CHAPTER SEVENTEEN

*L*eila's face paled. "Why isn't it good?"

McBride's eyes narrowed. "His family is here in St. Louis. I know Manning, he's vindictive and is searching for his runaways."

Joshua gaped at him. He rubbed his bearded jaw. "How do I avoid him?"

McBride laid his hand on Josh's shoulder. "Leave St. Louis. If Manning finds you, you're a hanged man. I'll find clothes to give you a presence. Not all people of color are slaves. We must stop Manning from recognizing you."

Leila's stomach churned. "Go to Pennsylvania. The Anti-Slavery Society will help you. You will need a new name."

"What about Formby?"

"Perfect."

Joshua grinned. "I'll need papers."

"I'll request papers for a new slave at the courthouse. With the identification, you can take the train out of here."

~

Five days later, footsore and weary, Joshua appeared back at the hospital. Leila stared at him in dismay. "What are you doing here? What happened?"

"At the train station, I waited to board, staying close in the crowd. I kept my head down and thought my clothes and the wide brim of my hat were enough of a disguise. Manning mingled in the crowd. He stood between Rebels, arms flailing. I had to forget the train and get back to the barracks. I hailed a nearby buggy. Too late."

He started yelling, "There he is! My runaway!" The Rebels, led by Manning, bore down on me. I threw the driver into the seat next to me and flicked the reins. The buggy swayed and tilted on the potted streets, the horse foaming at his bit. I guided the rig through the crowd and broke free.

I continued driving and veered left down a side street, turned right, and stopped at a random boarding house. I gave the buggy back to the driver and started walking along the dusty road to Benton Barracks. Trees along the road gave me a place to hide whenever a carriage passed."

"You are brave. What's next?"

Joshua slumped his shoulders. "Manning will guard the train station. I can never leave."

"I'm going out west to look for Hank, and Cornelia wants to take Michael to his family in California. Come with us."

Joshua's eyes brightened. "Is Michael well enough to travel?"

Leila glanced across at Cornelia sitting by Michael. "He can't make sense of things yet, but Cornelia believes he'll heal with familiar surroundings."

Leila smiled—the corners of her eyes crinkled. "Dr. McBride agrees Michael taking the trip is best. Even in twenty-four hours, his arm has improved with Cornelia cleaning the wound regularly."

"It's a long journey, Leila. And grueling," Cornelia frowned. "Rebels are prevalent."

Joshua shook his head. "If I come, it'll endanger all of you."

Leila scowled at him. "You can protect us. Come, please come. With your new identity as my slave, I can protect you as well."

He compressed his lips. Joshua hesitated at Leila's glance and agreed to the idea of him as a guardian. "Sounds smart."

"That's decided. We'll see when we can move Michael. In the meantime, stay in my room at the boarding house."

A smile lit Joshua's face. "Thank you, Mrs. Dempsey."

"Please call me Leila. Take the carriage that's outside. Alf knows where to take you." She hurried off to consult with Cornelia.

Pounding on the door dragged Rork to awareness. "Yes?" he said in a croaky voice. He flung back the blankets and clutched his aching shoulder. Staggering to the door, he yanked it open.

"I'm sorry to disturb you, Mr. Millburn. A courier asked me to deliver this letter immediately."

He glared at the scrawny clerk. "Damn, couldn't it wait until morning?"

The clerk thrust the letter at him and scurried off.

Rork kicked the door closed behind him and winced. His shoulder wasn't healing in a hurry. Sleeping was a chore. He missed Leila and damned himself for moving too fast with her. Putting the letter on a desk, he used one hand to splash cold water on his face. He ran his fingers over the stubble on his chin. Shaving was another nightmare. Half on, his nightshirt hampered his efforts as he tore the letter open, accidentally tearing it in two. He cursed and laid the pieces on the desk and turned up a kerosene lamp.

Rork tilted the lamp and scowled. What the hell does it say?

Sliding the torn edges together, he squinted at the words. Cornelia wants—what? He slammed a fist onto the desk and winced as a sharp pain shot through his shoulder. His knees gave way, and he leaned his good hand on the desk, took a deep breath, and pieced the letter together. *Dear Mr. Millburn, Leila is going to Atchison by steamer within a week or two. I believe she returns your affection. Cornelia Hancock.*

Rork stared at the letter. He folded it, ripped open the door, and took the stairs two at a time down to the lobby. His head swollen with thoughts of Leila—he cornered the clerk. "How often do the trains run to St. Louis?"

The clerk stared at him. "E-early morning and late afternoon."

"Get a porter to take my luggage to the train within the hour."

"Yes, sir."

"Thanks." Rork slapped his back. "Didn't mean to stomp you earlier, boy, but this injured shoulder is a bear."

The crowd gave way to Rork's careening carriage. Wincing with pain, he jounced on the back seat, holding onto his hat. The sun pushed up beyond tall buildings with a splashy sunrise in a symphony of pink rippling across the white mist of a morning sky. Rork breathed a sigh of relief when the carriage stopped. He unbuttoned his long morning coat, checked his pocket watch and stepped from the carriage.

A colored boy ran up to him. "Ya need help carryin' yer baggage, sir?"

"I do indeed. Come on, lad, let's get my things onto the train."

An elderly, groomed gentleman fell in step with Rork.

"Aren't you the artist, Millburn?"

"Yes, I am."

"Met you in your Tenth Street studio in an exhibition with the other artists. Your work is splendid. Where are you headed?"

"West."

"Are you going to paint scenes of the battles?"

Rork laughed. "I may do that."

The man lifted his hat. "I'll keep an eye out for your work. Good Day, Mr. Millburn."

His reluctance to join the war bothered him, mostly since he supported the emancipation of slaves. He let out a breath and beckoned the boy to follow him to his compartment.

CHAPTER EIGHTEEN

*C*ornelia sat on the Benton Barracks hospital floor at Michael's side, speaking in a voice as soft as a feather. "I'm proud of you and your fight for freedom. We will have the life we promised each other before you left." Cornelia pressed her cheek to his. She rose, her shoulders slumped.

Leila put a hand on her arm. "I'm so sorry, Cornelia."

Cornelia swallowed her tears. "I hope the war has not crushed his heart. He's burning with fever. I need to cool him."

"I'll get cold water, alcohol, and cloths, anything else?"

"Thank you, that will do." Cornelia sagged to the floor.

Leila returned. "Cornelia, let me help."

"Please, your help is welcome."

Leila pressed cold cloths on Michael's face while Cornelia rubbed him down with the alcohol.

Cornelia glanced at Leila. "I need to get Michael to his family in California. I'm sure it will help him recover."

"Joshua also intends to travel out west. I hear there's a paddle steamer taking some soldiers from this hospital to Atchison. Perhaps we can join them. At least Atchison is in the right direction. They need space at the hospital for a new flood of injured men coming from the battlefields."

Cornelia's lips curved into a smile, and her eyes brightened. "Perfect. We can stay together."

Cornelia stood and pulled a blanket over Michael. "Let me ask Dr. McBride."

Leila looked up a few minutes later when Cornelia returned. "So?"

"He doesn't have a problem with us going." She knelt next to Michael. "It's a chance, but we hope his fever abates before we leave." She smoothed his hair and choked back tears. "He still doesn't recognize me."

"Give him time, dear. He will come around."

Leila stood with an arm around Cornelia as the men carried Michael on a stretcher up the steamboat's gangplank. Cornelia left to show them where to place him and went to find Leila.

Walking along the deck, Cornelia put her hand on the staircase rail. "Michael is in the ballroom with other injured soldiers, and Joshua stayed to keep watch. Come on. Let's go see how they are doing."

Leila stopped to admire the staircase. She gasped as she looked up into a round dome with intricately carved wood and painted angels floating in a heavenly sky inside the dome.

"Isn't the decor splendid?"

Cornelia looked up and continued up the stairs. "Oh my, yes."

Leila followed her. "This boat is remarkable. Father took me to Europe on a colossal ship, and this one is every bit as opulent."

Cornelia spread her arms as though gathering the opulence of the ship. "It's sad the army had to use this magnificent ship for war."

They stepped onto the landing and made their way into the ballroom. "Oh, joy," Leila clapped her hands. "This ballroom is gorgeous. There are gold and carvings everywhere." Crystal chandeliers illuminated the space crammed with injured men lying on pallets. The gasoliers added luster to the highly polished wainscot. Imported tapestries lining the walls muted the sound of the men's voices. The poignant notes of a harmonica played "Home Sweet Home."

Melancholy settled on Leila like a dark cloud. "Righteous or not, war is a waste of lives. Thankfully, music is a panacea for sorrow."

"I'm blessed. I got my Michael back."

Leila clapped as Josh joined in the lively Virginia Reel music, encouraging others. "It's sad we must sacrifice so many lives. Pray that it's worth the loss." Soldiers sat up on pallets, smiling. Others lay watching, too ill to move. Those more able-bodied danced and clapped to the reel.

Leila squeezed through the soldiers.

A boy played a fife, accompanying a man with a harmonica. He paused and grinned at Leila. "Do ya like music, ma'am?"

"It's lovely. How old are you?"

"I am twelve. So why ain't ya dancin'?"

"Ladies, come, dance with us," yelled a soldier. He grinned and put out his hand to Leila. "C'mon, dance the reel with me."

Leila smiled and took the soldier's hand. She enjoyed being able to dance again. They finished the last swing of the reel and sashayed to the front of their set.

A smiling Cornelia watched for a while and returned to Michael's side.

Leila eventually stepped back from her partner. "Please excuse me. I need a breath of fresh air."

"You take care out there," he said, bowing. "The steamer has just entered the junction to the Missouri River. Plenty o' Rebs on this river."

Leila nodded and made her way out onto the companionway. Holding the rail, she gazed at the trees lining the banks of the

Missouri and drew a deep breath. She lifted her face to the light breeze—her thoughts centered on Rork.

Is he still in New York? Has he recovered? She missed him but wasn't sure she would ever see him again. His words echoed in her head. As soon as I am healed—*I will find you.* She released a shuddering sigh.

"Why the sigh, lovely lady?"

Gasping, Leila spun around, her legs turning to jelly. "Rork." Her hand flew to her chest, and her heart pounded. "Oh, my soul. Where did you come from?" She tried to catch her breath.

He chuckled. "New York. The train arrived this morning, and I came straight to the docks." He took her hand and held it against his heart. "I told you I'd find you," he whispered. "I would find you anywhere in the world." He kissed her fingertips and held her gaze for what seemed a lifetime.

"You would?" Mesmerized by his eyes, she swayed toward him, her lips parted.

"I would." He drew her close and cradled her head against his chest. "I've thought of you every moment of every day you were away."

"How did you know where to find me?"

He buried his face in her hair. "Cornelia sent me a wire."

"I should have guessed she'd contact you. She's a wonderful friend."

"Tell me you're pleased."

"You forget I'm still married, Rork." She swallowed hard, wishing it were not so.

He lifted her chin, leaned forward, and lightly traced her lips with his tongue. "It doesn't matter. I'll wait for you until the world ceases to exist."

She lowered her eyes and sank against him as he claimed her mouth. He pulled her tight against his body and deepened the kiss. Heat raced through her blood, and she clung to him.

He finally broke the kiss. "Will you come west with me?"

"I'm married, Rork."

"So, you keep saying. Will you come with me or not?"

"I cannot."

"I will go wherever you go. It's as simple as that." He put his hand on her back and pressed her against him.

Her mind was spinning, and she fought to regain her composure. "I-I'll be happy to accompany you when the time comes."

"What is that supposed to mean?"

She laid her palm on his cheek. "I have to resolve things with Hank. He must sign the divorce papers. I'm not sure he will."

Rork grimaced. "I'll damn well force him to."

A flash of light followed by a blast shattered the moment. Leila stopped breathing. "Did you hear a gunshot? Please tell me I'm wrong."

"No, you're not wrong. Let's go." Keeping his arm around her waist, they ran.

Looking at the shore, Leila gasped. "More gunfire."

A bullet slammed into the wood near their heads.

"Get down!" They ducked and ran. Bullets peppered the steamer. They catapulted into Joshua and fell, taking him with them.

"Everyone get down!" Rork yelled.

Leila grabbed Joshua's arm. "Where is Cornelia?"

He pointed. "Over there, crouched over Michael."

Joshua looked at Rork. "Who's he, Leila?"

"Rork Millburn here." Rork stretched out his hand.

"Joshua Formby." He shook Rork's hand.

Another barrage of bullets hit the ship.

"We must get to the center of the room!" Rork shouted above the commotion. He grabbed Leila and scrambled away as bullets smashed windows and sent shards of glass and wood flying.

An explosion lifted the ship, shattering wood, along with screams of pain and distress, as men and pallets slid to the starboard side.

"They're bombarding the ship with cannons!" Rork yelled.

Air left Leila's lungs as they slipped along the polished floor and slammed into a wall. Rork fell on top of her. The ship listed, and water rushed into the ballroom.

"The ship is sinking." Rork grabbed Leila and staggered to his feet. "We must get off."

Leila struggled in his arms. "Cornelia's betrothed can't move. We must help her."

Rork stared at Leila. "He's alive?"

"Yes, I'll tell you the story later. Help her."

"Of course, get down and stay down!"

Joshua rose to his knees and turned to Rork. "You stay with Leila. I'll get them." Within minutes, he returned, carrying Michael, Cornelia stumbling after him.

Rork herded the women to the door and pushed, but water held it shut. He slammed his boot into the barricade. It shattered, and water poured in. "Hurry! Ladies, take off your petticoats or you'll sink."

Needing no further encouragement, they hiked drenched skirts and unhooked their petticoats, kicking them off.

Rork urged them out and forced the women over the rail. "We must swim, make for the north shore. It isn't far." He followed them into the water and looked back. "Are you all right, Joshua?"

He nodded and slid over the rail, hanging onto Michael.

Fighting the drag of her dress, Leila shivered in the freezing water and struck out, swimming to the shore. Waves of water washed over her, filling her mouth. Fear rippled through her as memories of the Catskills flashed into her head.

"Keep going!" Rork yelled.

"M-my dress is dragging me down."

Finally, her feet touched the bottom, and she waded to the bank and collapsed. Rolling onto her back, she lay panting.

Rork helped Joshua drag Michael to dry ground and knelt beside Leila. "Are you all right?"

She nodded.

He urged her up. "Get into the trees and wait for me. I'm going back to help the injured men."

"Wait." Joshua ran to the trees with Michael and put him down. "I'll come with you." Rork nodded, and together they waded in and swam back to the sinking steamer.

"Please don't die," Leila whispered as they disappeared. Through the dwindling daylight, she stared at hundreds of bodies floating in the water and soldiers frantically making for the shore. She crawled to Cornelia. "We need to keep him warm, Cornelia."

Leila ripped off leafy branches to cover Michael. "We've been on the water since early morning, and the sun is setting, so we must have come a fair distance."

Teeth chattering, Cornelia worked with Leila to cover Michael.

"According to the Captain, we should be near Boonville," Leila said. "And he mentioned a settlement on the south bank. How can we get across the river for help?"

Cornelia stroked Michael's cheek. "Please live. I pray."

Leila wrapped her arms around herself and tried not to shiver. "One can't attempt to cross the river here anyway—too many Confederates roaming about." Leila jutted her chin. "I'm going to fetch help."

Cornelia glanced at her. "Maybe the soldiers' commanding officer could go with some of his men. It'll be dangerous."

Leila scowled. "The explosion injured most of the men."

She swept an arm around at the men in the water and many strewn on the shore. She swallowed. "O-or killed them."

Cornelia grabbed her arm. "Please wait for Rork and Joshua."

"There is no time to wait. I must get help no matter the

danger. I'll pick up a weapon from one of the injured men." A million thoughts rushed her mind though she couldn't make sense of a one. Was she doing the right thing? A lonely tear breached her will, and she wrung as much water as she could from her sodden skirt and struck out, heading west.

CHAPTER NINETEEN

*R*ork panted, spitting water as he and Joshua dragged men from the ship that had settled on the riverbed. "Let's look in the decks underwater. Air pockets could trap some men." He waded through debris with Joshua.

Almost zero visibility in the fading light when they returned to the stricken ship. Rork swam into the lower deck. No one appeared to have survived.

"Over here! We're over here!" a man yelled. Voices screaming for help skimmed across the water.

"Let's get them," Joshua said as he and Rork followed the voices. Men clung to an overturned lifeboat.

Rork reached the boat first. "Help me right it."

"Need to get them off it first." Joshua ripped their hands off the hull.

"Are you mad?" a man cried, trying to regain his hold.

"Let go, damn it!" Rork barked.

"Okay, let's flip this thing." Breath rasping, Rork ground his teeth and ignored the pain in his shoulder while righting the lifeboat.

One by one, the exhausted men clambered into the boat, murmuring their thanks.

"We need to find planks to use as oars," Rork hollered.

"Way ahead of you." Joshua tossed planks into the boat.

The lifeboat pulled away while the men chanted the strains of "Amazing Grace." The boat rose and fell in rhythm with the makeshift oars sweeping through the water.

Surrounded by moonlight and silence, Rork and Joshua crawled onto the shore and lay on their backs, staring at starlit heaven. The moon slowly crept higher into the sky. "You all right?" Rork croaked, hacking up water.

"Yeah."

Joshua sat up, head hanging. "We need to set up a watch to deter Confederates from sneaking up on the survivors."

Rork nodded. "I'll check if Leila, Cornelia, and Michael are safe." He rose beyond exhausted, clutching his throbbing shoulder.

Rork glanced around at soldiers propped against the trees and his small group of friends in a huddle.

"Cornelia, do you know where Leila is?"

"Leila went for help. She's headed for Boonville."

Rork's heart tripped. "Alone?"

She nodded. "I couldn't stop her."

"I'm going after her." He turned to Joshua. "I need a weapon. Any idea where I can find one?"

"I helped a captain from the ship. He insisted on keeping a haversack. Said it had his gun in it. Perhaps he'll give it to us."

Rork put a hand on Cornelia's shoulder. "How is Michael doing?"

"He seems alright. His wounds might get infected without medication."

"Joshua can search the ship for medication at first light. I need to find Leila before renegades do."

Joshua returned and handed Rork a Remington revolver. "Here you are. He also gave me a handful of paper cartridges and nipples. Be careful about how many shots you fire. This was all the ammunition he had."

"Thank you. Hopefully, I won't have to use it at all." He stuffed the gun into his belt and hung the pouch of ammunition on it. "How did the man keep it dry?"

"He had it wrapped in a tarred bag. He escorted his troops to Kansas and wanted to join you but thinks he's better off staying here with the survivors."

Rork nodded. "Fair enough."

Joshua handed him an army greatcoat from one survivor in the lifeboat. "He said to give you this."

"Give it to Cornelia for Michael," Rork said.

"Will do, thanks. I'm going deeper into the forest to light fires. The captain and I will move the injured there. He already has men posted on watch. Every soldier not seriously injured must answer the call to duty," Joshua said.

"I better be on my way." Rork took off at a run, heading west.

Leila quelled the fear curdling up from the pit of her stomach, but she scampered, keeping warm. Ominous shadows appeared as moonlight filtered through the canopy of the dark forest. Dead leaves and branches crunched under her wet boots. She slowed down to listen. Her flesh crawled, and the hairs stood up on the back of her neck. Her former life of ease and luxury seemed a million years away. "You can do this, Leila. You can do this."

A low growl filtered through the undergrowth. Leila's legs turned to jelly, and bile rose in her throat. She glanced up at the trees. She could scale one, but she didn't know if the animal could climb. A sob escaped. The animal gave another rolling growl—the sound stabbed her like a sliver of glass. Cold was no longer her problem. *Dear God, I'm going to die a virgin.* A nervous giggle seeped from her lips. Heavens, Leila, that's your last thought on this earth?

Crouching, she groped around. Her hand landed on a log, and she snatched it up, holding it in front of her. She crept closer. In the distance, firelight flickered through the trees. She hesitated. No fear, Leila. The rough, low growls weren't comforting.

When she moved again, her skirt caught, and her heart seized. A boot had her skirt trapped. A scream ripped from her throat, and rough hands grabbed her arms.

"Rork, thank God. I thought death would consume me."

"It's a wildcat, could be a cougar," Rork whispered, "Leila, drop."

She complied and fell to the ground.

The cougar charged. Rork fired. The bullet hit the animal, and it ran off. "We aren't safe if that cat isn't dead, and dead if there's more than one cat."

"I should have never left. I'm so sorry. I put us both in danger."

"Your intentions were noble. We will find help."

Rork surveyed their findings. "Something, maybe a cougar, attacked this camp and dragged the man to the den—it probably had cubs to feed. We'll know if there are more hungry cats. They don't scare easily. The man was probably a bushwhacker. If he was the cat's dinner, we have a lucky find."

He rummaged through the haversack.

"You saved my life again."

Sitting cross-legged next to her, he gazed into her eyes to see if the same hot, dark depths were there as he remembered. "Purely selfish. I can't bear the thought of losing you." He moved a strand of hair from her cheek.

"I thought you'd be busy rescuing soldiers all night."

He shook his head. "A shroud of darkness surrounded us. I doubt there were any left to save. We noticed boxes with red crosses floating in the water. We lost sight of them. Joshua will organize the search for medicine at first light."

"You are fearless."

"So are you." He winked and squeezed her hand.

"Are you hungry?"

"Heavens, no."

"I found a bottle of whiskey in the bedroll. I think you should drink some." She nodded, and he rose to fetch it. Holding her head, he tipped the bottle to her lips.

She swallowed and pushed the bottle away. "Enough, or I'll be drunk."

Rork took a few swigs. He put the stopper on the bottle and set it down. "I think we should stay here until first light."

She shuddered, her eyes skittering to the foliage.

He followed her gaze. "Do you think there is something in the bushes?"

She grabbed his arm. "Maybe it's that cat."

Rork searched and found the dead cougar. He launched him into the undergrowth.

"We don't have to worry about that cat. Let's get some sleep."

"Please lie next to me."

"I'm not sure that's a good idea." But he complied, put out the bedroll, and lay down with her, holding her in his arms. Her even breaths brushed his neck. She fell into a deep sleep.

For a long time, he lay listening to the night sounds. Crickets whirred, and somewhere a mockingbird sent out a melodic song.

Rork quietly built up the fire as Leila slept. He reloaded the revolver and leaned against a log, keeping watch.

CHAPTER TWENTY

*R*ork woke with a start. The first rays of sunlight filtered through the trees. He released a long breath and stumbled to his feet, walked to Leila, and smiled. Sleeping beauty.

He found a can of beans and biscuits. Building up the fire, he set about heating the food in a battered frying pan.

Leila sat up and stretched. "How long have you been up?"

"A while. Are you hungry?"

"Starving."

"We should get a move on soon." He nodded at the haversack. "You'll find a shirt in there and breeches. It might be easier to walk without that dress."

Leila nodded and took out the clothes. "I'm not going into the bushes. I have no desire to stumble across that carcass. Please turn your back."

"Good idea." He concentrated on the beans boiling in the pan, anything to avoid thinking of her naked body and the irresistible temptation to pull her into his arms and kiss her breathless.

"I'm done." She walked around and stood in front of him, spreading her arms. "Do I pass muster as a boy?"

Swallowing hard, he turned, and his eyes traveled down her slender body to impossibly long legs. He put the pan aside, stood, and walked to her.

"Well?"

"You make a terrible boy."

Her eyebrows arched. "I do?" She smiled with her finger on her lips. "I thought I looked pretty debonair."

"I agree with pretty. Well, gorgeous and . . . delectable." He put his hands on her hips and pulled her against him. "Bending, he captured her mouth in a searing kiss."

She broke the kiss and laughed. "Do you make a habit of kissing boys?"

His hoot filled the empty spaces between the leaves on the trees. "No, but I could spend my life kissing you."

Pressing her hands against his chest, she leaned back in his arms. "Rork, men are dying. We need to get to Boonville." He consented and released her, gathering the bushwhacker's supplies. "Let's eat and go. It can't be much farther." Leila scooped food onto tin plates.

They crept to the river's edge, keeping to the trees. Boonville seemed quiet on the opposite bank. "We can't swim across."

"What if Rebels control Boonville?" Leila sat and pulled off her boots, wincing as they peeled off the skin from multiple blisters.

"It's a chance we must take. We can pretend to be Confederates and make our way to Kansas."

Her eyes popped. "Kansas?"

"Or the next place controlled by federal soldiers." He knelt and touched her bleeding feet gently. "I'm sorry. I wish we had a salve for your poor feet."

"I can't believe we've been walking through this inhospitable terrain only to find we can't get across."

"There has to be a canoe or something. People cross to Boonville all the time, or so I've heard." He crept closer to the edge. Leila clenched her teeth, putting her boots on again. She followed Rork. "What if we swim across holding onto a log? I saw some back in the forest."

He blew out his cheeks. "The current is strong, and the water is too cold. We wouldn't survive." He searched the bank, finding nothing. "Let's get back into the forest and think of a way across." He glanced up at the horizon's sinking sun. "We'll camp for the night, and maybe by morning—we'll come up with an idea."

"Another night under the stars." Leila's mouth twisted. "Just what I envisaged for a joyous evening."

Rork chuckled and put an arm around her waist. "It hasn't been that bad, has it? I've enjoyed our time together."

She stared at her grimy hands and split nails.

"Hey." He stopped and lifted her chin. He held her gaze. "We'll get across the river. Prayfully, it'll all be over."

She sniffed and stared. "It will only be over when I get Hank to sign those papers." A sigh escaped. "And that may never happen at this rate."

"Such little faith." He drew her close and held her head against his chest. "I promise we'll soon be on our way to Atchison." He put his arm around her waist again and led her deeper into the forest. "Let's make a fire and cook the last of our provisions. Things will look better in the morning."

Rork registered the loud click. His eyes snapped open, and he stared into the barrel of a rifle. Shifting his eyes left and right, he swallowed. There was a dozen or more rifles aimed at his head. Blue uniforms—He sagged with relief. "Thank God, you're Union soldiers." He slid his arm from under Leila, who slept on peacefully. He tried to sit up.

A rifle slammed into his chest. "Stay right where you are."

Rork scowled. "Who the hell do you think I am?"

"A bushwhacker."

Leila woke and stifled a scream.

Rork put an arm around her and drew her close, his eyes on the soldier. "Our paddle steamer came under fire, and the Rebels sank the damn thing three or four days' walk from here. We were transporting injured Union soldiers to Atchison." He glanced at Leila. "My intended and I left to find help, but the Rebels are everywhere."

The soldier lowered his weapon and held out his hand. "I'm Captain Webb."

Releasing a long breath, Rork rose slowly and glared at the other soldiers and civilians still pointing rifles at him. "I'll thank you for putting your weapons down, gentlemen."

Webb signaled his men to comply.

Rork helped Leila to her feet. "We looked for a way across to Boonville."

"The Rebs took it in a battle, but I heard they left the town today. No idea why, but I know they're intent on taking control of bigger towns."

"I think there could be bushwhackers. A cougar killed one. The same cougar was about to attack my fiancée." Rork avoided looking at Leila, sure she glared at him for lying. "I killed the cat."

Webb's eyebrows rose. "Do you know how many bush-whackers there are?"

"I don't know. We found a campsite that appeared to be from the one killed by the cat."

"That's why I'm here. We're after bushwhackers who are terrorizing folk in smaller towns. You're damn lucky you didn't run into more."

"Glad to hear the army is protecting the towns," Rork said in a confident voice. He asked Webb a question in that same voice.

"How can we get help to the soldiers and nurses from our paddle steamer?"

Webb called a civilian and murmured. The man took off at a run. "My tracker will hail a steamer that's on its way to St. Louis with troops."

Rork rubbed his cheek. "They took the soldiers on our ship from the hospital in St. Louis to make room for more. I doubt they'll be happy to see them return."

Webb nodded. "I'll speak to the pilot. I could use more troops here. Perhaps their commanding officer will assist. I hate to admit it, but Johnny Rebs are gaining the upper hand in this war."

"I need to sit," Leila said in a soft voice.

"We must get down to the river, miss."

"I'll carry her. I'm afraid the long walk has taken a toll on her feet." Rork scooped her up.

Leila leaned to his ear and whispered. "What possessed you to say I'm your betrothed?"

Rork grinned while following Webb and his men.

"Because soon you will be, and it's easier than trying to explain."

Rork stood on the paddle steamer's deck, towering over the commanding officer, hands on his hips. "Major Jones, why can't we turn the boat once we pick up the injured soldiers. And St. Louis isn't an option."

Jones bristled. "Young man, don't take that tone with me. I have my orders."

Rork rubbed the back of his neck and glared at the small, gray-haired man. "Fine. What do *you* suggest?"

"I have wagons on board. I'll let you have three."

"There must be at least two hundred survivors. At least half can't damn well move, let alone walk. How the hell will you fit that many men into three wagons? Another problem, how can I get three wagons, single handedly, back to the injured? I'll wait for another steamer. Maybe the pilot and commander will have a heart."

"You whippersnapper." Jones balled his fingers, head tilted back to glare at Rork.

Captain Webb stepped in. "Major, I think you should reconsider. Fighting for the Union injured those brave men. The least we can do is aid them." He laid a hand on the incensed Major's shoulder. "And I could use help here. I think St. Louis has sufficient troops for now. Bushwhackers are causing trouble in this area. They are robbing and killing civilians." He looked at Rork. "Why, this man encountered a cougar that killed a bushwhacker. He shot the cougar about to pounce on his fiancée."

"Fortunately for us, the bushwhacker left behind his campsite and supplies. There could've been more bushwhackers, but we didn't see or hear any."

Jones smoothed his mustache, his eyes sweeping Rork's length. "Very well, but we will only pick them up and bring them back to Howard County. They have a hospital facility at Boonville. I had word that Price fled with his Reb army the day after they took the town."

Rork inclined his head, delighted to have succeeded even partially. "Thank you. I'm sure we'll find another steamer to take us to Atchison once they've attended to the soldiers."

"I'll inform the pilot." Jones bowed briefly and strode off.

Rork grinned at Webb. "Thank you, Captain. I was ready to force him at gunpoint."

Webb chuckled and glanced at armed troops milling about on the deck. "That might not have been a wise move."

. . .

Her eyes bright, Cornelia waited at the foot of the gangplank to greet Leila and Rork as they left the ship. "You made it." Cornelia hugged them. "Well done."

"How is Michael?" Rork asked.

"Not well, but when I get him dried out and have access to medication, I'm sure he'll rally. Joshua couldn't salvage anything. The Confederates helped themselves." She folded her arms over her chest. "Quite a few soldiers died."

Joshua gripped Rork's shoulder. "A few men made it to shore alone and found our camp in the forest." He looked across at men being carried off.

Rork rubbed his stubbled face. "You did what you could. Let's get the injured off the ship and bury the dead."

For the next three hours, men loaded the injured into wagons and transported them to the ferry.

Joshua and Rork worked in silence, digging graves. "This could have been someone we loved," Joshua murmured.

"I cannot imagine losing Leila." Rork glanced at Joshua. "Has she told you anything about us?"

"Just that she's married but seeking a divorce." He grinned. "She doesn't talk much about herself. She said her husband was a womanizer."

"The man is a prick and mistreats her. Besides his despicable addictions."

Joshua tossed a spade of dirt on a pile. "He should rot. Leila is a kind woman and deserves better." He slanted a glance at Rork. "What's the future look like with her?"

"Right now, it doesn't look promising. Some sort of honor won't allow her to admit how she feels about me."

"That's too bad."

Rork buried the last body and grimaced. "Thank God. Done." He put his hands on his hips and looked around. "I think we're almost ready to depart. I'll find Captain Webb."

Instead, the Captain found him. "I hear that you and Mr.

Formby showed exceptional courage rescuing men from the steamer. Thank you, sirs." He shook their hands. "I wish you'd both consider joining the Union army."

Joshua shook his head. "I'm going to assist the underground in rescuing slaves."

"Good. You have my blessing."

"Thank you, sir."

Webb looked at Rork and tilted his head. "You said your name is Millburn. Aren't you a well-known artist?"

Rork nodded. "I was actually on my way west to paint scenes of remote areas."

"Would you consider painting war scenes instead?"

Rork shrugged. "I wouldn't mind. I guess the west can wait."

"Good. I'll speak to General Grant when he gets back in a week or two."

"I would also like to help Joshua with rescuing slaves. I see no reason I can't do both."

Webb smoothed his beard. "Why didn't you join the Union?"

"I'm sure my participation could add more value by recording events. I know nothing about soldiering."

Webb laughed. "Few men do when they join up. But so far, you've done remarkably well for a man with no fighting experience." He bowed. "I must get these men across to Boonville. I'll ensure you all find suitable accommodation."

"That's kind of you, Captain," Rork said.

Joshua gripped Rork's shoulder. "Did you mean that about helping me?"

"Of course. I wouldn't say something I don't mean."

CHAPTER TWENTY-ONE

*S*teamers from Boonville to Atchison proved challenging to find. Webb and his small force remained in Boonville, searching for bushwhackers. Jones followed orders and went back to St. Louis—while Michael recovered at the rented boarding house with an attendant who works there.

The morning after they arrived, Leila finished putting her hair up and knocked on Cornelia's door. "It's me, Leila."

"Come in, it's good to have your company."

"I would like to talk to you about an idea I have."

"I'm listening."

Leila took a breath. "I've been thinking about the youngsters we see running about and how they are getting schooled."

"Heavens, what made you think about schooling?"

"A minister stopped in to greet us. You were busy with Michael. The minister asked if we would have the interest to teach. He could give us a room in his church to hold classes."

"Oh, Leila, that sounds wonderful, but I don't want to leave Michael all day."

"It's only for the morning. We'll finish by noon."

Cornelia gave Leila a hug and a smile. "I like that. The timing works well. I can get back to Michael."

The word spread fast. Two days later, children came with smiles on their faces. The small room had two windows facing south, and in front of the room, there was a chunk of black slate and chalk to write the lessons. The children sat on benches at long tables to accommodate several little bodies. At noon, after class, the women sank into chairs and watched the energetic children file out.

Cornelia smoothed her dress. "How do the children stay so sunny? Most don't know where their parents are or if they are alive."

"Such enthusiasm to learn, it's heartwarming. We make a wonderful team, don't you agree, Cornelia?"

"Yes, let's also teach them some spiritual songs like *Amazing Grace*, to break up the time with their grammar, composition, and arithmetic."

Leila gathered her cape and bonnet. "Let's get back to the house. I hope the men are back. I worry about them trying to find and help escaped slaves."

Cornelia's mouth pulled down. "Me, too. I detest the night searches the most."

Leila gazed at the trees, its leaves changing color. "It's quiet on the road."

She breathed in the scents of apple pie permeating the air with cinnamon and freshly baked bread.

A child shot out from among the buildings, screaming. Her tattered blue dress flapped around her skinny legs. Her eyes wide, she scrambled away from a rotund man following close behind. With a growl, he lunged at the girl. "Come here, ya brat. I'll peel yer darkie hide off."

Cornelia and Leila stopped and stared at the altercation.

Squealing, the girl zigzagged to escape his enormous hairy hands. "No, master." Legs pumping, she raced onto the road, looked over her shoulder, and ran straight into Cornelia. She knocked Cornelia flat onto her back and fell on top of her.

The man bore down on the child. "Now see what ye've done to the lady, ya miserable little bitch."

Rising to her knees, Cornelia wrapped her arms around the child and glared at the man. "Keep your hands off her, you brute."

Leila held her breath.

His eyes narrowed, and he reached for the child. "The brat is my property. Her mama's my slave."

Leila grit her teeth. "You despicable slaver."

Growling, he lunged for Leila and grabbed her wrist. "I'll teach ya for buttin' in." He brought his arm back.

"You don't scare me." Trying to free her wrist, Leila stared into his fat face. A day's growth of stubble sprouted on his jowls. His small, green eyes speared her with rage.

"Leave the child alone." Cornelia pushed the frightened child behind her and surged to her feet, a rock clutched in her hand. She smashed it against his temple.

Blood trickled down his face. He released Leila and rounded on Cornelia. "Bitch."

Just then, a familiar voice rang out, "Stand back, fellow."

Leila sagged with relief. "Captain Webb. Thank God."

He kept his eyes on the man. "What's your name?"

"What's it to ya?" The man scowled and stepped forward to take the child. "I want my slave back and I'll be on my way."

Webb raised one eyebrow. "I take it you haven't noticed my uniform, fellow."

"Yeah, I noticed ye're a damn Yankee. Now get outta my way."

Webb shoved him. "I detest slavers, so best you watch your step."

The man stumbled back, scowling at Webb. "Ya have no rights here, Yankee, and hands off my property." Sloan roared.

Leila looked from the child to Sloan. The resemblance was uncanny. Her voice dropped to a whisper. "My God, is this little girl your flesh and blood? How could you abuse your own child?"

Sloan dropped his head, eyes slits of venom. "I don't sleep with no darkies."

Webb touched Leila's arm. "Let's go, Mrs. Dempsey. This man isn't worth talking to."

Leila took off her cape and wrapped it around Martha. "The child is shaking like jelly."

They turned and walked away. Webb bent and took the child's hand. "Don't worry, honey. I won't let the man take you."

"He after my mama, suh. She an' me done gone an' run away from Masta Sloan. He catch me where my mama hid me in an old empty barn. Said he was gonna use me to get her back."

Sloane fired a shot, missing Webb, who threw his arms around the women and flung them to the ground. The breath left Leila's lungs—pain jarring her as she hit the hard ground.

Webb rolled onto his back and drew his pistol. "Desist, Sloan!"

"Go to hell, Yankee." A shot exploded, and Sloan crumpled.

Rising to his feet, Webb walked to the slaver and rolled him onto his back. "I would've preferred to take him into custody. I'll wager he's a bushwhacker." He took Sloan's weapon and stuffed it into his belt. "Ladies, get to your residence. I'm sure Mr. Formby and Mr. Millburn will find the child's mother. I am going to find the sheriff to remove the body."

Leila rose and glanced at Sloan. His inert body seeped blood into the ground from a chest wound. She shuddered and helped Cornelia and the child up. "Let's get home. The men might have returned."

Cornelia picked up a weeping Martha. "Hush, sweet girl. You're safe. Mr. Formby will find your mama."

The men bumped into the women on the road. Joshua put his hands on his hips and looked at Cornelia, grinning. "Have you adopted a child?"

"Martha ran into us on the road, trying to escape from her slave owner, who shot at us as we walked away with his little girl. Captain Webb returned the shot and downed the slave owner. We are taking Martha with us. Hopefully, you can find her mama."

Rork's eyes swept over Leila's stained dress, his lips twisted. "Are you okay?"

Leila collapsed against him and explained. "Some people are just plain mean." They walked arm in arm. She glanced up at him, savoring the warmth and strength of his arms.

"Bet Martha's mother is one of the women we found and brought to the Safe House."

Leila looked up at Rork. "Safe House?"

"We met Anya today. She runs the House. Been in operation for months, right under Reb noses."

Leila's eyes sparkled. "Let's go."

Rork ran his fingers through his hair. "It's right by the boarding house."

"I'll carry her." Joshua took Martha from Cornelia.

The child's eyes went from Cornelia to Joshua. "Who he be?"

Cornelia smiled. "Our friend, Joshua."

"You a free slave, missus?"

Cornelia chuckled. "I'm not a slave, little one." She stroked Martha's cheek. "Soon, there will be no more slaves." Martha stuck her thumb in her mouth and nodded.

Rork held onto Leila. "Shall we join them to the safe house?"

"Of course."

Rork kissed her forehead. "This sort of life is foreign to you, isn't it?"

Leila brushed his chest with her fingertips. "I have news for you, mister. I'm no spoilt miss."

His eyes danced. "Oh, aren't you, now? I recall a certain lady who couldn't wait to get to Tiffany's, shopping with a vengeance."

Her mouth quirked up in a smile. "That was then."

"Alas, your innocence lost in the haze of war."

"I like to think I'm the better for it."

"I agree. Just don't let all of this harden you."

Heat crept into her cheeks. "Thank you, I'll try not to let it."

Joshua looked back. "Are you two coming?"

Rork turned, "We're coming." He guided Leila down the road.

A thrill ran through her as his hand rode her hip. She turned to face him, putting a hand on his chest.

"Rork, be patient with me. I am attracted to you, but the timing is wrong."

A grin lit up his face, and he brought her hand to his lips, kissing her fingers. "Hope at last. That will suffice. For now." Leila's heart set up a clamor, and it seemed every nerve in her body was alive to his touch. "Thank you."

"Let's get to the Safe House." With a jaunty step, he took her hand and followed Joshua and Cornelia. Her skirt raised dust as she walked.

Leila smiled. "It doesn't take much to make you happy."

He looked down at her, his eyes dancing. "Even one crumb to a starving man is a banquet."

In a voice stripped of passion, Leila said, "You make me sound mean."

Rork grinned. "Perhaps it will encourage you to give me a slice of bread. Although I'd prefer the whole loaf."

"Stop, Rork Millburn."

"If you bestow one of your heart-stopping smiles on me, I'll stop—momentarily." He poked her in the ribs. "Come on. One smile can't hurt."

Giggling, she scooted sideways. "Stop, I'm ticklish."

"Mmm, are you now?"

She glanced up at him, unable to keep a smile off her lips. "Don't you dare."

"Ha, there's that smile. Thank you. Was that so difficult?"

She laughed. "You're incorrigible."

His fiery gaze settled on her, and heat coursed through her veins. Her eyes fixed on his mouth, a mouth that had claimed her with a passion she yearned for.

"Keep looking at me like that, and I shall have to kiss you," he whispered.

Leila averted her gaze. She concentrated on following Joshua and Cornelia.

The small, nondescript house tucked between other buildings needed paint. Broken green shutters hung from grimy windows, and weeds pushed through the paving leading to a sagging porch. In contrast, the door gleamed with fresh red paint.

"Outward appearances can deceive," Rork said, as though reading her mind. "They identify the door by its color. Escaped slaves know to come to the derelict house with a red door."

Leila shook the dust off her dress. "That makes sense."

Joshua opened the door and greeted a plump woman. "Hello, Anya. We have a child seeking her mother."

Anya ushered them to rooms at the back of the house. Putting her hand on a doorknob, she looked at Leila and Cornelia. "Don't ya be gettin' a shock now. Some of these poor souls are in a bad way." Her eyes danced, and her fat, pink cheeks lifted as she chuckled. "They don't need sympathy, mind. Treat them with respect as equal human beings. Ya ain't ever seen a braver, prouder lot than these poor slaves. Their journey to this safe house has been long and hard."

Cornelia smiled. "My friend's father was a slaver. If he knew she'd married one of his slaves, he would likely kill her."

"I also married a colored fella. Wonderful man he was, too," Anya said.

A bronze-colored child raced down the passage, screaming with laughter as she chased a Negro lad. Her brown curls flew behind her. She touched his shoulder. "Tag." She spun and ran back.

"Oi, Jenny. What did I say about runnin' in the house?"

The children stopped, and Jenny hung her head. "We just havin' fun, Mama."

"Well, ya can have fun in the backyard."

"Well, hello there. I'm Joshua. These are my friends, Rork, Leila and Cornelia—we've traveled together to get here."

Anya tapped the skinny child's backside. "Say hello to our guests, the both of ya and take yerselves outside to play." The boy smiled and bowed. "I'm Joe Junior and pleased to meet y'all." Jenny followed suit, bobbing a curtsey. "Now off with ya," Anya said with a grin.

"They're wild like their papa. God rest his soul."

Leila blinked. "Your husband?"

Tears gleamed in Anya's eyes. "Aye, slavers caught and hanged him last year."

She put a hand to her mouth, Leila's eyes filled. "I'm so sorry."

"I was pregnant with our third child, and they beat me, leaving me for dead. I lost the baby." She swiped at the moisture on her cheeks. "My Joe was a free slave, had been for years. He was a fierce abolitionist and died for the cause." She swept out a plump arm. "That's why I do this, to honor his memory and fulfill his dream to see all men and women treated equally." She opened the door. "Come and meet our latest escapees." She pushed a stray red curl into a frilly mobcap. "Maybe little Martha's mama is amongst them."

Crammed into the room were eight iron beds. A woman in a crisp white apron attended to their needs. Some bore wounds—others emaciated from starvation and illness. A stench of unwashed bodies and despair permeated the atmosphere.

Leila steeled her lips to stop a gasp. Rork put an arm around her and squeezed her shoulders. She leaned against him, drawing strength.

Anya glanced at her with gentle eyes. "It's a shock the first time one sees the cruelty of man. Food in the South is scarce. Some have been on the run for over a year." She pointed at a man lying on his stomach, his torso wrapped in bandages. "His owner whipped him with a cat-o'-nine-tails, took the flesh off his back. They left him for dead." She smiled at Leila. "Your husband found him near the river. Poor fella was lucid enough to tell his story."

Leila liked the sound of Rork being her husband. He grinned and winked at Joshua.

Cornelia walked to the beds, holding Martha. "Do you see your mama here?"

Martha's wide eyes scanned the occupants of the room. She shook her head.

Anya touched her cheek. "Don't ya fret, honey. There are three more rooms like this. What is your mama's name?"

Martha stared at her. "*Mama.*"

Anya chuckled. "We'll find yer mama." Leila was not sure she could face more human misery, but she took a big breath and followed the group. Rork had an arm firmly around her waist.

CHAPTER TWENTY-TWO

They stepped into the last room. "Mama!" Martha squealed, squirmed out of Leila's arms, and ran to her mother, a tall woman with smooth bronze skin. She dropped an empty bedpan, held out her arms, and cried out, "Martha, my baby."

She held her daughter, tears rolling down her cheeks. Martha had her arms around her mother's neck. "Don't cry, Mama, I here now." Martha kissed her mother's tears.

Anya beamed. "I insist y'all have dinner with us. The victuals are plain but will fill your bellies." She waved a hand. "Come, I'm going to the kitchen to cook. Everyone in the house meets there for our meals."

They followed Anya to a warm kitchen with an enormous oak table and plain wooden chairs in the center. A thin, blue checkered curtain hung over a small window. Anya slipped an apron over her head to save her blue and her yellow flowered sack type dresses. One for church and one for everything else. She tied the apron around her protruding belly to protect the front of her dress.

Aware of Rork's hip pressed to hers, Leila gazed at the cheerful faces around the table.

Rork tweaked a plait of her hair. "What are you thinking?"

Her smile gave her eyes a moment of glitter. "I prefer this setting to the way I grew up."

"Dinnertime in my parents' home was chaotic. I can guess what meals were like in your house, having met your mother."

She grimaced. "Silence reigned."

Passed around the table were tin plates piled with grits and beef stew.

"Let's give thanks," Anya said in her bubbly voice. After the prayer, she clapped her hands. "Pass the bread, Jenny." Two steaming loaves of bread, the aroma intoxicating, made the rounds.

Leila stared at the bread. "Is there a bread knife?"

Anya hooted, her massive bosom wobbling like jelly. "Honey, we never cut bread here. We break off chunks to remind us of Christ breaking bread."

Heat crept into Leila's cheeks. "Wonderful idea, a good way to teach the children about spiritual things. For every meal?"

"Whenever we have bread."

Rork chuckled. "Different?"

"No tin plates and utilitarian cutlery for my mother, only porcelain crockery, silver cutlery, and crystal glasses. And she kept a bowl of yellow roses in the middle of the table." Leila took a spoonful of the rich stew. "No surprise, I never had an appetite at home in that stilted atmosphere." She broke off a chunk of bread and bit into the fresh, aromatic, airy treat. "This is so good. It has a chewy texture and a crisp, crackly crust. I love the crunchy the best."

Anya ate with relish and mopped up the thick gravy with the bread. She smiled at Leila. "I see ya gently reared." Anya picked up an infant and spooned food into his mouth. "I'm afraid war strips most folk of pretenses."

"When I think of the person I was, it makes me cringe." Leila toyed with her tin spoon.

"Yer education has given ya the ability to teach the less fortunate. And that ain't somethin' to sniff at." Anya pointed her spoon at Leila. "Don't ya ever have regrets about what ya had in life. That's what molds ya into what ye've become, a fine and compassionate lady."

"Thank you," she whispered. Compliments were rare in her life.

Rork regaled them with the sinking boat, Leila going for help, and the cougar's death threat.

The children stared at Leila, wide-eyed. "Ya must have been real scared with a cougar prowlin' about," Jenny piped.

Leila giggled. "Terrified!" Admiration shone in Joe's eyes.

Leila shook her head. "I thought the cat was hungry."

Joe's mouth tightened. "Ya was still brave." His expression softened. "And ye're pretty—real pretty."

"Thank you, kind sir," she said, looking down.

Rork swept a strand of hair behind her ear. "You need to learn to accept compliments, my love."

"Listen to yer husband, honey."

Leila opened her mouth to tell Anya that Rork wasn't her husband.

Rork squeezed her hand and leaned closer. "Say nothing."

"Why on earth not?" She looked at Anya. "Mr. Millburn is not my husband."

"Well, he should be." Anya tilted her head. "Where is yer husband?"

"I warned you," Rork whispered. "Now you've opened yourself up to an inquiry."

Leila scowled at him and turned back to Anya. "I am married to Hank Dempsey. I must find him to sign my divorce papers."

Anya tapped her misshapen teeth. "Hank Dempsey, ya say. Is he with a loudmouthed redhead?"

Leila leaned forward, her heart racing. "Yes. I take it you've met him?"

"Aye, I had the misfortune. Not surprised ya want to divorce that dimwit." Anya's mouth quivered. "I had a young lady helpin' me. Dempsey saw her at an inn where she works when she's not here. He was drunk and tried to molest her. One of her children saw it happen and ran here to get me."

Leila put a hand over her mouth, her eyes wide. "Oh, my soul."

Rork's mouth set in a hard line. "What happened?"

"I stopped him. But he had ripped her dress, exposin' the poor girl's bosom for all to see." Anya blew her nose with a huge handkerchief. "Poor lamb was a virgin, and the shame was too much for her." She stared at her hands. "I could've helped her get over feelin' dirty. That's what she called herself—dirty." Anya's head sagged. "But I never got the chance. The child hanged herself. I found that damn Dempsey and told him she died because of his abuse."

She looked at Rork and Leila, and anger seeped into her voice. "He said he was sorry she's dead, but it weren't his fault. His hussy says she didn't think one less mulatto made any difference. Then he up and agrees with her. Those two fit each other perfect."

"I'm ashamed of what he did. His addictions make him violent and irrational. Not that it excuses his behavior." She slinked in her chair. "My husband opposed slavery. I can't believe the depths to which he's sunk."

"As ya said, it ain't no excuse." Anya sneered. "I pray he gets what he deserves—to burn in hell."

Rork put an arm around Leila, but she pushed him away. "Anya, is he still in Boonville?"

"Nah, he took off like the weasel he is—hauled his miserable ass off to Kansas City. Took his woman with him."

Leila finished her food. "Then I'll go to Kansas City."

Rork fiddled with the top button of his shirt. "We must find a steamer going that way."

"We?" Leila rose slowly. "I can find my own way there."

"Not while I'm around." He patted her chair. "Sit. Too late to inquire about steamers now."

CHAPTER TWENTY-THREE

*R*ork cocked an eyebrow. "Are you coming, Leila?"

"Yes," she quavered and stepped onto the gang-plank, careful not to fall in between the cracks of the wooden planks. The fierce winds blew against Leila's face, pushing her down the gangplank while she walked up to board the ship. Her clenched fingers turned white holding onto the ropes for fear the wind would blow her off.

Rork couldn't resist. "Ah, you're afraid." He swept her up in his arms and carried her aboard the steamer. "It's just as well I insisted on coming with you to Kansas City. If you'd denied me, I'd have followed you, anyway."

She avoided his gaze.

"You have impossibly long lashes. They're like black butter-flies on your pink cheeks." He opened his mouth to say more.

She put her fingers on his lips. "Please don't, not yet. You promised."

"Did I? Must have slipped my mind." He set her onto her feet. "When the divorce is final, I envision you'll marry me."

"I don't know if I could marry again. People change after marriage."

"We'll have children and grow old together. You must believe I'll always be there for you."

She pushed him away. "Let's wait and see." She laughed. "You might well become bored with me before it gets to marriage." Turning, she strode along the deck. "We have a long trip ahead of us."

He had a roguish grin on his face, following Leila and enjoying the sight of her swaying hips.

The riverboat pulled smoothly from the wharf, smoke billowing from its tall stacks.

The rumble of engines reverberated under Rork's feet. Leila stumbled. "Oh, my."

Rork caught her. "Got you. The gods must favor me."

Dimples played on Leila's cheeks. "It's a good thing you were close by—again. You can let me go now."

"I was rather enjoying holding onto you." Rork released her.

"I'm fine." She scrambled to her feet, brushed soot off her dress, and tucked away stray tendrils of her hair. "I would like to freshen up."

He took her arm firmly. "Let's get you to your cabin." He cocked one eyebrow. "I'm willing to be your maid."

Leila's mouth quirked up at the corners. "I don't think so, mister."

He laughed and steered her to a deck below. "It was worth a try. I never told you how wonderful you were braving the attack on our steamer."

"Thank you. I didn't know if I would survive. She glanced up at him from under her lashes. "I wouldn't have made it if you hadn't shown up."

"I told you, I will follow wherever you go." Rork led her to the stairs, and a nasal voice halted them.

"What have we here?"

Rork turned slowly, eyebrows raised. He took in a squirrel-like man in a uniform. "I assume you're the captain, sir."

The man doffed his hat. "I am." His eyes fixed on Leila. The hard lines of his face and a long nose with a meager mouth gave him a predatory look. He smoothed his hair, graying at the temples. "Captain Iliad Johnson at your service, Miss . . ."

Leila smiled. "Mrs. Ashburn Dempsey."

"Ah, Mrs. Dempsey. I'm delighted to meet you, madam." His beady black eyes slid over her, and he moved closer, taking her hand. Rork hid a smile. Leila jerked her hand away as though scalded, and she wrapped her arms around her waist.

"I'm rather cold and wet. I tripped on the slippery deck. Please excuse me, Captain." Leila looked up at Rork.

Rork gave her his arm, more than happy to rescue her. "Shall we continue?" He bowed. "Good day, Captain Johnson." Rork turned with Leila and scowled. The fawning captain followed.

"Oh, Mrs. Dempsey, before you go," the captain gushed, "it would give me great pleasure if you'd join me at my table for dinner tonight."

Leila raised delicate eyebrows. "I wouldn't dream of deserting my traveling companion, Captain."

He shook his narrow head. "Of course not." He gave Rork a cursory glance. "You're welcome to join us if you wish, sir."

"I will join Mrs. Dempsey at your table. I never leave the lady's side," Rork spoke in a deep voice, relaxed.

Johnson all but ignored him and turned back to Leila, an obsequious smile ferreting across his lips. "Is your husband the famed journalist, Hank Dempsey?"

Leila lifted her chin. "Yes, Captain." She looked at Rork. "And this is Rork Millburn, the famous artist."

He barely looked at Rork. "Oh?" He laughed. "I thought at first that he was your husband—until I heard your name. Where is your husband?"

Leila's eyes narrowed. "I don't think that's any of your business. Shall we go, Rork?"

"It's a pleasure to meet you, Mrs. Dempsey. So, will you join me for dinner tonight?"

Leila glanced at Rork. He gave her a nod.

"I suppose so, Captain."

"Well, tonight can't come swiftly enough." He bowed and scampered off.

Leila blew out a breath. "What a vile man."

"I couldn't agree more." Rork walked her down the stairs. "Perhaps I should feign seasickness tonight."

"It's up to you, Leila, but it's good to befriend the captain of a ship, and I'll be there with you."

"So you think I should accommodate the captain?"

Rork shrugged. "We'll get a decent meal and if we need anything, he'll comply."

She slapped his arm. "So, I'm sacrificing so you can have a good meal?"

"A man my size needs plenty of sustenance." He chuckled and escorted Leila along a corridor below the saloon deck. A crewman ran after them.

"Excuse me, madam." They turned, and Leila raised her eyebrows. "Yes?"

He stopped to catch his breath. "The captain allocated one of our luxury suites for your comfort." He sidled past them. "This way, please," he twittered, scurrying ahead.

Leila hung back. "Why would he give me a luxury cabin? I don't like the attention that man lavishes on me."

Rork patted her hand on his arm. "I won't let it get beyond what it is now. Enjoy the luxury. It may be the last you have for a while."

The scrawny crewman led them to the lowest deck and showed Leila to the cabin the captain had set aside for her. "Here you are, ma'am." He pinched his nose and slid a glance at Rork. "I'll show you to your cabin now, sir."

Rork scowled down at him. "I know where my cabin is, thank you. And I don't need help to get there."

The crewman cleared his throat. "Ah, the captain gave me specific instructions to escort you there."

Rork clenched his jaw. "Young man, I know well that your captain is intent on dispensing with me." He stepped closer to the crewman. "But I have no intention of being shunted about. Now, get the hell out of here and tell your slimy little captain that he will not manipulate me." He put an arm around Leila. "Nor will he corner the lady. She will always have me at her side. Always." He thrust a thumb over his shoulder. "Now scoot."

Eyes popping, the crewman bobbed his head and scuttled off.

Leaning against the cabin wall, a hand pressed to her stomach, Leila gave way to uncontrollable laughter.

Rork smiled and rubbed his cheek. "I suppose that was a poor reaction on my part. But I detest Johnson's transparent ploys to get rid of me and get his grubby paws on you." He looked at her flushed cheeks and eyes sparkling with amusement. "God, you're beautiful," he whispered.

She stopped laughing and held his gaze.

With a groan, he drew her into his arms. He captured her mouth, and she opened to him, taking his breath away. Their bodies melded, and his world spun into a realm of pure pleasure. He maneuvered her toward a plush double bed draped in white lace testers. Leila wrapped her arms around his neck, and his heart raced as they fell onto the bed.

Trembling, he undid the tiny pearl buttons running down the front of her dress. "I will give you pleasure beyond your wildest dreams," he whispered.

A small sob escaped her, and she pushed him away. "I want you, too, but this is wrong, Rork."

Disappointment assailed him, and he ached with need. "I can wait," he growled. He touched her lower lip and smiled. "It's hard to resist you, my innocent one." Rising, he leaned down and planted a tender kiss.

She wound her arms around his neck. "And I want you, but this is not the time."

"Do you think you could ever love me?"

Leila nodded. "Give me time."

"That I can do . . . I think." He grinned and ran a finger down her cheek. "I'm on fire for you, my lovely Leila." He adjusted his jacket. "I'll leave you to rest and freshen up for dinner."

He walked out before he lost the ability to resist her.

"Painful business being around that lady," he said and strode to his less opulent cabin. He stopped short once inside. A tray on the table had a bottle of champagne and a glass containing a note. Rork picked it up with two fingers and read it. *With compliments from Captain Johnson.* Rork snorted. "Now he's trying to gain favor with me. What a prick." Johnson had already uncorked the bottle. Chuckling, Rork poured the bubbly libation into the glass and downed it, pouring another. "May as well make the most of it." He stripped off his jacket and plucked at the bottom button of his waistcoat. His fingers went numb, and his head swam.

"What the hell?" Rork staggered, lurching toward the door. "I think the bastard drugged me. Got to warn Leila—" He collapsed, and oblivion claimed him.

CHAPTER TWENTY-FOUR

*L*eila lay on the bed, staring up at the canopy, and sucked in a breath. Somehow, she'd resisted Rork. Every nerve in her body still tingled with desire. Rising, she roamed around the room. It was reminiscent of the elegance of her parents' home. She ran her hand along the cream colored walls, moved to the furniture, and fingered the fine damask, lace, and velvet. In an armoire, she found shimmering silk-colored gowns of all sizes hung from satin-wrapped hangers. The faint fragrance of those who came before lingered. To whom did they belong? Did that revolting captain keep these gowns for women he intended to seduce?

A knock at the door shook her from dark thoughts.

It must be Rork. "Come in."

The crewman opened the door. "Ma'am, I am sorry to interrupt you. The Captain sent me to escort you to his cabin."

"I am not ready. I'm sure Mr. Millburn will be here shortly to accompany me. I'll wait."

"I'll be here in the corridor should you change your mind."

Leila shut the door, poured water into a porcelain basin, and washed her face. I won't wear one of those dresses, mine will do just fine. I miss Biddy. Oh, bother. She dragged a brush through her hair, leaving it loose over her shoulders. Leaning forward, she examined her image in the mirror. She pinched her cheeks, released a sigh, and opened the door.

The crewman's face turned red. "M—Ma'am, you're beautiful." He gave her his arm.

She ignored it. "We'll fetch Mr. Millburn on the way."

"No, ma'am, I believe the captain has taken care of him."

"Taken care of him?"

"That was all the captain said."

She braced her shoulders. Must I confront that captain alone?

The crewman knocked on the captain's door and bowed.

"There you go, ma'am."

Johnson beamed at her. "Could you be more beautiful? You didn't avail yourself of the lovely dresses. Why not?"

She raised one eyebrow. "They aren't mine."

He took her arm and pulled her into his cabin before she could protest. "I wish you had."

She shook his hand off, and her mouth tightened. "What on earth for?"

He shrugged, retook her arm, and led her to a couch.

"Unhand me." Leila pulled from his grasp, setting distance between them. "I assume Mr. Millburn is coming shortly."

"I expect he's on his way." He handed her a glass of champagne.

Leila glanced at a table set for two. Her heart sank. Dim candlelight created long shadows crossing the floor.

Platters of hors d'oeuvres and canapes adorned a sideboard emitting a spoiled smell of uncooked day-old fish. She moved farther away from him. "Captain, tell me about your steamer."

"We serve in the war effort." He took a smelly canape and moved closer to Leila.

She turned away. Ugh, he is disgusting. Loud banging on the door interrupted them.

Johnson spun around, choking on a shrimp. He wiped his mouth with a napkin and opened the door. "Mr. Millburn, were you disturbed from your sleep?"

Leila released a breath. "Thank goodness."

Rork stumbled in, unshaven, his eyes ringed with red. "Sleeping? You mean drugged, you underhanded son of a bitch."

Johnson stiffened. "I beg your pardon, sir. What are you accusing me of?"

Rork grabbed Johnson's jacket lapels in one huge fist and lifted him off his feet. "You know damn well what I'm talking about, you slimy little worm."

Leila grasped Rork's arm. "No! He isn't worth going to jail for."

"You're right." Rork threw Johnson on the couch. "Come near this lady again, and you're dead meat!" He took Leila's hand. "Let's get the hell out of here."

"I know what your game is—you want her!" screamed Johnson. "I'll ensure her husband hears about this."

With a growl, Rork turned and bore down on him. "You have no idea what the hell you're talking about."

"Rork, no. Please, let's go." Leila glared at the disheveled captain cringing on the couch.

"My husband no longer exists. We're divorcing."

Again, Rork took her arm. "No need to explain anything to this prick."

The steamer docked at Kansas City, Leila and Rork stood at the rail. She drew a deep breath of air laden with the pungent perfume of pine trees and the first snow drifting down in white flurries.

Rork reached out, took Leila's hand, turned it over, and pressed his lips to her palm.

Electric currents permeated her from his hot lips and pulsed through her body in a tide of desire. Trembling with need, Leila submitted to the passion as he captured her mouth. She tried to withdraw.

"Don't pull away, Leila. I need you."

"Need me? Rork, you can have whatever you want, but it can't be me—not yet."

Tight-lipped, he released her and ushered her down the gangplank. Crewmen hoisted bags onto the roof of a four-horse carriage. Rork handed Leila into the vehicle. She avoided his intense eyes. "Please stop looking at me like that." There was a note of exasperation in her voice. She sat and stared ahead. "Where will we live?"

"At a friend's house. A mansion. It's the Alexander Majors Mansion. It isn't far."

For the first time, Leila noticed the elaborate trappings of the carriage. "You didn't mention the trip to your friend's place."

"I know the owner. I sent a letter telling him we were on our way to Kansas. At the start of the war, he visited me in my Tenth Street studio to commission me to paint war scenes." Rork sat opposite Leila. "But when was I to paint? I haven't been in one place long enough."

Leila gave him a sidelong glance from under her lashes and murmured, "Why not paint while we're at your friend's manor?"

His eyes traveled to her lips, and he smiled. "You're good for me."

She looked down. The heat of his gaze thrilled her. At least he appreciated her.

"I doubt there will be time, though." He squeezed her hand. "I don't think we need to prolong this visit. We'll find Hank and move on."

"We can't go west until spring. We have nothing but time."

"You're right. Perhaps I can get some work done."

"Before we go, I need my valise. It's in the boot." She alighted from the carriage.

"Stay there, I'll get it." Rork jumped out and strode to the back of the carriage. Leila followed him.

A sailor approached. "Sir, take care on the wharf. The authorities reported that bushwhackers are accosting people."

Rork tipped his hat. "Thank you, but I can take care of myself and the lady."

The man chuckled and scanned Rork from head to toe. "I imagine you can."

Opening the boot, Rork hauled out her valise. "Here you are."

Shadows flickered near buildings that loomed ominously in the dawn light. Leila drew closer to Rork. "I think we should get out of here."

Two figures moved behind the carriage.

Leila's eyes widened.

One figure emerged, unshaven, his clothes threadbare. A tall man with a short, fat neck followed. He hunched over, his hands in pockets of a trench coat. The short man leered. "Where do you think you is goin', mate?"

Rork pushed Leila behind him and ripped off his hat, flinging it aside. The man's fetid breath assailed him. Rork's lip curled. "It has nothing to do with you where I'm going, you piece of crap."

The man growled. "Who do you think you're sayin' that to, smart ass? No one that don't meet with me approval steps into my territory."

"I don't need your damn approval. Now move aside."

"Get back on your ship and steam out of here."

"Like hell. Back off, low life."

A feral smile exposed tobacco-stained teeth as he pulled out a knife.

Rork's knee came up and slammed into the man's crotch. The knife flew from his hand, and he buckled, clutching his crotch. "You son of a bitch!"

"Back off, bastard," Rork snarled and shoved him.

The taller man lunged forward and grabbed Leila. His arm snapped around her waist, and he pulled her against his chest, holding a knife to her throat. "One move an' this li'l lady gets the blade."

Rork held up his hands and backed away. "No harm done, gentlemen."

The tall one relaxed his hold on Leila.

Leila jabbed her elbow into his ribs. He grunted and doubled over. She spun away and brought her parasol down onto the back of his neck.

Rork chuckled and brought his fist up, sending the man flying. "Well done, Leila."

"I cannot stand bullies." Leila scowled and dusted off her skirt and adjusted her bonnet.

Rork strolled to the prostrate men and pulled out his revolver. "You have a choice. I can shoot you both and claim self-defense, or you can take your horses and get your sorry asses out of here."

"We don't have any horses."

"Then you'd better run."

Crewmen, standing at the rail of the steamer, clapped and cheered. "It's about time someone taught them a lesson."

Eyes riveted to the deserters, Rork fired a shot at their feet. "I said get the hell out." He pulled the trigger again, and dust flew up near them.

"We goin.'" They ran, weaving and jumping as more bullets hit the ground at their feet.

Rork shoved the revolver into his belt and put an arm around Leila. "Are you all right?"

"I am. Just a little shaken."

"You can be on my team anytime." He brushed his fingertips across her trembling hand.

"Let's get out of here." He swept her up in his arms and put her into the carriage.

She giggled. "I can still walk."

"I know." He grinned. "But holding you is more my fancy."

They strolled through the estate gardens. Rork stroked Leila's hand resting on his arm. "One is almost unaware a war is raging near here."

Leila glanced back at the mansion. "The house is exquisite."

He leaned down and kissed the top of her head. Her hair gleamed in the dull light. "Put up the hood of your cape, so you don't catch a chill." He pulled the hood over her head.

"Thank you."

"I'll build you a home like this one day."

Despite the gray light of early evening, the four tall chimneys and white trim of the house defined its charming character.

Leila chuckled. "I don't think I want a mansion like this. I appreciate glorious beauty, but I'm over displays of opulence."

"My, how you've changed." He tapped her short nose. "I like this new Leila."

She laughed. "Why, thank you, sir. I'm delighted you approve."

A buggy passed them on its way to the house. "I didn't know Alex was expecting guests. He didn't mention anyone." His eyes fixed on a figure alighting from the vehicle. Something was familiar about him. The man took a woman's hand and helped her out. Her red hair curled from beneath an elaborate bonnet.

"What is it?" Leila asked.

"Not sure," he grunted. With speed reminiscent of a thoroughbred racer, he ran over the rough road to the carriage. He grabbed the man's shoulder and spun him around. "Hank, you bastard."

Hank's eyes dilated, and he tried to squirm from the iron grasp. "Rork, I thought you were dead."

"I'm sure you did. You should have hung around after you shot me, you coward."

"I sent someone to fetch an ambulance."

"Big man, but that's crap. Someone else called for help."

Hank avoided Rork's intense eyes. "I-I meant to."

"What the hell were you thinking, shooting me?"

"Mistake—I made a mistake."

"Shooting someone is more than a mistake. It's a lifetime error." Rork wrapped a hand around Hank's throat and shook him.

Choking, Hank cringed beneath the onslaught of Rork's rage. "Didn't you ever make a mistake?" he croaked, clawing at Rork's hand.

"Of that magnitude? No. You don't have a shred of decency, Hank. You turned tail and ran." Rork flung him to the ground. "You aren't even worth my anger."

"Rork, what in the world is going on?" Leila stared at Hank and put both her hands on her cheeks. "You."

Scrambling to his feet, Hank tried to brush off-road dirt and gravel from his suit. He glared at Rork—his lip lifted in a sneer. "Well, well, it didn't take you long to fill the space my absence left."

With a growl, Rork bore down on him, hands clenched. "You miserable little snot, who are you to point fingers when you have your whore in tow."

Sissy huffed and pressed her back to the carriage. "H-how dare you? Hank, punch him or something." she screeched.

Hank swung his head and gaped at her. "Are you insane, woman? One punch from him, and I'm dead. Get into the damn buggy."

Rork grabbed his arms. "Since you've conveniently fallen into my hands, Leila has divorce papers for you to sign. Doesn't seem that Pinkerton ever found you to have you sign."

"What the hell are you talking about?"

"You know damn well what I'm talking about."

"That bastard Pinkerton? I threw him out and burned the papers."

Rork looked over his shoulder. "Leila, you have an extra set. Where are they?"

"I must fetch them. They're in my valise."

He nodded. "Get them. I'll hold onto this bastard." Leila ran to the mansion.

Hank lashed out at Rork. "You're in love with my wife. You've lusted after her since you met her at the Catskill Mountain House."

Snarling, Rork shook him as though he were a rat. "If you want to live, you'd better shut your damn mouth."

Despite the threats, Hank blustered like a bantam cock. "I could call you out for screwing my wife. The little slut has panted for you from the moment she set eyes on you."

Rork smiled coldly. "Please name your second. I welcome a duel with you. Then I don't have to go the messy route of tearing you apart." He released Hank.

He staggered back, pouting and rubbing his arms. "So you have screwed my wife."

"Don't align her with your filthy dallying. I would never dishonor her."

"I don't believe you. I know my wife is spreading her legs for you."

"You miserable bastard, you don't deserve her."

"And you do?" Hank sneered.

Rork shook his head. "I am not having this discussion with you."

Hank drew a pistol, his lip lifting in a snarl. "This is the only type of discussion you understand."

"So, you would attempt to kill me again?" Rork folded his arms. "You sniveling coward. You failed before, and you will fail again."

Leila came with her copy of the divorce papers, panting. "Just sign these, Hank. Hank! What are you doing with that gun? Rork?"

"If you think I'm going to waste time on divorce maneuvers, think again."

"Cut out this crap, Hank. Kill me, and you'll hang unless you plan to shoot Leila as well." Hank's raw, mirthless laugh raked Rork's nerves. "Put the damn gun away. It won't solve anything," he breathed, holding Hank's wild eyes.

Hank cocked the hammer and swung the gun from Rork to Leila.

A shot rang out.

CHAPTER TWENTY-FIVE

*H*ank spun and fell like a skittle.

Alex stood a short distance away, a smoking revolver in his hand. "Seems I arrived in the nick of time."

"Dear God." Leila cried and ran to Hank, falling to her knees. Hesitating, she leaned down, putting her ear to his mouth. "I think he's breathing."

The driver's eyes dilated. "Bugger me." He leaped from the buggy and ran.

"What happened?" Sissy poked her head out the carriage window and emitted a piercing scream. "Hank." The carriage door flew open, and she raced to his side. "My poor man, what have they done to you?" She sagged to the ground in a billow of blue satin and lace, grasping Hank's hand.

"Your lover got shot, dear," Rork drawled and walked to Alex. "You saved our lives, my friend. Thank you."

"You're welcome. I always thought his habits deranged the prick." Alex smiled and stuffed the revolver into his belt. "Who is the redhead bawling like a banshee?"

Rork jerked his head toward Hank. "His mistress. What was

he doing here, anyway? I had no idea he was an associate of yours."

"He's not. I don't know why he came calling."

"Rork," Leila cried. "I think Hank is alive."

"Well, he should be," Alex said. "Only shot the fool in the shoulder."

"Oh." Leila turned back to Hank. "Perhaps we should get him inside."

Alex laughed. "I'm not coddling that cur in my house. Toss him into the carriage. His slut can drive him to a hospital."

Hank grabbed Leila's cape with a bloodied hand. "Listen, my darlin'. I deserved this."

Leila took off her cape and stuffed it under his head.

"You need to keep still, Hank."

"I haven't treated you well. Please forgive me."

"I forgive you."

He reached up and grabbed her hand, leaving a bloody smear. "Does that mean you won't divorce me?"

"Why? Because you got shot? You threatened to shoot us." She shook her head. "I want a divorce more than ever now. You need help with your addictions."

Groaning, he reached up and pulled her head down, capturing her mouth.

She jerked away and glanced at Sissy, who glared at her.

Leila wiped her mouth. "Your mistress will attend to your needs."

"I don't want the bitch," he whined, clutching at Leila's bodice. "I want you. I've always loved you. You love me, too. I know you do."

"You couldn't be more wrong. You killed any love I had for you. I cannot abide by your abusive behavior and dissipated life-style." She tried to peel his fingers off her bodice. "Let me go, Hank."

"I'll change, Leila. I swear."

She rose and glared down at him. "I've heard that before. You'll never change. Marry Sissy, or don't. I couldn't care less what you do with her. Just sign the divorce papers."

Hank grabbed the hem of Leila's dress. "Please, darlin', don't divorce me, I beg you." He scowled at Sissy. "Go away. Piss off, bitch! You ruined my life."

Sissy rocked back on her heels. "I am the one who stood behind you through all the hard times."

Hank wrapped his arm around her legs. He pulled her feet out from under her, sending her onto her back. "I said, piss off!" Again, he squirmed toward Leila. "Don't leave me—please."

Leila stepped out of his reach.

Sissy scrambled to her knees. She grabbed Hank's gun—her face contorted with rage. "You treacherous bastard." Leveling the gun at his head, she fired and swung the weapon to Leila. "Now you die, you sniveling bitch."

Rork lunged forward, grabbed Sissy's arm, and twisted the gun from her hand. With an upward thrust, he jabbed his elbow into her jaw, knocking her senseless.

Alex put an arm around Leila. "Don't look, honey."

Leila's breath escaped in labored gasps. She pressed a fist into her mouth. "This is my fault." She stared at the bloody mess that was Hank's face.

"Don't talk nonsense, Leila," Alex said, guiding her to his villa. "How could you possibly have known she'd shoot Hank?"

Tears snaked down her cheeks. "I've just witnessed the death of a great mind. Perhaps I should have stood by him, whatever the cost. Now Sissy's ruined."

"Who gives a damn? You're being ridiculous, Leila. Those two engineered their fate."

She tore away from his protective arms. "I can't just walk away. He was my husband." Leila brushed at her tears. "The least I can do is to be with him," she sobbed.

"Oh, for God's sake, the man is dead."

"You don't understand," she mumbled and hurried back. Kneeling beside Hank, she swallowed a sob and touched his lank, bloodstained hair, smoothing it back with trembling fingers.

Binding Sissy's wrists with his stock, Rork picked her up and carried her to the carriage.

She revived and struggled against the strain of her bonds. "What happened? Let me go."

Rork dumped her on the seat. "You're not fooling anyone, sweetheart." He slammed the door and strode back to Leila, holding her. "I think you should go to the house with Alex."

For a moment, she snuggled against his broad chest, drawing strength from him and sobbing uncontrollably.

"Please go. I'll deal with this."

"How can you refer to Hank as *this*?"

"You're overwrought. I'll take Hank into town and plan for his funeral and ensure to imprison Sissy."

Leila pushed Rork away. "They'll hang her."

"Well, yes."

"She doesn't deserve to hang."

"What are you suggesting, Leila?"

She turned her back on Rork and whispered, "Let her go."

He took her arm and turned her to face him. "You can't be serious."

"I've caused enough pain by asking for a divorce. I think she honestly loved him."

Alex approached, shaking his head. "Honey, none of this is your fault."

Leila's eyes went from Alex to Rork. "I still feel responsible." Her eyes skittered to Hank's corpse, and she shuddered. "Sissy has always been hotheaded." She twisted her bloodied hands. "Can't we say Hank took his own life?"

Alex and Rork exchanged glances, and Rork shrugged. "If that's what you want."

Alex rubbed his cheek, his eyes resting on her. "Will it make you feel less responsible?"

She nodded.

"It's your call. I'll release her." Rork walked to the carriage, opened the door, and untied Sissy's bonds.

"W-what is going on?" Sissy said, staring at him wide-eyed, cringing against the seat cushions.

"Leila wants to let you go. We're telling the authorities Hank shot himself." His eyes hardened. "I want you to stay out of her life. Do you understand me?"

Sissy's red curls bounced as she nodded. "I promise she'll never see me again."

"Good." Rork turned from the carriage, and Leila pushed past him, moving toward Sissy.

He grabbed her arm. "Damn it, Leila. The woman just killed Hank."

Sissy leaned forward and grasped Leila's hand. "Thank you. I didn't mean to kill him. I swear."

"Alex, could you ask one of your servants to find the driver? Or perhaps we can use one of your men to take the body into town?"

"I'll call my driver. The fewer people involved, the better," Alex said and strode off to the stables.

Leila ran after him. "Please send Sissy to town in another carriage."

Alex smiled. "You are too soft for your own good, madam, but I shall do as you ask."

Rork covered Hank's mutilated face and guided a weeping Leila to the villa.

"Thank you," she said, her sobs muffled in a lace handkerchief.

"I hope this act of kindness doesn't come back to haunt us."

CHAPTER TWENTY-SIX

*R*ork stood on the patio of the mansion—icicles hung from the eaves. Kansas City's buildings outlined an angry late afternoon sky. He walked down the steps and wiped a drop of icy water from his neck. Brave spears of green grass poked through melting snow. Catching a whiff of lavender and vanilla perfume, he strolled to greet her.

Leila pulled her fur cape tighter around herself. "It's still rather cold."

He took her hand, tucking it into his arm. Their feet crunched the snow underfoot. "We'll be able to travel west in a few weeks." The cold brought a pink bloom to Leila's cheeks. She'd never looked lovelier to him. "Have you given any more thought to marry me?"

"No, Hank's death still haunts me."

Stopping, he turned and took her shoulders. "You never had a proper marriage with him. How long must I wait, Leila?" He suffered the sorrow in her eyes. "He's been dead for months."

"I know, but I can't help what I feel."

Rork released a long breath. How can I break her melancholia? He touched her cheek. "I love you. I want to marry you before we head west."

A scowl marred her smooth forehead, and she brushed his hand away. "Stop it! Stop pressing me. Why can't you just let me suffer the loss of my husband?"

"For God's sake, Leila, less than five months ago, you were hell-bent on divorcing him. What's going on with you?"

"I'm grieving for my husband. That's what's going on." She slapped his chest. "How can you be so insensitive?"

He grabbed her hand. "How can you be so hypocritical?"

She dropped her chin and sighed.

His heart fell. "I'm sorry. I didn't mean that."

"Yes, you did." She spun and ran back to the villa.

He ran his fingers through his hair. "Damn, now I've gone and done it." Scowling, he watched her skirt sway from left to right as she stormed up the steps and disappeared into the house. He shoved his hands into his pockets and milled about. "I need to make this right, but how do I get through to her?" He kicked clumps of snow. "Damn you, Hank. It was impossible competing with you alive but dead, you're an unmanageable fortress. But you will not win."

He took off at a run, boots pounding across the wooden patio floor and into the villa. Breathing heavily, he stopped at her suite door and knocked.

"Go away!"

"If you don't open this damn door, I'll break the thing down." He strained to hear her muffled response.

"Get out of my life!"

He leaned against the oak door. "I'm sorry I called you a hypocrite, Leila. I'm upset you won't marry me and jealous of Hank's memory."

Movement, then silence.

"Leila?" He turned the doorknob, and it swung open a fraction. Putting his shoulder to the door, he pushed harder. A squeal emitted from inside, and he stumbled through to see Leila fall on her backside in a welter of silk petticoats. He stared at her long legs and cotton bloomers edged with lace.

Leila looked up at him, scowling. "Get out."

"No." He bent, scooped her up, and carried her to the bed. The scent of her perfume and the heat from her body aroused him. Laying her down, he held her wide-eyed gaze and slowly undid the buttons on her bodice.

"I told you to get out," she said and yanked his fingers away.

"You don't mean it."

"I-I do . . ." Her sobs stoked the fire in him.

Tears streamed down her cheeks. She gazed into his eyes through the blur. "Rork, I love you, and I want you, but—" Letting those words out was like the first taste of something hot and delicious, as though it were a safe secret that she didn't have to share with anyone. "I am weary. I'm tired of rejecting you." She closed her teary eyes and wrapped her arms around Rork's neck. "I can't make you any promises, Rork. Will you allow me to mourn my way? If I do this, will you love me through my pain?"

He nodded. Leila loved his nod, for it had wisdom that spoke to her when she needed it.

He put one hand on her nape and lifted her face to his, kissing her tenderly. "You enslave me."

He lost his breath, pulled his shirt over his head, and tossed it aside. The silk shirt fluttered down like snowflakes blowing in the wind.

CHAPTER TWENTY-SEVEN

*R*ork gathered her in his arms. "My darling—I need you in my life, want you to be my wife."

He knew what she felt, but she bit the inside of her lip and said nothing.

He lay on his side, head propped up on his hand. "Hey, what's wrong? Will it be so onerous to marry me?"

"Hank is barely cold in the ground, and I'm sleeping with another man."

"That's ridiculous, Leila. He treated you like dirt, and you were filing for divorce."

She reached for her chemise and held it against herself.

"I know, but somehow this is wrong."

He spread his hands. "What is wrong with our making love?" He reached for her, but she evaded him. "Damn it, the man didn't honor his vows or consummate your marriage." He ran his fingers through his hair. "What is it about dead people? Now wonderful and flawless."

"I didn't say that, but a brilliant mind died because I wanted my freedom." Bitterness bled from her words.

Rork threw his hands up. "Great! Why don't you shoulder all

the blame for his dissipated, substance-induced life?" He rose and donned his clothes. "I want to marry you, Leila. I love you, but I will not share you with a man whose ghost isn't worthy of you." He shoved his shirt into his trousers and glared at her. "Let me know when you finish grieving for that prick."

He pulled on his boots and draped his jacket over his shoulder. "I'm going for a walk before dinner." He turned at the door, and his heart tripped.

She sat cross-legged on the bed. A tangle of wavy locks fell about her shoulders and reached to her waist. Her empty eyes stared at Rork with cheeks still flushed from lovemaking. He wanted to run back, gather her in his arms, and tell her to take as long as needed. His resolve strengthened. No. A damn ghost will not control me. He ripped the door open and strode out.

Leila gathered her hair, pulled and twisted it over her shoulder, and stared at Rork departing. The door closed with a sharp click of finality. "Please don't go," she whispered.

She hugged herself, reliving his hands and mouth on her body. The fire of desire coursed through her. Heat crept into her cheeks. She touched her fingers to her tingling lips for a moment and closed her eyes to capture her new self-image. She slid off the bed and drew the draperies aside.

A full moon lit the garden below and added sparkle to the icicles dancing on the trees. Rork's tall form crossed the icy terrain.

Leila's stomach churned, and heat surged through her again. Her head sagged. "Hank, I'm sorry you died." She ground her teeth and slammed her fist down on the windowsill. I can't stop thinking—I caused his death.

She threw her head back and groaned, pressed her fingers against her temples, and wrestled with unresolved emotions.

She glanced at an ornate rosewood clock on the mantel. The next hurdle—dinner with Rork.

Alex offered Leila his maid to help her bathe and dress.

"Thank you," Leila murmured. The maid nodded and left. Leila stared at her reflection in the cheval mirror. I look the same, but I feel so different. She splashed perfume on her neck and wrists and smoothed the pale green dress with overlays of cream lace. The off-the-shoulder decolletage revealed her cleavage in a froth of lace. Her thoughts caressed Rork, raising goosebumps on her skin. Spinning, she walked out. The hem of her skirt whispered against the wooden floor, walking into the drawing-room, head held high.

Rork stood with his back to the fire, legs wide and hands behind his back. His eyes held her captive, and his wide mouth tightened into a hard line.

Alex smiled. "Ah, here you are, honey." He poured sherry into a crystal glass and handed it to her. "The cook announced dinner is ready."

"I'm not hungry," she murmured, trying to escape Rork's intense eyes. Her hand shook, spilling her sherry onto the Persian carpet. "Oh, I'm sorry."

Alex waved the apology away and rang for the maid to clean up the spill. "You seem out of sorts, Leila"

"I-I don't feel very well."

"Shall I send for a physician?"

Heat crept into her cheeks. "No, I'm just a little indisposed. Perhaps fresh air will help."

"Yes, good idea." He offered her his arm. "Allow me."

Rork stepped forward. "Alex, thank you. I'll escort her."

Protest hovered on her lips. The last thing she needed was to be alone with Rork. But he took her arm and whisked her through French doors leading onto the patio.

Her heart drummed against her ribcage. She drew a sharp breath as the cold air hit her.

Rork took off his jacket, draped it around her shoulders, and led her down the patio steps into the garden.

"I don't think this was a good idea after all," she said, trying to withdraw her hand.

"Why not? Because Hank's ghost won't approve? It was an excellent idea. We have issues to discuss."

Anger came to her aid. "I told you I might have regrets. Perhaps you didn't understand. We made love, but that was a mistake."

He placed his hands on either side of her head. "I think you need to know something regarding this trip."

She glared at him. "What is that?"

"When you joined us on the train for our trip west, Hank asked me to distract you, flirt with you, so he could carry on with Sissy, unhindered by your presence."

Betrayal jolted through her. "What? I don't believe you."

"I have never lied to you. The man was a degenerate of the lowest order. Get that into your damn head." He maneuvered her to a tree, pressed against her, and captured her mouth with unbridled passion. The cold was no longer a problem. Fire shot through her, and she fought desire. A faint taste of whiskey on his lips, the smell of his masculinity breached her resistance. Leila was vaguely aware of being lifted. Her heart pounded.

"Please don't. I can't fight you."

"Don't." His words came out delicate, a simple saying wrapped in a whisper.

"Stop. This cannot happen again. It's too soon."

He lowered her slowly and said, "When will this end, Leila? It's been months. What is wrong with you?"

"I need more time."

"Enough." He adjusted his clothes and walked away. Still leaning against the tree, she watched him walk away.

CHAPTER TWENTY-EIGHT

*L*eila stared at Alex. "What do you mean Rork has left? Where did he go?"

Alex ran a hand down his cheek, avoiding her eyes. "He said to give you this." He handed her a sealed missive. "I'll leave you to read it."

Fingers trembling, Leila cracked the seal and opened the note.

I'm heading out west alone. I will be away for a year, perhaps longer. Hopefully, when I return, you will grieve no more. But I presume a great deal can change in a year. R.

She touched his initial. "He didn't even bother to write his name." She balled her hand into a fist, crushed the missive, and walked in haste to her suite.

"That bastard. He makes love to me and leaves. And then he wants more." She slammed her door and leaned against it, fighting disappointment. Sinking to her knees, she opened the crumpled note and laid it on the floor, ironing it with one palm and rereading it. She gleaned nothing more by trying to read between the lines. With her skirt spread around her in a pool of blue velvet, she lay down, pressing her hot cheeks to the cool wood and pounding the floor with her fists.

~

"Leila."

She struggled from disturbed, uncomfortable sleep and rolled onto her back, staring up at Alex. "What?"

Alex knelt and took her hand, his face filled with consternation. "What are you doing on the floor, honey?"

"You did not answer my knock. I let myself in. I hope it's all right. You frightened me." He ran one finger over her cheek. "Your eyes are red as beets. You've been crying. Want to talk about it?" He pulled her up and wrapped his arms around her. "Rork told me everything."

She leaned back in his arms, searching his face, her eyes wide. "Everything?" Heat invaded her cheeks.

"Yup. Even men need to confide occasionally. Rork and I go back a long way. He's like a son to me. You missed breakfast and lunch. I worried and came for you." He led her from the suite. "Come on. A little sustenance will help you think more clearly."

She followed him to the dining room, where delightful aromas of clam chowder and freshly baked bread permeated the air. Servants filled goblets with hot cider, the steaming beverage releasing a cinnamon fragrance. Leila took one spoonful of the creamy chowder but picked at her food. *What am I to do? Do I miss him? He's like all men—only concerned for himself.*

Alex took her hand. "You have one decision to make. Marry Rork or don't. This business of blaming yourself for Hank's death is senseless. After all, you didn't pull the trigger. I shot him, and Sissy finished him."

"I know, but why do I feel guilty?"

He leaned forward. "Your entire life, you've been told the fault lies with you if you fail. I have a rather liberal way of thinking about how to rear children." He sat back and stared into the distance. "Which is the reason I never married. I believe my methods would have made life difficult."

Leila stared at him and whispered, "What do you mean?"

"Simple. Don't conform mindlessly, ever."

"But one has to get on with society, or you'd be an outcast."

"Not at all. You assumed I meant to conform to the social dictates of dress and manners. I would teach a child to be discerning. Your mother doubtless told you to obey your father no matter what he demanded or how he treated you. The same applied to the man you married and took the unthinkable step of wanting a divorce. That was a wonderful decision for you."

"Not according to my parents. They told me it was up to me to make it work."

"Exactly. They taught you to be responsible for the success or failure of the marriage." He sat back and smiled. "You perpetuate this ridiculous state by saying Hank's death is your fault."

"You don't understand, Alex. Speaking to Hank when he was drunk or hallucinating incurred his wrath. I should have chosen the time to tell him more carefully."

"Why should you choose the right moment? The man was intoxicated most of the time."

"I suppose."

"So what are you going to do about Rork?"

Leila shrugged. "If he is going west, he'll probably go to Atchison to get the coach." She moved the silver spoon around the soup. She jumped to her feet, dropping the spoon and spilling chowder on the lace tablecloth. "I'll follow him."

"Good girl. Now sit and finish your soup while we discuss your plan of action."

Buoyed by her decision, she sat and ate. "I might not find him."

Alex buttered a thick slice of bread and placed it on Leila's bread plate. "Yes, you will. He must find a stagecoach willing to let him join them." He chuckled. "It isn't like boarding the next train to New York. If not, he'll have to purchase a wagon with a team of horses and a driver. He'll need supplies. He'll not be leaving in a hurry."

She clapped. "Of course." She picked up the bread and bit into the crunchy crust. "Oh, my, this is delicious, thank you.

He touched Leila's cheek. "It's good to see you smile again."

Her smile disappeared. "I had an unfortunate experience with the captain of a steamer. Rork rescued me." She related the incident and sighed. "What if that happens again?"

"Think of a plan to combat such events." He waved the knife up and down. "It isn't as if you're big enough to defend yourself against a man intent on rape."

"I'm quite resourceful."

"I'm sure you are, honey." He pushed aside his empty bowl and sat back. "So, what will you do?"

She rested her chin on one hand. "I could dress as a boy."

"Brilliant. I have clothes left by a friend. The outfits belong to his son, who often joined him. I'm sure he won't mind if you take a few of them." He rose and gave her his hand. "Come on. Let's see if we can fit you out with some fashionable male clothes. I would accompany you to Atchison, but I have friends coming to stay."

She followed him. "I'll be fine."

Leila swaggered into the drawing room arms outstretched. "So, do I pass muster?"

Alex guffawed and slapped his thigh. "You make a very delectable boy. You may have a problem from a different quarter. Best keep that neat backside to a wall. I think every molly within a mile will be after you."

She frowned. "Molly?"

He coughed lightly. "Ah, men who like men."

"I thought all men got on with each other famously."

Alex threw his head back and hooted with laughter. He

stopped and scratched his head, smoothing his mop of silver hair. "My sweet ingenue, I'm talking about men who sleep with men and shun the delights of women."

Heat crept into her cheeks, and she sat on an armchair, her eyes wide and a smile hovering on her lips. "Really? Do some men prefer to, ah, sleep with men? How do they do that?"

Now Alex turned red. "Ah, perhaps Rork can explain it to you." He jumped to his feet and pulled her up. "Let's have a good look at you." He touched her hair, pulled back into a braid. "You may have to style your hair to tuck all of it into a hat."

"Do you have a pair of scissors?"

"What?" He gaped at her. "You aren't seriously thinking of cutting these gorgeous long locks, are you?"

Leila shrugged. "Why not? It will be cooler in the Nevada desert. One has to cross it on the way."

"Well, it's up to you. I thought women shunned the idea of cutting their hair."

She grinned and raised one eyebrow. "Now, who believes everything their parents said?"

"Touché. I'll get a pair of scissors." He returned, wielding a pair of scissors, and showed her to an ottoman. "Sit. I'll be your barber. How much shall I cut off? Many young men have their hair at shoulder length or even longer."

She sat and pulled a blue ribbon from her hair. "Cut it short —collar length."

He sighed. "It's almost a crime to cut this lovely hair."

"This is the new me." Leila giggled. "People will think Rork is a molly."

"How will you contain your bosom?"

For a second, she stiffened. A woman's bosom was taboo. He'd asked so casually that it was far from offensive. "I hadn't thought of that."

He cut steadily until chunks of long sable hair lay on the Persian rug. "I suggest strips of cloth bound around your chest.

I'll cut up an old muslin sheet." He chuckled. "You're pretty well-endowed. Not sure you'll be able to hide them."

Again, she squirmed at his comfortable familiarity. Leila tilted her head back to look at him. "You can help me."

"It will be my pleasure." His smile disarmed her. "Not sure Rork won't be baying for my blood."

Laughing, she jumped up and ran her fingers through the riot of short tresses. "This feels wonderful—liberating. I shall go into town tomorrow and see if my disguise works." She pulled a face. "Hopefully, the captain isn't a molly this time."

Alex chuckled. "One look at you, and most men might change." He rang for a servant to clean up the hair and escort her out. "Let's get some more clothes packed for you. I'll join you on the trip into town. I'm intrigued to see the reactions you get. What will your name be?"

"What about Leland Jameson? It's close to my name, and Jameson is my mother's maiden name."

"Perfect."

Alex strolled into a tavern with Leila. He leaned down and whispered. "This should be entertaining."

"Alex, how are ya?" A trapper dressed in moccasin boots and a long ornate hide coat approached. He pumped Alex's hand and looked at Leila. "Starting the lad on the road to debauchery so soon?" He held out a hand to Leila. "I'm Thomas Tobin."

She took his hand and winced as his callused fingers closed tightly over hers. "I-I'm Leland Jameson."

Tom adjusted a fluffy, wide-brimmed beaver hat, turned up at one side with a spray of bluebird feathers on it. "Well, young Leland, where ya from?"

"New York, sir."

Alex clasped Leila's shoulder. "Leland is going to Atchison to head out west. Don't suppose you're going that way, Tom."

Tom pursed his lips and stroked his gaunt olive cheeks. "Matter of fact, I am."

"Would you mind if the lad traveled with you?"

"You talk a lot, boy?" Tom's yellow eyes bored into Leila. "Cain't abide chattering.'"

"No, sir."

Alex slapped Leila's back and sent her staggering and coughing. He grabbed her arm, steadying her. "Boy spends his life with his nose in a book or writing in his journal."

Tom scratched his chest, rocking on his heels. "I can see he spends little time outdoors." He studied Leila's face. "Ya don't even shave yet. How old are ya anyway, boy?"

Leila looked down and scuffed her feet on the wooden floor. "Fifteen, sir."

"I was a year younger when I started trappin'. Think ya can keep up?"

"Yes, sir."

"It ain't a walk in the garden out west. Don't call it the Wild West for nuthin'. Life is hard on the trail." He shoved his thumbs into his belt. "Ye'll have to pull yer weight—grow a pair of balls."

Leila almost choked. "I'm no slouch, sir."

"Good. Now, let's get somethin' to wash the dust from our gullets." He sauntered to an oak bar stained dark with ale and whiskey.

The stale smell of alcohol and sweat permeated the smoky air and caught in Leila's throat. She suppressed a cough and tried not to wrinkle her nose as she followed.

"Two whiskeys and lemonade for the lad," Thomas barked at the bartender, leaned an elbow on the bar top, and looked at Leila. "Do your ma and pa know where you are, boy, or did ya run away to seek adventure?"

Alex threw an arm around her shoulders. "They asked me to help Leland find his way west. His father thinks he needs to live rough for a bit and become a man."

Tom expelled a grunt that passed for a laugh. "I'd say his pa is right. The lad is skinny as a whip. Nothin' like roughin' it in the wilds to make a man of a boy." He quaffed the whiskey and slammed the glass down. "Fill 'er up."

The barman slopped whiskey into the glass.

Leila sipped the lemonade and watched Thomas covertly. His distinct Indian features were uncompromising—grim. She sensed she could trust this man. It was some comfort that Alex knew him. She cleared her throat and tried to deepen her voice. "How long have you known each other, Alex?"

Alex downed his drink and gestured for a refill. "Tom and I go back years. I dealt in the fur trade for a while, and Tom was trapping with his brother Charles." He twirled the amber liquid in his glass. "Must be close on twenty years, eh, Tom?"

"Yup."

"Are you still trapping?"

"Some, but I work with the army, helpin' them track criminals, insurrectionists, and such. I'm the liaison with the Indians."

Alex laughed. "Have you become a bounty hunter?"

"Turns a good profit, and I like takin' out scum."

"You know about those men that killed thirty Englishmen a while back."

"Yup. Colonel Tappan, stationed at Fort Garland, has been after the Espinosa boys since last year." Tom's yellow eyes fixed on a point in the distance. "I could find the varmints."

Alex sipped his whiskey. "In that case, why don't you?"

"I'll see." He glanced at Leila. "If I'm takin' the boy along, it may not be a good idea. They're mighty dangerous."

Leila's eyes dilated.

"Good point." Alex put an arm around Leila.

Tom hoisted a haversack. "I'll see if Tappan contacts me. They may have found them by now." He smiled. "Or be a good experience in trackin' for the boy."

"I don't need to know how to track things—men," Leila said, twisting her hands.

Alex chuckled. "Tom will look after you, son. He's one of the bravest men around, and his skill with a rifle is legendary. He's one of the best mountain men we have."

"That's good to know," she mumbled, misgiving curling through her.

Please, God, let me find Rork quickly.

The dull thud of the paddle steamer's engines reverberated in Leila's head along with Tom's words.

"We're meeting Colonel Tappan in Atchison. I got a message that he can't find Espinosa's gang." Tom sat back and picked his teeth. "That was a fine meal."

Leila lost her appetite and pushed her plate of stew away. "I suppose that means we aren't going out west right away." Tom shrugged. "What difference does it make? Yer with me to get experience. This will be a way to improve yer skills in trackin' men."

"I don't think I want any experience at being a trapper or anything related."

He chuckled. "Can't disappoint yer pa now, can ya?" He rose and stretched. "Ya better get some shuteye. We dock at Atchison tomorrow first thing in the mornin' an' see Tappan right after."

She blew out her cheeks, staring at her congealing stew.

"I didn't join you to hunt and kill men."

"I'll leave ya at Atchison. Ya can go snivelin' back to yer pa like a good yellowbelly." He sauntered off.

"I'm no coward," she snapped, shouting at Tom's back.

"Then buck up, lad," Tom called out over his shoulder to Leila as he left the dining area.

"Oh, Rork, where are you?" she whispered.

CHAPTER TWENTY-NINE

*R*ork stood in a line that snaked along the wharf. He waits for the steamship burdened by the musky, rotten smells of dead fish and green murky water—his hands sweating, while the deckhands placed the passenger gangway. Would she come today? Unease rolled through him like a stinging dark wave—he made his way back to the carriage. Joshua met Rork halfway. "Still no sign of Leila?"

Rork shook his head. A trapper walking with a youth caught his eye. The boy looked familiar—looked like Leila. Twitching his shoulders with irritation, he opened the carriage door. God, I see her everywhere. That can't be Leila. Why would she dress as a boy? Why would she be in the company of a questionable-looking character?

"Maybe tomorrow." Joshua followed Rork into the carriage.

"This must be my tenth trip here in three weeks." Rork laughed. "Like a lovesick fool, I've met every boat arriving from Kansas City."

"Even if you miss her here, I'm sure she'll at least visit Cornelia and you can talk to her there."

Rork stared at his clasped hands. "Hank's memory has infiltrated Leila. She refuses to let go. But I messed up. I should never have threatened her by leaving. I could go back to Kansas to be with her, but my leaving would have seemed indecisive."

Joshua laughed. "And that's a bad thing?"

Rork scratched the back of his head. "I don't know."

"It's done." Joshua patted Rork's shoulder. "Find something to paint. It'll cheer you up and take your mind off Leila."

He sat back and stared out the window. There was that boy and the trapper again. He stared at the lad's backside, dressed too fashionably for a trapper's son. His thoughts drifted to Leila dressed in trousers when they'd stumbled on those renegades. God, her legs seem to go on forever. He groaned. Hank's dead, but how the hell do I get him out of her head?

Joshua's compassionate gaze settled on him. "Hard to get the person you love out of your head?"

Rork shook his head and pulled up his coat collar to keep warm.

They lapsed into companionable silence until they reached the boardinghouse. It was ideal for a brief stay. Single rooms off the long hallway stretching from the front door to the back door, big enough for six guests and a kitchen. The small house accommodated six guests and the landladies and boasted excellent food, but the place was not always free of lice.

Cornelia, all smiles, returning from teaching at the same time Rork and Joshua's carriage arrived, waited on the front porch. She didn't see any trace of Leila as the men stepped out of the carriage. She lost her smile.

"Rork, I see no Leila again? I'm so sorry."

Rork walked up the stairs, embraced Cornelia and gave her a peck on her cheek. He stood back his shoulders drooped. "I cannot figure out where she is."

Cornelia shrugged. "This is unusual. I hope she's all right. The children ask for her every day."

"I don't know how I missed her. Will you understand if I leave? I'll paint. It will take my mind off things."

"Yes, good idea."

"I'll talk with Michael and pack up and go."

"I'll go in and get Michael." Cornelia said. She supported him with an arm around his waist, and he placed an arm around her shoulders. He had folded his left trouser leg and safety pinned it over his stump.

Rork smiled and patted him on his shoulder. "Good to see you up, Michael."

"You call this up?"

Cornelia glanced at him, pain in her eyes. "Remember, we talked about being positive."

"I'm positive—positively eyeless and legless." He laughed, his eyes empty, no light, no joy.

"Michael, stop that."

"If you don't like who I am, end our betrothal."

"I will not stand here and listen to you wallow in self-pity."

"I'm not asking you to. Please leave me the hell alone."

Rork glanced at Joshua and jerked his head toward the front door. Joshua nodded. They walked past Michael and Cornelia. The couple seemed oblivious as they glared at each other. Cornelia stepped away, depriving Michael of her support.

Using only his crutch, he wobbled and almost crumpled. "Damn it, woman, at least warn me."

Rork grit his teeth. "Cornelia does nothing but support you. Show some gratitude. What happened to your battlefield bravery, your strength, and your courage?"

Michael growled and jerked away. He tumbled down the steps and lay on his back, pounding the ground with his crutch. "Shit, shit, shit!" He lifted his head and glared at them. "Just get out of my sight. All of you." His angry gaze settled on Rork. "You haven't volunteered to fight, you damn coward."

Hand clasped to her mouth, Michael's remark mortified Cornelia.

Rork walked down the three steps and hauled Michael up. He slung his frail form over his shoulder and carried him into the house.

"Put me down. I am not a damn child." Michael pounded Rork's back as he strode to Michael's quarters.

"Stop behaving like a child." Rork opened the bedroom door and launched Michael onto the cot-sized bed on wheels. He loomed over him, hands on his hips. "You're right. I haven't joined up. Maybe I do lack courage. You, however, showed immense bravery against impossible odds. Then you lapsed into this state of self-pity. What the hell is wrong with you? Cornelia adores you. She's loyal, isn't she?"

Michael struggled to sit. He hung his head, tears slowly coursing down his gaunt cheeks. "Truth is, I'd rather be dead than half a man."

"Shoot yourself. You're damn lucky you didn't lose your arm as well, thanks to Cornelia's nursing."

Michael gaped at him. "You unfeeling bastard."

Rork's mouth twitched. "Which do you prefer, living or dying?"

"I lack the courage to take my life, but I'm no damn good to anyone."

Rork sat next to him. "Michael, you know what it's like to lose a limb and half your sight. You could help other soldiers." He put a hand on Michael's shoulder. "Drummer boys in the hospital have lost limbs, and their fathers and mothers. Life must seem pointless to them. Instead of feeling sorry for yourself, help them."

Several minutes passed before Michael spoke. "It's difficult to get over the shock and the terror of war. I don't imagine you ever get over it. You just learn to live with it." Michael glanced at Rork. "Sorry I called you a coward. I heard you showed incredible bravery when that steamer went down." His eyes slid from Rork. "Why didn't you join up?"

Rork shrugged. "I've agonized over that. I thought painting the war was more valuable for the folks at home." He snorted. "I've not done much of that either. I keep getting caught up in events."

Michael bent to grab his crutch and struggled to stand upright.

Rork took his arm.

"No, let me do this myself." He stood, leaning on the crutch. "Thanks. Nobody dared say anything to me." He moved to a corner and picked up a second crutch. "I'll make things right with Cornelia."

Cornelia and Joshua waited at the doorway. "Gentlemen, may we come in?"

Michael's voice came soft and sweet. "I'm sorry, my love."

She wrapped her arms around Michael's neck, her face aglow, and kissed him. She looked at Rork. "Thank you."

Rork nodded.

Joshua reminded them he took up residence at the Safe House and will continue his work with the abolitionists.

Rork walked to the door. "We'll leave you two. I must sort out my art material, pack, and go."

Leila sat with Tom in a bar near Atchison wharf, avoiding any woman-like posture that could expose her. Tom leaned forward with his elbows on his knees, holding Tappan's gaze. "The Espinosa clan is still on the run?"

"They are." Tappan sat back and ran a hand through his shoulder-length hair, eyes fixed on Tom. "We need your tracking skills to apprehend them. We killed one brother, but cousins have joined the remaining sibling. We had tracked them headed for

Mexico. Unfortunately, we lost them." He rose and slapped on his hat. "Will you help us?"

"Sure will."

Tappan stroked his trim beard and looked at Leila. "The boy will hamper your progress."

"That's *my* problem." Tom rose, prodding Leila lightly on the shoulder. "Let's get movin', lad."

Eyes wide, Leila hurried after him. "How long will this take?"

"As long as needed to find an' kill 'em."

Leila's eyes widened. "I thought you weren't going after the killers?"

Tom halted, and Leila collided with him. "Ya a coward, boy? Ya sure soundin' more like one every day."

"No, I'm not." She planted her hands on her hips. "But neither am I a fool." She flapped her hand. "I don't stand a chance in a confrontation against these-these murderers."

"There won't be a confrontation." He jammed his hat over his eyes. "They don't stand a chance against me. You're welcome to go snivelin' back to yer pa."

Jaw clamped—Leila glared at his back as he strode away before running after him. "I need to see a friend of mine before we leave."

"What friend would that be?"

"A lady."

Tom stopped and lifted one heavy eyebrow, his yellow eyes dancing with humor for the first time. "Seems I underestimated ya." He laughed. "Most boys yer age don't know what to do with that little thing between their legs."

Heat invaded Leila's cheeks. "She's my sister's friend, and I have a message for her."

Tom shoved his thumbs into his belt and rocked back on his heels, lips pursed. "Sure, ya do. I'll get horses. Go talk to yer lady."

"She's not *my* lady," Leila said and spun on her heel, marching off. She stopped and turned. "Ah, I'm not sure where she's staying."

Tom laughed. "I guess ya ain't gonna see yer lady."

"I have to see her. Aren't you the know-all tracker? Help me find her."

"I follow tracks, lad. I don't hunt for dwellings."

Leila's breath exploded. "You are so damn difficult." She spun and walked away.

"Go to the wharf and make inquiries. I'll see ya back here at the hotel in two hours, an' don't be late," he yelled.

Expelling a sharp breath, Leila hailed a coach. "Take me to the wharf, please."

"Where ya goin', boy?"

"I'm looking for a friend and hoping someone remembers her. She's with a soldier who lost a leg and an eye. There is also a negro gentleman accompanying them."

Leila relaxed and smiled. "Do you remember them or heard anything about them?"

"Aye, a buddy of mine took 'em to a boardinghouse in town. Hop in. I'll take ya there."

"Thank you." She climbed into the coach and fell back against the hard seat. "Please, God, help me find Rork." She took off her hat and ran her fingers through her short hair. The carriage stopped at a white and pale green wooden house with walkout windows. She jumped out. "Please wait for me." She opened the gate and walked up the stone path.

Cornelia flung open the door and ran out to meet her. "Leila, is that really you? I didn't recognize you at first. Your outfit! And your hair! What happened to your hair?"

"I had to cut it. My long hair didn't fit my disguise. I love it. Do you like it?"

"No question. You look like a pretty boy!"

"Oh, no. Does my disguise hide the real me?"

"*I* think so."

"Whew, I worried for a minute."

"But why the disguise?"

"I'll explain everything, but right now, I need a cup of tea." They linked arms and walked into the house. "I wasn't even sure you were in Atchison."

"We left shortly after you. Michael responded well to treatment and recovered enough to travel." Cornelia's eyes danced. "Why are you dressed like a boy?"

"It's a long story." She hugged Cornelia. "Is Rork here?"

"No."

Leila's heart fell. "Has he gone out west?"

Cornelia took Leila's arm and led her to the kitchen. "Come and have that cup of tea. I also have many things to tell you."

"I have little time. I traveled here with a trapper, Tom Tobin, and he expects me back in less than two hours."

Michael hobbled into the kitchen on crutches and grinned. "Who is your boyfriend?"

Cornelia moved to his side and kissed him. "You were sick and not of sound mind when Leila worked with us at the army hospital." She filled him in. "Why this charade? Well, she must enlighten us."

Leila peeled off her sheepskin jacket and tossed it on a peg. For half an hour, Leila, her mouth dry and palms sweating, explained the circumstances around Hank's death. "I take responsibility for destroying a great mind." Her shoulders sagged. "My pitiful regrets about Hank's death drove Rork away. By the time I came to my senses, he'd left."

Cornelia waved a hand. "Are you having an identity crisis?"

Leila cocked her head. "What do you mean?"

"Your outfit is strange."

"It's true, strange is correct. On our trip to Kansas, the steamer's captain tried to seduce me, but Rock intervened. Without Rork's protection now, I didn't want to take any more chances."

She shrugged. "To keep me safe, Rork's friend, Alex, gave me boys clothes to disguise myself. They belonged to a friend's son. Just so you know, Alex invited us to stay with him for the winter. The plan was to go west.

"That makes sense."

Leila stood, her lips turned up at the corners to a smile, and spun around with her hands on her hips. "Do you like it? My trousers are knickers. They have a zipper right here in the front. Easy to get them on and off—and the best part, no more corsets. It would horrify Mama."

Cornelia felt the fabric and ran her hand over the suspenders fastened on the trousers. She pulled them out and laughed. "Guess you need these to hold up the trousers." Cornelia let them snap back.

Leila laughed and slapped her hand. "Stop that."

"I want you to be careful."

"The trapper is running the show. All I can do is follow."

"At least you dressed the part, like Daniel Boone."

Leila ran her hand over her shirt's billowy long sleeves. "I'm getting used to these fashions, much easier to wear than ours."

"Do you have warm underwear?"

"I do. I'm all set. My coat is warm too."

Cornelia turned Leila round. "You look wonderful, and your bosom is only a slight bump. How's that?"

"Have a look." Leila unbuttoned her shirt. "A couple of strips from an old sheet of Alex's, wrapped about three times and pinned on the side with a couple of big safety pins."

"Clever. Does the wrapping hurt?"

"It's snug but practical, better than a corset."

Cornelia folded her arms. "I like your trouser pockets. Perfect to harbor a gun."

Leila's eyes widened, she gasped. "Oh, no. Will I need a gun?"

"Ask your trapper."

Leila sipped her tea. Staring at Michael and Cornelia, she set her cup down. "Rork and I made love," she blurted.

Cornelia gasped. "What did you just say?"

Michael's eyes widened and kept silent.

"Where did Rork go?" Leila asked.

"First, tell me again," Cornelia said.

"Yes, we made love. But I still couldn't shake my heartache over Hank's death, so Rork left."

"Heavens, Leila. That is monumental. How do you feel? Was it wonderful?"

"I don't feel too different, maybe more complete as a woman."

"Do you know if you love Rork? Did the intimacy draw you closer?"

"I do love him—he was gentle and gave me great pleasure. I think it's part of learning the depths of a marital relationship."

"I'm so sorry, but we don't know where Rork went. Perhaps only for the day, or he's headed west. He said he was going to paint but didn't say for how long or where. He left on horseback with a mule for his equipment."

"I think he has gone out west." Michael smiled. "Aren't all artists a little deranged?"

"Perhaps, but Rork isn't like other artists." Leila rose, her heart aching. "I've made a mess of things. Now I'm stuck with this morose and rather mad trapper."

"Why not stay with us until Rork returns?"

"If Rork took all his things, I'm guessing he *will* head west. The man I'm with is an expert tracker, and after he's apprehended these killers, he'll help me find Rork."

Cornelia's brow furrowed. "It's dangerous for you to accompany the tracker. Ask him if he'll come back for you after his hunt is over."

Leila's mouth tugged down. "No, he won't do that. Tom is heading west after he's caught the murderers. He answers to no one and is intractable." She smiled at Michael. "I like the eye patch. It gives you a roughish air."

"Thanks, it feels like I've been to hell and back."

"You have, but here you are up and able with a smile on your face."

"I agree. And he was handsome before, but now he's positively devastating," Cornelia said.

Michael took her hand and kissed it. "Flatterer."

"Not at all. It's true."

"I must go. Mr. Tobin told me not to be late." Leila picked up her broad-brimmed hat.

"Please be careful. We will miss you."

"I'll do my best." She shoved the hat on her head and touched Michael's shoulder. "Goodbye."

He struggled up, took her hand, kissed it, and kissed her on the cheek. "I owe you and Rork a debt of gratitude for your help and your friendship."

Leila chuckled. "It was all Rork. If he had left anything to me you would all still be languishing in the forest." She walked out arm-in-arm with Cornelia. They hugged. She climbed into the carriage, turned, and waved.

CHAPTER THIRTY

*L*eila rubbed her eyes, yawned, pulled on her native-tanned deer hide gloves with fringe, and swung onto her horse. Cold mist curled through the grasses—she rubbed her arms and focused on the horizon's rising sun. The expected warmth would melt the overnight frost. She was past caring about her skin tanning or the freckles that dotted her nose.

The horses snorted and tossed their heads, vapor rising from their nostrils. Tom controlled his mount and looked at Leila. "You all right, boy?"

"Why shouldn't I be? I mean, life is grand. I'm on my way through a barren land with a mad trapper to engage a group of cold-blooded murderers."

He chuckled and ejected a stream of brown tobacco spittle. "Only two days, and ye're griping already. I take it our luxurious sleeping accommodations last night didn't meet with yer high standards."

Her mouth twitched. Hmm, he has a sense of humor. "Not at all. It exceeded my expectations. How can one not enjoy checking the bedding for scorpions or finding comfort among rocks?"

"At least I saved ya the trouble of removing the rattler from yer bedding."

She lifted one eyebrow. "Is that what we had for dinner? I wondered."

"You ride well."

"That's a rare compliment."

A plume of dust climbed skyward in the distance.

Tom reined his horse and shielded his eyes. "Someone's in a mighty hurry." His back stiffened, and he drew his rifle from a scabbard on the saddle and laid it across his muscular thighs. "Stay behind me, lad." His shoulders relaxed.

"Damn, I sure hope the colonel didn't send me a posse of soldiers to help find the Espinosa clan."

Leila's spirits rose. "You are mad, but I'm thrilled if soldiers join us."

"I work alone," Tom grumbled. He took his penknife and a rope of chewing tobacco from his pocket, cut a wad, and popped it into his mouth.

Leila maneuvered her horse until she was next to Tom. "You're so ornery."

Tom chortled. "That I am. Wait until I turn ya into a trapper. Ye'll also get to like yer own company."

She shuddered. "I doubt I'll ever be one." *The man is crazier than a haversack full of desert-rats.*

"It's a good life for a man."

Leila shot a glance at him. "I will grow up, you know."

"Will ya now? Into what?"

Soldiers, followed by the cloud of dust, drew closer. She rolled her shoulders to ease the tension in the back of her neck. The soldiers came to a halt, enveloping them all in the dust. Tom leaned on the pommel, chewing tobacco methodically and scowling at fifteen Union soldiers.

One of them tipped his hat. "I'm Sergeant Winkler. Colonel

Tappan ordered us to join you to help find Espinosa and his gang."

Tom grunted and spat out the wad of tobacco. "It wasn't necessary, but you're here now, so get behind me." He flicked the reins and set off at a trot. "An' no jabberin'."

The rhythmic pounding of hooves was comforting. Leila relaxed in the saddle as the sun slid past its zenith. The rolling plains, fringed with a distant blue haze of hills, surrounded them for hundreds of miles. Swathes of long, dry grass bent to the wind's will. Few trees graced the prairie.

They rode up a steep hill. Leila took off her hat, sighing as a stronger breeze cooled her.

The earth rumbled.

She looked around. "What is that?"

Tom held up his hand, halting the procession on the summit. "Ye'll soon see." They overlooked grassy plains that merged with a wide band of green trees that hugged a broad, muddy river. "That's the Platte River. We'll camp there tonight." He pointed east. "After we bag dinner."

A massive dust cloud billowed up, and Leila's eyes widened as a dark, undulating form emerged.

Thousands of bison thundered across the plains to the river. The calm water became a boiling cauldron as the beasts plunged into it.

"I've never seen such a spectacular sight," she roared over the sound of the thundering hooves.

"It sure is. Time to get dinner." Tom pulled his rifle from the scabbard and glanced at Leila. "Come along, boy. Ya need to learn how to hunt."

Leila shook her head. "I can't kill one of those magnificent animals. I don't want to kill anything, thank you."

Tom shrugged. "Ye'll starve in the wild." He tapped his horse. The soldiers made to follow, and he fixed them with cold yellow eyes. "Stay put. I don't need ya to spook 'em."

Leila dismounted and sat on the ground, chewing a blade of grass.

Tom rode away, moving downwind of the herd until he was a speck in the distance, and finally disappeared into the trees.

A short time later, two shots rang out. Leila flinched.

The bison bellowed and took off, racing up the opposite riverbank, fanning out as they galloped across the plains. Tom emerged from the trees and rode halfway back to the soldiers.

He cupped his mouth, yelling, "Get yer asses down here and butcher the bison."

Leila followed reluctantly, even though her stomach grumbled with hunger. Jerky and hard biscuits became more unpalatable with each passing day. Visions of perfectly grilled steak swirled around her head, and she wondered for the hundredth time why she put herself through this hell for a man when she could relax in luxury and enjoy gourmet meals. She smiled. Life wasn't dull anymore.

Sweat trickled down Leila's face, staring at the granite rocks rising from the desert. Green trees, hugging the base, offered the only relief to the barren vista. She brushed gnats from her eyes and wiped her face on her sleeve, leaving a brown streak of dust. "What mountains are those? Do we have to climb them?" she croaked, coughing up dust.

"Laramie Mountains. Nothing compared to the Rockies, but we don't go over them. A canyon runs through it." He grinned, appearing unaffected by the grueling trip. "Ya wiltin', lad?"

"Of course, I'm damn well wilting," she snapped.

Winkler chuckled. "You gotta get some guts, boy, if you want to survive this godforsaken land."

"I have plenty," Leila scrunched her face and tapped her horse, riding ahead. She looked up, and her heart skipped a beat.

A line of Indian horsemen blocked the trail.

She reined her horse, pulse racing. They didn't seem aggres-

sive, and she relaxed, struck by their regal bearing. Lifting one
hand, she wiggled her fingers. "Hello."

In a magnificent feather headdress and intricately beaded
hide clothes, an elder lifted his hand, palm out in greeting.
"*Hao*."

The metallic click of the pistol's cocking resounded in the
still air. Leila stiffened. Oh, God, what now?

Tom galloped past her toward the Indians.

Leila's horse danced aside, and she controlled it. She feared a
battle would ensue. But Tom and the elder greeted each other,
grasping forearms and speaking in a tongue Leila had never
heard. She released a long breath.

Tom turned in the saddle after a lengthy exchange. "Come
here, boy. I want ya to meet Chief Little Raven, peace chief of
the Arapaho people."

Smiling with reserve, she dismounted, walked to the elder,
took off her hat, and struck a courtly bow. "I'm happy to meet
you, your majesty."

"He's not a king, lad." Little Raven said something. Tom
threw back his head and hooted with laughter. He studied Leila,
rubbed his cheek, and conversed briefly with the chief again. He
wheeled his horse and rode back to the soldiers. "Put yer damn
weapons away, unless y'all wants spears in yer chests." He
looked at each soldier. "Little Raven's warriors commented on
y'all having fine heads of hair."

The soldiers scowled and put away their guns. "I don't trust
redskins," muttered Winkler.

"The feeling is mutual. They don't trust white men either, but
watch yer tongue. Little Raven speaks English. Oh, and ya might
want to cast yer eyes to the north." He shaded his eyes.

"At a guess, I'd say about two hundred Arapaho warriors just
appeared on that there rise."

The soldiers drew their horses closer to each other.

Tom chuckled. "We camp with the Arapaho tonight." He

rode back to Chief Little Raven and set off with the chief and his men. He glanced over his shoulder. "Get a move on, boy."

Leila sat cross-legged next to Tom on the grass. In the distance, an owl hooted. Sparks swirled up as a warrior tossed a log on the blazing fire, crackling and hissing yellow and orange flames. Leila's cheeks warmed from the heat of the fire. She enjoyed the intoxicating aroma of aromatic smoke and pine needles. Firelight shimmered on eagle feathers hanging from a pipe stem. Leila stared, the light reflecting in her dark eyes, the smoke rising high and dissipating between the mountains. Rork would love to paint this. The soldiers sat opposite, keeping their distance.

Little Raven took a stone pipe stem, a bowl and stood. He sprinkled a little tobacco on the ground and put an equal amount in the bowl. He pointed the stem eastward.

Little Raven chanted and repeated the process, pointing the stem south, west, and north, each time sprinkling tobacco on the earth and adding a little to the pipe. His musical voice rose and fell. He touched the stem to the ground and lifted it high, pointing at a sickle moon hanging on the horizon in a star-studded sky.

Finally, he pointed up, smiled, and said in halting English, "Now Wakan Tanka favor us—we one with the earth, sky, and all living things." Little Raven joined the bowl and stem, he bent and ignited a piece of bark from his pouch and lit the pipe, blowing smoke in six directions. He passed the pipe around.

Leila leaned closer to Tom. "Who is Wakan Tanka?" she said in a low voice.

"The Great Spirit—like your God."

"What is the pipe ritual about?"

"I'll tell you another time." Tom took the pipe and puffed it, blowing the smoke heavenward. He gave it to Leila. She held up her hand. "I don't smoke."

"If ya refuse, they will see it as an insult." His yellow eyes bored into her. "If ya don't want to smoke the peace pipe or want yer scalp hanging from a warrior's belt, ye'd better start runnin'."

Eyes dilated, Leila nodded and took the pipe, sucking the end. The tobacco, mixed with herbs and willow bark, filled her mouth. Eyes watering, she expelled a cloud of aromatic smoke, trying to contain the urge to cough.

"Good, lad. Now give it to the warrior beside you."

Leila glanced at the tall, stony-faced Indian and handed him the pipe.

His chiseled face revealed nothing, taking the pipe and drawing on it, immediately releasing the smoke upwards. He said something to Tom in a deep voice.

Tom smiled and nodded.

"What did he say?"

"That you're a girl."

Leila's eyes flickered. "I'm just a boy." The warrior snorted, speaking in his deep rumbling voice.

Tom chuckled. "He says, 'Yer grandfather didn't teach you well.' Indian boys become warriors at fifteen, after their first bison kill."

Leila glared at the handsome warrior. "What has my grandfather got to do with it?"

"In Indian culture, grandfathers teach boys to hunt and train them in the ways of a warrior. The fathers are too busy hunting or warring."

"Oh."

They cooked Bison steaks from an earlier hunt on hot stones set in the coals. Tom handed her a nearly raw steak on a stick. "Eat up. We have to get some shuteye and make an early start tomorrow."

She took the steak. Blood dripped onto her pants. "Could I have it done a bit more?"

"Eat. It's more nutritious undercooked."

Gagging with every mouthful, Leila ate it. Minutes later, she jumped up and ran to the bushes to throw up. She came back, wiping her mouth on her sleeve.

"Sorry about that. But I told you I couldn't eat it."

Tom's eyes narrowed, and he cooked another steak. "This time, see if ya can keep it down." He handed her a chunk of flat cornbread. "Eat the bread first."

She nodded, nibbling on the bread. "Will the Indians help us find the murderers?"

"Nope. They leave at dawn."

Keeping the food down, Leila bid everyone goodnight. She curled up in a bison hide and fell asleep to the drone of voices.

Tom shook Leila. She woke with a start. "Time to go," he whispered.

She sat up, shivering as the warm fur fell away. She sulked and looked around. "But it's still dark."

"Come on," he hauled her up. "Just get on yer horse. It's saddled an' all."

Rubbing her sleepy eyes, she followed and wished she could at least brush her teeth. But Tom didn't brook any arguments when he decided on a course. She realized the Indians were with them. Once away from the camp, she glanced at Tom.

He scowled, forbidding conversation.

Leila shrugged. He was half-Indian, after all. *Perhaps he is more comfortable around them. The soldiers acted like idiots yesterday.*

The sun peeped over the Laramie Mountains, and the Indians bid them farewell.

Hunger gnawed at Leila. "When can we stop for breakfast?" Tom handed her jerky and cornbread. "No time to stop."

"Why sneak away from the soldiers? They were to help you apprehend the killers."

"They talk too much." He veered south.

"I don't think it's a good idea to take on these killers alone."

But Tom simply increased the pace.

"Little Raven said they found tracks that could belong to the Espinosa clan."

Leila's gall rose. "Oh, damn." She reined her horse, retched, and wiped her mouth, grimacing. "I'm likely getting sick."

"Maybe ye're pregnant."

She gaped at him and laughed. "Oh, amusing. I'm sure I'll make history if I am."

He held up his hand. "I hear something." He dismounted and put his ear to the ground. After a few seconds, he leaped up and remounted. "It could be Espinosa."

"It could also be Indians."

He gave her a scathing look. "There's a difference. Indians don't shoe their horses. Get back and hide between those boulders. The riders are coming toward us."

Men's voices drifted faintly through the undergrowth. Leila froze.

"Don't ya ever listen?" he hissed. He grabbed her horse's halter and dragged them both between a crevice, putting a finger on his lips.

Within half an hour, five horsemen appeared. Tom shoved her down, pressing her flat on the horse's withers as he pulled the rifle from his scabbard.

CHAPTER THIRTY-ONE

*P*erspiration ran down Leila's face, and the acrid smell of horse sweat filled her nostrils. The glimpse she caught of the desperados' faces chilled her. Her heart pounded in her chest as the drum of hooves and the metallic rattle of spurs and tack resonated through the bush, then grew faint.

Eventually, birdcalls and the rustle of a breeze sighing through the trees was all that remained.

"We must follow them," Tom whispered.

"We?"

"Yes, we."

Leila straightened slowly and shuddered. "What use will I be?"

Tom scowled. "I need backup. Ye'll never find yer way out of the mountains if they get me first."

She mopped sweat from her face. "What do you expect me to do as *backup*?"

"Watch my back, of course." He pulled a revolver from his bag and thrust it into her hand.

Holding the trigger guard with two fingers, she gaped at him. "I don't know how to use this thing."

He moved out of their hiding place. "Point and pull the damn trigger."

"Maybe I should practice first."

He cocked one eyebrow. "Good idea, that should flush 'em out and see us killed." He tapped his horse. "Come, an' keep quiet."

She trotted her horse behind Tom and looked up into the tree canopy. The sun filtered through new green leaves, and the grass emitted a sweet aroma as it crushed beneath hooves.

"It's a nice day. Good day as any to die, I suppose."

"Quit carpin' about everythin'."

"Oh, I'm not carping. I'm just commenting that I'm glad to have a pleasant day to die." She pulled out a piece of jerky and chewed it. "I'm heartily sick of dry food."

"Like I said, quit carpin'."

She clapped a hand to her mouth, leaned over and vomited. "I can't keep anything down. Maybe the jerky is rotten or something." She wiped her mouth and drank water from a leather flagon.

"Ye're pregnant."

Leila slid a glance at him. "I'll make history."

He chuckled. "Cut the pretense. I know ye're a woman."

"What?"

"Ya heard me."

Her shoulders sagged. "How did you know?"

"I could smell ya."

She wrinkled her nose and stared at him. "I stink?"

"Ya smell like a woman."

"Oh." Heat crept into her cheeks.

He looked at her, his yellow eyes sparkling. "Ya forget I'm a trapper and rely on my senses. Also, ye haven't had yer flux in the six weeks we've been on the trail."

Now her cheeks burned. "That should have made you think I was a boy. And why didn't you say anything before?"

"I didn't trust the soldiers to keep their pants on if they knew ya were a woman."

Leila hung her head. "I'm sorry I deceived you."

"I wouldn't have taken ya if I'd known at the outset. Now keep yer mouth shut. If Espinosa and his boys hear us, we're dead."

"Where are they headed?"

"Probably Mexico."

"Well, I don't need to bind myself anymore, thank God." He scowled her to silence.

Leila pouted, fell back, and pulled up her shirt, unwinding the bindings. She sighed with relief. She had ached more than usual.

Leila gazed up at massive, snowcapped mountains and breathtaking surroundings. They had only stopped briefly to rest and eat. It was already two weeks of trailing the Espinosa gang. "What exactly are we waiting for?"

"The right moment to take 'em all at once. But ya need to keep quiet."

"Where are we? These mountains are immense, but that peak there towers over the rest," she whispered.

He scowled. "Natives call the peak *Heey-otoyoo*—long mountain. Now shut yer mouth, gal."

She ground her teeth and glared at him. She confined herself to studying the magnificent terrain.

Tom held up his hand and dismounted. "We stop here until dusk. They camped up ahead near the springs." He pointed at a spiral of smoke rising above the trees.

Leila nodded and slid off her horse. Every bone and muscle in her body ached. "I read in *Harper's* that there was a gold rush here. Perhaps that's a mining camp and not the Espinosa gang."

"There ain't much gold, and I avoid areas where folk pan for gold. It's Espinosa all right." Throwing a fur on the ground, he lay down, settling into a depression between rocks. "Get some shuteye." He pulled his hat over his eyes and fell asleep.

As always, Rork was on Leila's mind. She stared at the snowcapped peaks. She put the revolver down and pressed her hands to her belly. Am I really pregnant? That didn't occur to me. Is it possible to fall pregnant after making love once or twice? The thought of having a baby alone and out of wedlock seemed a grim future. Tears squeezed up, and she swiped them irritably. I might not even live beyond today. Stroking her tummy, she fell into a deep sleep.

Tom shook Leila and pressed a callused hand over her mouth. She woke with a start and pulled his handoff. "W-what?" "Time to go," he whispered. "We're walking to their camp. Horses make too much noise."

She rose and winced as a sharp pain shot through her abdomen. If I don't die, I still could lose the baby.

He bent and picked up the revolver he'd given her. "Keep it in yer belt at all times. It ain't a purse." He shoved it into her hand. "If ya need to shoot, drop to one knee first so that yer a smaller target."

She stumbled after him. The pungent scent of pine trees permeated the air and lifted her spirits—the smell of a fire filled her nostrils.

They were close to the killers.

Tom held up his hand, cautioning her to tread lightly. He moved into denser undergrowth, barely making a sound.

Creeping after Tom with the revolver in her hand and her pulse racing, Leila tried to ignore the gnats flying around her face.

The sun sagged and seemed to rest on the mountains, casting a yellow and pink hue on the granite.

Gnats flew into Leila's mouth and crawled up her nostrils. She gagged, flapping a hand to get rid of them, earning a yellow-eyed glare from Tom. Clamping her lips—she tolerated the irritating little insects and the sweat running into her eyes.

Tom hissed and held up one gnarled hand.

Leila marveled at his ability to negotiate the dense undergrowth silently. She cocked her head and listened. What on earth did he hear?

He motioned for her to stop and pulled a second rifle from a sling on his back.

She held still, her heart slamming till she thought a rib might crack. Her blood roared in her ears. The revolver slipped in her wet palm, but she clutched it tighter against her chest and listened.

Tom moved through the bush, stepping forward one moccasin-clad foot at a time, using a rolling motion as he set each foot down.

Leila heard the hum of voices. *I can't let him go alone.* Gathering her courage, she followed Tom's example, with less success.

He turned and glared at her.

She stopped.

Emitting a war cry, Tom charged from the undergrowth. Men cried out, and shots exploded.

Leila hesitated and ran to where he'd disappeared. *I have to help him.* She entered a clearing and dropped to one knee, holding the revolver in trembling hands. Her senses shut down.

Tom looked over his shoulder, and a rare grin split his face, his even teeth gleaming in the dwindling light. "Ah, the cavalry has arrived."

She shook uncontrollably and stared at four bodies sprawled around a fire. One man lay face down in flames. Her gall rose at the stench of burning flesh. "Shouldn't you pull him from the fire?"

"He cain't feel much, that's for sure." Tom walked to the burning man and pulled out a huge hunting knife. He lifted the man by his hair and brought the blade down, severing his head.

"Oh, my God!" Leila vomited until all that remained was bile burning her gullet.

Methodically, Tom administered the same treatment to the other three, emptied one of their bags and dumped the bloody heads into it. "Right, let's get to Fort Garland before these head rot."

She sank to the ground, her eyes wide. "Th-that was horrible," she whispered. "Why?"

Ripping out a grass stem, he put it in his mouth and chewed. "I ain't gonna lug their bodies to Fort Garland, and I need proof that they're dead."

Rising on jelly-like legs, she pressed one hand to her stomach that threatened to rebel again. "Of course, how foolish of me. Heads are all we need. What a wonderful idea—carting heads about." She stepped back as he passed to avoid touching the bag. Blood dripped from it, leaving a trail. "This is so revolting—so savage." She squeezed her eyes, shuddered, and walked after him.

"Not half as savage as what they did to thirty Anglos, and God knows how many other poor souls." He glanced at her. "Ya did good."

"Thank you. That's a rare compliment."

"Would ya like to bathe in the springs?"

"I would love to bathe."

"Let's get back to our horses, and I'll take ya." He picked up the pace.

Spirits buoyed—she ran after him. "I've heard of springs around here. Apparently, the waters have healing properties."

"They do." Tom hooked the bag on his saddle and swung up. "Must've stuck in yer craw not bein' able to bathe posin' like a boy."

Leila mounted her horse and rode at Tom's side. You have no idea."

An hour later, a full moon washed over a basin valley.

Tom led her through the forest to a ring of boulders enclosing a bubbling spring.

"The springs are sacred to the Ute Indians. They say the bubbles burstin' up from the water are the breath of the Great Spirit. They make offerings every year of beads and such to thank their god for their health and ask him to make their hunt successful." He dismounted.

"Get yer clothes off an' bathe."

"I am not stripping in front of you."

"I'm not askin' ya to. I'll turn my back."

"No. You must leave."

He shrugged. "Fine. You can deal with a grizzly if it comes callin'."

Her eyes skidded back and forth across the bushes. "Th-there are bears here?"

"And cougars aplenty."

"S-stay, but keep your back turned."

"Ya ain't my taste, gal, so relax." He sank to the grass and sat cross-legged, the rifle on his knees and his back to her. Clothes discarded, Leila stepped into the effervescent pool and submerged herself. She surfaced and floated on her back, sighing with pleasure. She gazed up at the magnificent Pike's Peak and surrounding forest washed in the soft moonlight. "This is like a piece of heaven. Do only the Utes use it?"

"No, the Cheyenne and other Plains tribes also make offerings here. Anyone can enjoy the gift of these waters without fear of conflict. The bears and cougars don't feel the same way." Tom chuckled. "They were here first." He rose. "Best ya get yer ass out. We must make camp."

"Why can't we camp here?"

"Get yer ass out there, gal." He moved toward the horses.

"Fine." Climbing out, she hesitated. No towel. She shrugged, brushed off the water, and put on her clothes, wishing she could wash them. All the outfits she'd packed were filthy. "When we get to Fort Garland, is there a town nearby with a hotel?"

"Ya decent or not?"

"I feel clean, but I had to put on my filthy clothes."

"Stop griping.'" Tom mounted and hurried Leila.

She ran to her horse and raced to his side. "God, you're so evil-tempered."

"I don't pander to a fussy woman's needs. Get a move on. It's a long way to Fort Garland."

"Fussy? I can't believe you said that. Hell, I've obeyed your every command." She swung into the saddle and followed him.

Leila stared at Fort Garland, an unimposing gray building surrounded by flat, treeless terrain and ringed by distant mountains. "This is it?" She wiped the sweat from her face onto her sleeves. Once more bound at Tom's behest, she twitched under the discomfort of the tight wraps.

"Sure, this is it. What did ya expect? Soldiers live rough, sweetheart."

"Where will we sleep tonight?"

"Where we've slept every night for weeks. On the damn ground." He dismounted and walked on bowlegs to a water pump over a horse trough. Pumping vigorously for a minute, he took off his hat and held his head under the steady stream of water. He shook himself like a dog.

Leila slid off her mount and went to the pump, grabbing the handle and throwing her weight on it. Nothing. Tom chortled. "Ye're too light in the breeches." He took the handle and pumped it.

Leila put her head under the jet of water and gasped. It was icy but refreshing. She longed to wallow in a tub of hot, scented water.

Tom took the bloody bag off his saddle. "C'mon, let's collect the ransom."

Her eyes widened. "You did it for the ransom?"

"Well, I ain't gonna do it for nothing'."

"Clearly." She walked behind him, repulsed by the stench emanating from the bag.

Tom walked into Colonel Tappan's office without knocking. "Howdy, Colonel."

"Ah, Tom. You dumped my men."

"They're a noisy bunch."

"How did the trip go?"

"So-so." Tom opened the bag and tipped it, sending the heads rolling across the floor.

Leila gagged. "It's disgusting."

"You got 'em all," Tappan said.

"Told ya I would."

Tappan rose, beamed, and shook Tom's hand. "Great job, thank you. The army is indebted to you." He opened a drawer and drew out a bag. It jingled as he handed it to Tom. "I'll send my aid to instruct the purser to give you the rest of the ransom." He walked to a gun cabinet and took out a rifle. "Please accept this Henry rifle as a token of our appreciation."

Tom took the rifle and ran his gnarled fingers reverently along the barrel. "Much obliged. This is a fine weapon." He tipped his hat and strode out. "C'mon, lad.

Leila bowed to Tappan and skirted around the blackened, decomposing heads, and ran after Tom.

He swung onto his horse and galloped off without a backward glance.

Leila mounted her horse and caught up with him. "What about the rest of your money?"

"The rifle is payment enough." He slowed the pace and made to toss her the bag of coins.

She halted him with a lifted hand. "I don't need the money. Keep it."

"Fine by me." He shoved the bag into his jacket pocket. "We're headed out to find Rork."

"At last," Leila mumbled.

CHAPTER THIRTY-TWO

*R*ork stared at Cornelia. "She was here? Dressed as a boy and with a trapper?" His tone cracked against the quiet air.

She wrung her hands. "Yes, it gets worse. This Tobin is after Espinosa—a Mexican and his brothers who killed thirty English people in cold blood."

Rork's heart faltered. "And she's with him, chasing after these killers?" Rork turned and rubbed a hand across the back of his neck. "What the hell was she thinking?"

Cornelia's eyes narrowed, and her brows shot up. "The right to take off isn't yours alone. She came looking for you."

He almost swallowed his tongue. "I must find her immediately."

"Of course, you must, but it's too late to go now. It'll be dark in a couple of hours."

"If I leave now, I can make it part of the way."

"We'll also go," Michael said, his face set with determination.

Veins throbbed in Rork's temples. Now there really will be a delay.

Michael scowled at him. "I suppose you think I'll be a burden?"

"Ah, no, not at all." Rork clenched his jaw. But that was the problem.

"I've been learning to ride again, and I'm doing well. I'll manage just fine." He spun on his crutches. "I'll organize our baggage."

Rork blew out his cheeks and headed for his quarters. Cornelia's voice rang out. "Not so fast!"

Rork stopped and turned. "What?"

She tapped her foot and shook a finger at him. "You assume Michael is a burden, and a woman along adds to the problem."

Rork's temper surfaced. "In a nutshell? Yes."

Cornelia flapped her hand. "You go on ahead, and Michael and I will catch up after you cripple your horse by finding a burrow in the dark or get attacked by the hundreds of deserters and bushwhackers roaming the countryside looking for fools like you."

His breath exploded. "Fine. I'll wait until first light, and we'll all go."

Cornelia grabbed his arm. "While you were away, Michael and I found out we are having a baby."

"You are? You've all been busy, haven't you?" Rork kissed her on her cheek and said, "I'm happy for you. When's the wedding?"

"Well, we don't have a wedding date yet. Does that make me a fallen woman?" Her eyes narrowed. "You didn't bother to marry Leila before taking her virginity. So, I guess she also classifies as a fallen woman." She folded her arms and tapped one foot. "Perhaps you don't intend to marry her at all."

Heat flooded Rork's cheeks. "How do you know about our intimate life?"

"It doesn't matter that I know, Rork Millburn. Do you intend to do the honorable thing?"

Escape became rather urgent. "Of course, I want to marry Leila. But I'll first have to damn well find her, won't I?"

Cornelia smiled. "That makes sense. Please, Rork, can you go over to the church and tell the pastor there's been a change of plans and ask him to come early tomorrow morning to marry us?"

"Of course."

Grinding his teeth, Rork stalked off.

Rork ran his hand through his hair and pushed the curtains aside, looking out the windows like an expectant father. The sun hadn't made an appearance yet. And the pastor took an eternity to read the marriage vows uniting Michael and Cornelia.

Michael drew Cornelia into his arms and kissed her. "Not exactly the grand wedding we'd planned."

"Michael, that's the last thing I care about. This is the most wonderful day of my life. A miracle. I thought I'd lost you forever."

Rork flipped open his pocket watch. "Could we please get a move on? The sun will be up soon."

Cornelia scowled at him. "Since when did you become so insensitive?"

"Since no one could keep Leila here until my return."

"Now you're pointing a finger? You didn't tell us where you were going or for how long." Michael poked his shoulder. "The blame for this lack of communication lies squarely on your shoulders, my friend."

Rork grinned and waved a hand. "We need to get going— sooner rather than later."

"Hell, Rork, give us a moment to enjoy our nuptials."

"All right." Rork offered his felicitations.

Cornelia glowed with happiness. Standing on tiptoes, she kissed Rork on the cheek.

"We'll find her. Stop fretting." She looked at Michael. "Let's change so we can be on our way."

Rork went out to check the horses and luggage. He raised one eyebrow. "I expected Cornelia to have more baggage."

Michael laughed. "She's a practical wife."

Cornelia returned. "Men's clothing suit you, Cornelia."

"More comfortable, don't you think?" Cornelia said and swung up onto her mount, her eyes dancing. "Close your mouth, Rork Millburn, or you'll catch flies." Her laughter bubbled up, wheeling her horse.

Leaving Atchison behind, they watched the sunrise slide over the horizon.

Exhausted and covered in dust, Rork and his party rode through Fort Laramie's gates.

An old soldier greeted them. "You came just in time. The gates would've closed an hour later."

Rork hawked up dust and spat. He swallowed. "We'd like to speak with your commander."

"Colonel Chivington took our commander's place while he's away. We've had problems with redskins attacking wagon trains. The Cheyenne Dog Soldiers are a bloodthirsty lot."

They dismounted and followed the soldier across the parade ground. Rork got his attention. "I heard about a peace treaty—no more attacks. I don't understand. When did this happen?"

"Ah, hell, this goes back to '58 when the Pike's Peak gold rush started. The redskins objected to the whites invading their land. They signed a peace treaty, but it didn't stop the Dog Soldiers. No siree."

"And this Colonel Chivington is here to stop them?"

"Well, he's a pastor, not a commissioned officer. Governor Evans promoted him to Colonel of the Colorado Volunteer army. Has seven hundred men under him." The soldier chewed a stick that he moved from one side of his mouth to the other. "Hard man, Chivington. Them redskins had better watch out."

Rork's heart contracted. And Leila is in the middle of all this? The soldier ushered them into an office.

A broad man with a trim beard and receding hairline rose from his desk, hard brown eyes piercing Rork. He extended his hand. "Colonel Chivington. What can I do for you, sir?"

Rork shook his hand. "I'm Millburn. Did a woman with a trapper by the name of Tobin stop here? Has there been any news about them?"

Chivington's disapproving eyes shifted to Cornelia. He nodded. "Madam." He ignored Michael and returned to his seat behind the desk. "Thomas Tobin is half Indian. Good trapper, though, and he wasn't in the company of a woman. I heard, via army reports, that he killed the Espinosa gang, and a boy helped him."

Rork's mouth fell open. "A boy helped him?"

"Yes. They intend to head west."

Rork's belly somersaulted. "Headed west?"

Chivington scowled. "You hard of hearing, son?"

"Where did they kill the Espinosa gang?" Rork sagged onto a chair, rubbing the back of his neck.

"Near Pike's Peak, I think."

"Nope, not a boy. I'm to marry her!"

"Dear God, what is the world coming to."

Rork glared at him. "Bet you heard a gang of Indian Dog Soldiers, on the warpath, penetrated the area to protect their land."

Chivington steepled his fingers. "I track the Indians. Damn any man who sympathizes with them. Kill and scalp all, big and little, I say."

"You advocate killing women and children?"

"Nits make lice." The colonel busied himself with papers. Rork shook his head at the barbarism of the man.

"I'll bid you a good day, sir."

Chivington looked up. "Good day."

Red-faced, Cornelia exploded. "What a horrible, bigoted swine." They headed for their horses.

Rork smirked. "Yup, I concur."

A stagecoach raced through the gates and stopped amid a cloud of dust. A cage on the roof, crammed with chickens, tilted precariously.

The stout driver leaped down, clasped a rolled whip in his hand, strode to the soldier, shook his hand, and grinned. "Tarnation. Thought we wasn't goin' to make it afore ya closed the gates."

The soldier laughed. "Trust you to make it by the skin o' your teeth, Charley."

Charley took off his wide-brimmed hat and slapped the dust off his buckskin-clad thighs. "Well, ya need to be fast in this business, an' Butterfield has a reputation to uphold."

Four travel-worn passengers alighted with groans. A portly man brushed his jacket. "I'm not going another mile in this bone-rattler."

Charley shrugged. "Suit yerself."

The passenger crossed his arms. "I'll be asking for a part refund, mind."

"Sure." Charley took a pouch from his pocket and counted out coins. "Here ya go." He handed the money to the passenger. "Don't know how ya think y'all gonna get to California."

The passenger herded his skinny wife and two plump daughters to the fort's office. "I'll find a way."

Rork looked at Michael. "Why don't we put Cornelia on the stagecoach? We'll take the horses and ride alongside."

"Smart, great idea." Michael put an arm around Cornelia. He

brushed off strands of hair stuck to her sweaty brow. "I'm not sure it'll be a comfortable ride."

Cornelia leaned against him. "No matter. I'll just be happy to relax in a coach."

Rork laughed. "I don't think you'll find a ride in that rattle-trap relaxing." Rork approached the driver. "Could we buy one fare?"

"Sure. Need to fill the space, anyway. Cost ya seventy-five dollars, plus $1 for ye meals." With his one eye, he studied Cornelia. "It ain't a comfy ride if that's what yer after."

"It has to be better than riding." Rork counted out the money to the driver. "Here you go."

"Ya can call me Charley. Nope, an' we don't make overnight stops. Stop for forty-five minutes twice a day, and ya have to walk when the terrain is bad. Victuals are extra and provided twice a day. We also stop at various way stations to change the team o' mustangs. Butterfield don't supply ya with arms. Ya need to carry that yerself for possible Injun attacks."

Rork blinked. "Do you expect Indian attacks?"

Charley spat a stream of tobacco juice. "Butterfields has a sign at the start o' the journey." He stuffed another wad of tobacco in his mouth and chewed vigorously. "Ye'll be travelin' through Injun country an' the safety o' yer person cain't be vouched by anyone but God," he rattled off. "So now ya know Butterfield's conditions." He pulled a stained handkerchief from his pocket and wiped sweat and dust from his sun-browned face.

"Right. When do you leave?"

"Soon as we change the team. The lady can board while we harness fresh mustangs."

Rork nodded and turned to Cornelia. "Don't worry. We'll be right alongside."

Michael handed Cornelia into the coach. Cornelia nodded and smiled at passengers sitting with their backs to the driver. She sat next to a family on one of the two seats opposite.

Cornelia smiled. "Goodness, four people disembarked, and there doesn't seem enough room for just me." She stared at mailbags, crammed into the foot space, and looked at Charley. "Do we put our feet on those mailbags?"

He spat out another stream of tobacco-stained spittle. "Sure do, li'l lady. Make yerself comfy." He strode away. Cornelia sighed. "I'd hoped we could rest here for the night." Rork patted Cornelia's hand as she sat. "I'm hoping with the speed of the coach and taking the usual route, we'll catch up with Leila. Once we have her, we can decide how we want to travel."

Charley returned with a groom and four mustangs. They quickly unhitched the horses.

"I'm getting Cornelia out of there," Michael said. "These animals are feisty."

"I agree." Rork opened the coach door. "Cornelia, please," he extended his hand. "You can get back in when they're done harnessing them."

She clambered out and withdrew to a safe distance.

Charley and the groom backed the horses into the traces, harnessing the back two. As they maneuvered the two lead horses into position, one of them reared and plunged, slamming his hooves onto the hard earth. The other horse panicked and lunged sideways, breaking the pole chain. It fell and pandemonium broke out. Charley and the groom tried to control the bucking animals. Passengers screeched and tumbled from the coach. The fallen horse scrambled to rise and got jammed between the two harnessed horses, kicking out wildly. Charley ripped off his coat and threw it over the distressed animal's face, calming it.

The groom unhitched the rear horses and led them a short distance away. "Ya cain't travel today, Charley. That pole chain is broke good. We need to fix it."

Charley nodded and urged the quivering mustang to its feet.

He looked over his shoulder at the passengers. "Y'all have to hole up here for the night."

Cornelia smiled. "Thank goodness we can stay at least one night."

Rork gave her a deadpan look. "This is all I need—another damn delay."

Michael grabbed his arm. "We're stuck, Rork. They have to make repairs. How would you travel anyway? You can't even think about leaving now, especially not with Indians roaming the plains."

"I know. But if I'd come alone, I would have taken my chances."

Cornelia glared at him. "You would have been a fool, Rork Millburn."

"I am a fool," he said, stalking off. "A fool in love."

CHAPTER THIRTY-THREE

*T*he early call of a rooster pierced the dawn, rousing
Rork from a night of disturbed sleep. He needed
proper rest, but impossible in a room filled with snoring, road-
weary men. The hard straw pillow offered no comfort. He threw
off a threadbare blanket and rolled out of the bunk, opened the
creaky door, and slipped through onto a low-roofed porch. Rork
groaned, flexed his shoulders, and rubbed the stubble on his
chin. He leaned on the porch railing, and a cool breeze caressed
him. The rising sun soaked the mountains.

"Pretty, ain't it?"

Rork glanced at the soldier and nodded. "Tell me, is this
Charley a skillful driver?"

"One-eyed Charley's one of the best." He stuck out a gnarled
hand. "Bobby's the name."

"Millburn." Rork shook his hand. "How did Charley lose his
eye?"

"Horse kicked him. But even havin' only one eye, Charley is
right nifty with four or six in hand. He leaned on the railing. "Ol'
Charley is brave, too. Last trip, Sugarfoot, a bandit what's been
robbin' travelers left an' right, demanded Charley hand over the

strongbox which he did, but now he has it in for Sugarfoot. Reckon that bastard won't be so lucky if he tries to rob Charley again." Bobby hawked up phlegm and spat. "No, siree. Once old Charley's dander is up, best watch out."

"Sounds like Indians are a bigger problem."

"Ah, redskins don't rattle ol' Charley. Long as the passengers do their bit and help keep 'em at bay." He straightened. "Ya want coffee?"

"You bet." Bobby strode off, and Rork stared at the distant snowcapped mountains. *Why the hell couldn't Leila wait for me? I'm a fool for leaving.* The strong aroma of coffee drew him from self-incrimination.

Bobby handed Rork a cup of the brew. "Thank you." Rork gazed down at the dark brown liquid and took a deep breath. "Ah, just what I needed."

"Yup, people come to blows wantin' to sit up front with Charley. It's an honor to share the spare driver's seat with him." He squinted in the early morning light. "There goes Charley. Fixin' on repairin' that pole chain an' gettin' an early start." Bobby drained his cup and set it down. "Charley needs help."

"I'll join you." Rork downed his coffee. He grimaced at the overly sweet, strong brew, but it gave him a jolt.

Charley gave him the good eye. For an hour, they worked in silence, repairing the damage. Dripping sweat, Rork sighed with relief. The mustangs hitched and ready.

Cornelia and the other passengers, and goods loaded, Charley clambered onto the driver's seat and looked around. "Y'all set?"

"Yes," Rork ground out, impatient to get going.

"Yah! Yah!" Charley cracked his whip just above the horses' ears, and the red canvas-roofed coach took off, raising a cloud of dust.

Rork wrinkled his nose. "Michael, best we ride alongside to avoid choking to death." They urged the horses to move faster.

The coach moved briskly over the grassy plains. Rork and

Michael settled into an easy gait. Warm sunshine blanketed the prairie and cast a golden glow over the grasses.

They crossed a vast stretch of the desert without mishaps. The horses breathed heavily, snorting sand from their nostrils.

Charley negotiated the coach through a narrow, winding road leading to vast plains. Five hours later, the grueling heat of the sun beat down on them. The horses struggled to pull the coach over the mountainous terrain. Charley's gruff voice urged the team on, along with deft cracks of the whip.

Rork ripped off his shirt, unhooked his water canteen, and drank deeply, slaking his thirst. He moved closer to the coach and handed the canteen to Cornelia. "The dust must kill you," he yelled above the rumbling of the stagecoach.

Pale-faced, she drank.

Rork kept a watch out for trouble. Veering toward Michael, he scanned the tall cliffs. "An ambush is possible here. You're a soldier. How about you ride shotgun on the coach?"

Michael nodded.

Rork tapped his horse and drew close to the coach again. "Charley," he shouted, "I'll pay another fare to have my friend, Hargreaves, ride shotgun."

"No need to pay." He slowed the coach to a halt. "Good idea." Charley glanced at Rork, his eye twinkling. "Mr. Hargreaves served in the army, right?"

"Yes, as a sniper."

"I could use a good gun upfront with me."

Michael slid off his mount and untied his crutches strapped to the saddle.

The passengers alighted. They groaned as they stepped away from the coach.

Cornelia came to him. "How are you holding up in that rattler?" Michael asked. She leaned against him. "Tough ride. My knees feel bruised. We sit so close our legs interlock and

261

bang against each other. But we agreed to sing and tell stories to pass the time."

"Sounds good. I'm going to ride up top with Charley." She raised her brow. "I'm riding shotgun. We're ready if we get ambushed. These mountains can hide the enemy."

They sat and ate jerky and dry, worm-infested biscuits. Cornelia and the lady passengers refused the biscuits. "I'll vomit if I have to eat those." Cornelia wrinkled her nose.

Michael grinned and hit the hard biscuit on a rock, dislodging worms. "Even if I get them out for you?"

"Even if you do."

"Folks, all aboard. Time's a-wastin'," Charley hollered. He ejected a stream of brown spittle. "Shame we don't have time to bag them prairie chickens grubbin' through the horse droppings. Let's hit the road, folks." The horses took off with a will, ascending the mountain pass leading to the next way station.

Once free of the pass, Rork surveyed the land with an artist's eye, itching to paint. Signs of human occupation disappeared, and prairie chickens became less abundant. The sun disappeared behind clouds, gilding the edges. Clouds piled on distant, jagged mountains and sharp stabs of lightning forked from the billowing mass, sending wild patterns across the massive cliffs.

Within an hour, the sky turned to a blinding mass of white flames, accompanied by thunderclaps. The wind increased, and dust devils swirled across the plains.

Jamming his broad hat down on his head, Rork lifted his coat lapel as rain pelted down, cursing as it ran down his back. The horses continued at full tilt, galloping fetlocks deep in water that rushed over the hard ground in a torrent.

After a lull in the storm, the magnificent display resumed, illuminating a deserted house. A raging river under tall cotton-woods careened past the house, dragging broken trees in its wake.

Charley halted the team. "We need light," he yelled. Rork

dismounted, and Charley handed him four kerosene lanterns. "Tell the passengers to light 'em. At least it's dry in the coach."

Leaning into the wind-driven rain, Rork carried the lamps to the carriage. Once lit, he made his way back to Charley. "Let's stop here."

"Nothin' stops me." Charley leaped to the driver's seat and sent the horses plunging into the stormy night.

Shaking his head, Rork mounted and followed. "That man is insane," he yelled.

The hours ticked by to the monotonous thunder of hooves. Sagging with exhaustion, Rork rode on doggedly. "Doesn't that old bastard ever sleep?" Rork yelled for anyone to hear. Gleaming with sweat and rain, he removed his hat and slapped it against his thigh to rid it of water.

Rork peered through the gloom and rubbed his gritty eyes. Exhaustion became a real problem as they ate up the miles, changing to Cornelia's horse to relieve his mount.

A farm appeared on the horizon as dusk washed over the waterlogged land. Charley spotted the farmer in the field, hauled on the reins, and jumped down.

He slid a glance at Rork. "Yer lookin' a bit worse for wear." He popped a wad of tobacco in his mouth. "I've been thinkin' o' ya ridin' nonstop and decided to break my rule. We'll ask to bed down here for the night."

Rork jumped off his steed. "Mighty generous of you. He swallowed his smile. "My backside is numb."

"Yup, ridin' a horse for so long is a real ball crusher." Charley roared with laughter.

"And you're the damn court jester."

Charley called out, "Hello."

The farmer meandered over. "Hello, what can I do for you folks? Where you headed?"

Charley chewed his wad. "We need a warm place to rest. We got a pregnant lady and her mate, who is ridin' shotgun, and a few others. We be on our way to San Francisco. Can ya help?"

"We sure can. Welcome to Comstock farm."

Rork found his smile and shook the man's hand. "Mighty glad to meet you. Our horses need water."

"Help yourselves. I have horses I could swap if need be." He pointed to a pen. "There are some mighty fine mustangs in the corral for the pickin'.

"Much obliged." Rork took off his jacket and dunked his head in the water. "Ah." He blew out a breath, shaking off the drips. "Good for a wake-up."

Michael, moving with caution on his crutches not to slip on the sopping ground, had spoken to the farmer's wife. "Comstock can set us up, but there are only two rooms for us all. The smallest is for the ladies."

Morning arrived to the roar of Charley's voice. "Rise an' shine, folks. Time's a-wastin'."

Still fully clothed, Rork groaned and rolled off the narrow, lumpy bed. He stood and stretched. "I've had better nights on a bed of rocks."

The Comstocks' had food waiting. Michael reached for his crutches.

"Grab somethin' and let's get going," Charley said. He shook the farmer's hand and slipped him some money.

"Dang. Looking forward to some of that chow." He grabbed a few griddlecakes and bacon. "I'll be damn glad when we reach our destination," Michael said. Want me to stay upfront with you, Charley, and ride shotgun?

"Sure do!"

Rork slapped on his hat and picked up his saddlebag. He strode out.

Charlie had the job to hitch the horses. "Well, Rork, 'bout

time ya showed. We need fresh horses. Comstock okayed the exchange for a small fee. Can ye take care of the exchange?"

"Will do."

As the sun crept onto the horizon, they were once more on the road and heading for the mountains. Upon entering a pass, Charley slowed. Cliffs soared above them. Horses slipped on the trail as they negotiated the narrow, rocky road.

"Keep close and eye out. This is Cheyenne country."

"This pass is airless," Rork said with apprehension. Charley's lead horses shied away and whinnied. Dripping with sweat, they struggled over the rough terrain.

Rork rode to the coach. He stopped and drew his pistol.

A man in a long, ragged coat leveled two revolvers at Charley. "Give up the strongbox like a good fella, Parkhurst." He pointed a gun at Rork, waggling it. "Now, fella, ya don't want to go bein' a dead hero. Just put away that there gun."

"You son of a bitch." Charley growled, slowly reaching for his rifle. "Ain't this off yer beaten track, Sugarfoot? Santa Cruz is yer usual pickin' ground."

Sugarfoot grinned, exposing a row of rotting teeth. "Aye, that it be." He moved a piece of straw to the other side of his narrow lips. "Needed a change o' scenery is all." He wiggled the revolvers and stomped a burlap-wrapped foot. "Enough idle chatter. Hand over the loot."

"Like hell." A shot exploded from Charley's rifle, held at his knee. "Ya got me last time, but this time, ye're shit out o' luck, ya scaly bastard."

The bullet slammed into Sugarfoot's side. He screeched, dropped his guns and staggered away, disappearing between boulders.

Pulling out a revolver, Charley fired four more shots. The bullets ricocheted off the rocks where Sugarfoot had disappeared. Shoving the gun in his belt, Charley lifted his whip and flicked it across his team. "Ya! Ya!" They took off across the uneven terrain.

Rork chased after the coach to catch up. "Aren't we going after him?" he yelled above the rack of hooves.

"No time. With a wound like that, he'll be dead before sunset."

"Sugarfoot is an odd name. How did he come by it?"

Charley chuckled and popped a wad of tobacco in his mouth. "On account o' the fact that he wears burlap on his feet and stomps to enforce his point."

"You said Sugarfoot robbed you before."

Charley slowed the coach. "Aye, on the run through Santa Cruz 'bout a year ago, the bastard took the strongbox off me." Charley spat a stream of brown tobacco juice. "I swore that day I ain't gonna let that happen again. An' I didn't."

"When do we reach the next way station?"

"Just beyond this pass." Charley cocked a bushy eyebrow at Rork. "You tuckered out already?"

Rork scowled and concentrated on keeping his horse steady. "No, I'm not tired. I'm looking for someone."

Charley slowed his team to a gentle trot. "Who ya lookin' for?"

"My betrothed."

"How did ya lose her?"

"Damn it, Charley. I didn't lose her, and it's got nothing to do with you why I'm looking for her."

"Well, women are ornery creatures. Ya must o' done somethin' to piss her off."

Rork dropped behind, glaring at Charley's back.

Charley yelled, "Move! Dog Soldiers!" He whipped his team into action, and the coach forged ahead, wobbling and swaying, threatening to lose a wheel on the next rock. "Separate and make for those trees up ahead."

CHAPTER THIRTY-FOUR

$\mathcal{T}$hey veered off and hadn't even made a hundred yards when triumphant howls erupted behind them. Rork Shouted, "We must draw them away from the coach!"

Dropping flat on his mount's withers, Rork scanned the forest ahead. He wasn't sure if they could make it. He looked back.

A dozen Dog Soldiers galloped toward them, waving spears and yelling. The feathers of the leader's headdress whipped like flames, and the black and white war paint on their faces presented a frightening visage.

Rork looped the reins around his hand, wheeled his mount around, and galloped toward the Indians with his revolver drawn.

He kicked his horse, increasing the pace as he headed directly for the middle of the group of howling Indians.

The Dog Soldiers veered from Rork's path. Their horses, spooked by the unexpected attack, skittered aside at full tilt and reared, dismounting several Indians.

Rork fired as he cut through them, hitting two in the chest.

Foam flew from his mount's mouth, the stench of horse sweat assailed Rork. He wheeled and repeated his tactic.

The Indian leader stopped and turned his horse, drawing his bow. The first arrow went wide, but the second one found its mark.

Rork grunted. The sharp, serrated arrow slammed into his left shoulder. Ignoring the pain, he fired, missing the leader.

"Son of a bitch." Rork rasped and fired his remaining bullet, hitting the leader in the side.

Bleeding profusely from his wound, the leader shouted a command.

The warriors took off, heading for the mountains.

Panting with pain and exertion, Rork reined in his mount and stared after them.

Charley ran toward them. "Damn fool! Could've gotten yerself killed!" "I can't decide if I think you're brave or an idiot."

"Since I'm wounded, probably an idiot."

Charley pushed his hat back on his head and whistled. "Best we get that arrow out o' yer shoulder, lad. Can ya ride to the coach?"

"Of course, I can ride to the damn coach," Rork growled.

Charley walked beside them, his eye twinkling. "Just as well ya routed 'em. Coach lost a wheel before we reached the trees."

Cornelia helped Rork down. "My bag is in the coach. Sit under that tree. I'll be there in a moment."

Michael joined them. "You loon, didn't you realize the danger?" Pretty courageous, if you ask me."

Clutching his shoulder, Rork laughed. "Only because it worked. If my ploy had failed, my epitaph would have read —*Here lies Senseless, who charged rather than ran.*"

Cornelia waved everyone away. "I need to get that arrow out and treat the wound before it becomes infected."

Charley dropped to his haunches beside her. "I'll take it out for ya. Done plenty in my time, an' I'm quick."

Cornelia scowled. "No offense, Charley, but you are rather rough."

He grinned. "No offense taken, honey." In one swift movement, Charley shoved the arrow through Rork's shoulder. He rapidly snapped off the shaft and pulled the arrowhead out from the back.

Rork arched, cried out, and collapsed.

"There. Told ya it was quick." Charley tossed the bloodied arrowhead in one callused hand. "I'll wash this and make a leather thong for it. He can wear it around his neck. Hope he doesn't decide to charge a grizzly next. Might not get to wear a claw or tooth." Chuckling, he sauntered away.

Cornelia glared after him. "I knew he'd be savage." She set about washing the wound and dressing it. She waved smelling salts under Rork's nose.

He came to, groaning. "What did that old bastard do? Felt like a damn hot poker going through my shoulder."

"Well, Charley has no finesse, but he got it done faster than I might have." She held a vial to his lips. "Drink this laudanum. It will dull the pain."

Rork pushed her hand away. "I can't ride if I'm half asleep."

Cornelia scowled. "You are not riding, my friend." Struggling to his feet, Rork swayed and leaned against the tree. "No damn way I'm riding in the coach. Charley drives that thing like a maniac."

Michael lifted one eyebrow. "Don't be an idiot, Rork."

Rork snorted. "I'd be a bigger idiot to ride in the coach."

"For God's sake, be reasonable. The women ride in the coach," Michael said.

"Enough." He lifted his good hand. "Nothing will persuade me to change my mind. Besides, the wagon wheel needs repairing. By then I'll be fine." He stumbled away, his head swimming.

They sat around Rork, who tossed and turned on a makeshift

pallet under the trees. Charley shook his head and ejected spittle. "I don't know if he's gonna make it, an' I need to get goin'."

Michael struggled up off the rock he sat on. "Go. We'll continue once he recovers."

"Like I said, don't know if he'll make it." Charley rose from his haunches. He popped another wad of tobacco into his mouth and eyed each passenger. "Maybe three o' the folk can ride an' we'll put him on one of the seats."

Cornelia glanced at Rork. "I'm happy to ride."

Three male passengers looked away. A slender man with thinning hair hooked his fingers into his suspenders. "I paid to ride in the coach. Besides, I don't fare well on a horse."

Charley glared at him. "We owe our lives to this fella an' his friend. Them Injuns would've had yer sorry scalp by now."

"And I'm grateful to him, but I paid to ride in the coach," he insisted in a nasal voice. He took out a pocket watch and flipped it open, tapping the face with a skinny finger. "I have meetings in San Francisco in a few weeks. We need to get going."

Michael stood over the man and poked his chest. "You ungrateful bastard."

The man's eyes dilated, and he stepped back. "How dare you touch my person, you cripple."

Michael's fist slammed into his face, sending him flying. The man landed on his backside and glared at Michael.

"I'll see you put in prison."

Charley strode to him and jerked him to his feet by his jacket lapel. "Shut up, ya little snot. Ya are a selfish bastard! An' just try an' lay a charge. I'll have yer guts on a platter." He shoved him, sending him to the ground again. "Now git yer scrawny ass outta my sight."

The little man scurried away and dived into the coach.

Charley dusted his hands together and glared at the other two men, and sneered. "Well, ladies, yer carriage awaits ya."

An elderly gentleman puffed out his chest. "I object to your tone. And how dare you insult us?"

"Ah, piss off, ya old goat!" Charley went to Michael. "I'll make the yellowbellies sit atop or ride a horse."

Michael shook his head. "I'm riding, and so is my wife. Those snivelers can squeeze into one seat. We obviously can't stay here. Get us to Fort Hall. They should have a physician."

Charley nodded. "Let's get goin'."

By the time Fort Hall came into sight six days later, Rork had a raging fever. Cornelia sat cross-legged on a mailbag next to him, swabbing his face with wet cloths. She sagged with relief when the incessant jolting and swaying stopped. "Help is at hand, Rork," she whispered.

Michael opened the door. "You all right, honey?" She climbed out, and he put an arm around her. "Some grueling journey."

She leaned against his broad chest, sweeping a strand of blond hair off her damp forehead. "Well, it's over. We must get a physician. Rork is not faring well."

Charley organized a stretcher for Rork and ensured he was safely in the care of the army physician. "Are ya leavin' him here an' movin' out with me, or are y'all stayin'?"

"We'll stay, of course."

Charley touched the brim of his hat. "I'll bid ya farewell."

Michael lifted one eyebrow. "You aren't resting here tonight?"

"Nope. Enough time lost already." He handed Michael the arrow on a leather thong. "Be obliged if ye'd give this to Mr. Millburn. Tell him I'll not forget his brave deed—if he makes it." He strode out, slapping the rolled whip against his thigh.

The friends stared after him and looked at each other. "Well, that was positive, if nothing else," Michael muttered, slipping the arrow necklace into his pocket.

Rork burned with fever for a week, and the friends wondered if he would make it. Cornelia hardly left his side, continually swabbing him with cold, wet cloths.

Michael walked into the infirmary, putting a hand on Cornelia's shoulder. "Have a break. We'll take turns keeping him cool."

"I don't think that will be necessary." She put her hand on Rork's forehead. "He feels cooler, and he's calmer. When the physician dressed his wound earlier, it seemed cleaner, and the inflammation has gone down. I think he'll be all right."

Rork's eyes opened, and he blinked, shying from the light. "What happened?" he croaked, running a tongue over cracked lips. "Thirsty."

"Thank God." Cornelia smiled and lifted his head, dribbling water between his cracked lips. "Your wound became infected, and fever beset you." He struggled up, and Cornelia pushed him down. "You are not going anywhere, Mister."

"I have to find Leila. Something is wrong. I can feel it."

"And you will, but you need to recover first. And Leila will be quite safe with that trapper."

"You're a bully," he said and fell into a deep sleep.

CHAPTER THIRTY-FIVE

*S*creeching and hollering echoed against the cliff face. Tom held up his hand, grabbed the harness on Leila's horse, and dragged them behind the boulders.

He dismounted, and she followed suit. He pointed up at the mountain.

She nodded, heart pounding as they slowly climbed rocks to the summit. Her foot slipped, dislodging a stone.

Tom glared at her, put a finger over his lips, and continued the climb.

Sweat streamed off her face, and her fingers slid off the boulders. She struggled up the steep incline after Tom.

He reached the top and waited for her to come alongside him. "Dog Soldiers," he mouthed, pointing and handing her a telescope. "It looks like a few have injuries," she whispered. As the Indians rode closer, she drew a sharp breath. They were a frightening sight.

"Keep very still. My guess is the Indians attacked someone and came out second best. We're dead if they catch us."

Leila nodded and handed back the telescope.

A man in an ornate headdress held his bleeding side,

galloping close to where they hid. Three Indians carried injured men slumped over their horse's withers. One of the Indians yelled.

Tom crawled around the boulder. "They've found our horses," he hissed. "Let's get to the cave backside of these rocks. Hurry and don't make a noise."

Panting, Leila scrambled after him, dislodging rocks. She had heard stories of atrocities carried out by Indians. She crouched low.

"Keep quiet, girl." Tom hissed and disappeared down the other side of the rocky hill.

Leila slipped on an outcrop of rocks and rolled into a massive rock. Agonizing pain shot through her as she hit bottom with a bone-jarring impact. Dazed and disoriented, she lifted her head.

Close by, Indians chattered, and bushes rustled.

Leila turned onto her stomach and clamped her mouth shut to muffle a painful cry. She ignored the pain and pushed up onto her knees to crawl toward the undergrowth.

Horses neighed, and the sound of men crashing through the bushes grew louder.

The ground sloped toward thickets. She had to hide. Sobbing, she crossed her arms over her chest and rolled down the incline, landing in a thick clump of thorny shrubs. She bit her lip to stop from crying out as thorns hooked into her flesh. Rocks rained down on her. She squeezed her eyes shut and lay still.

The Indians closed in, close to the place where she'd fallen.

They whooped triumphantly, and a hand grabbed Leila's hair, dragging her from the thorny hideout.

Screaming hysterically, she fought to escape. She glimpsed a knife flash in the sunlight and increased her struggles.

A sharp command from the leader stayed the warrior's knife. With a growl of discontent, he hauled her up and dragged her toward his horse.

Snarling like a trapped cat, Leila raked her nails down his face.

He shook her and grabbed a leather thong from his waist-band. He tied her hands in front of her with a length of yucca rope. He mounted his horse in one fluid leap and jerked the rope, forcing her to run behind.

Leila looked back. Her breath rasped in her dry throat. Unable to see Tom, her heart shriveled. She knew the cave hid him and shielded her abduction. Horrid tales of Indian torture swam in her head.

Leila's strength flagged, and she stumbled.

Reining his horse, the warrior turned, his dark eyes searing her with hatred. He barked something and jerked the rope.

She fell to her knees and glared at him. "I can't run anymore," she screamed. She turned her anger to the leader slumped on his horse. "Tell your Dog Soldier to stop his abuse—emphasis on the word *dog*," she spat.

"You say much, squaw," he rasped and clutched his side. Blood seeped through his long brown fingers.

Her eyes widened. "You speak English?" Hopeful, she said, "I must rest. Water. I need water. I'm p—" She stopped, recalling a story of Indians cutting out a woman's unborn child.

The leader issued a brief command. Her captor dismounted and thrust a hide flagon of water into her bound hands. Pulling off the leather stopper with her teeth, she gulped the water, spilling it down her neck, wetting her shirt.

The warrior growled and snatched it away. "No waste."

"No need to be so rude. Maybe you don't know how hard it is to drink tied up." Leila wiped her mouth with the back of her hand and looked at the leader. "My name is Leila. What is yours?"

"Hook Nose."

She grinned. His name fit. "Please release me. I mean you no harm."

Hook Nose issued a command, and her captor lifted her and threw her over his horse's withers.

Her breath escaped with a whoosh, and she winced. *How will my baby ever survive this abuse?* The warrior mounted, once more on their way. Arms crushed under her, she cried out with the impact of every jolt. Lifting her head, she tried to twist onto her side.

The warrior jerked her up and sat her in front of him—his sinewy arms trapped her. He said something in a deep voice.

"I don't understand."

"No jump."

"Oh, so apart from one word, you do speak a sort of English." His black eyes pierced her.

"Red Arrow, no speak."

"Of course, you don't," she said and settled into the rhythm of the galloping horse.

Conical trees hide tipis, starkly outlined against an orange horizon streaked with purple. The sun rested on the low hills.

They lifted the injured warriors off their horses. Their women wailed. A woman ran to Hook Nose, tears running down her smooth olive cheeks. She reached up to touch him. He pointed to Leila, eyed her, and compressed her full lips.

Hook Nose pushed her shoulder. She nodded, dragging herself to Leila. "Come," she mumbled.

Red Arrow shoved Leila off the horse.

She landed on her feet, but her legs buckled. She struggled to stand and held the woman's intense black eyes. She stretched out her hand. "I'm Leila. What's your name?"

The woman hissed like an angry cat, grabbed the rope attached to Leila's hands, and dragged her to a tipi. Untying her hands, she opened a hide flap door and thrust Leila into the tent.

Leila fell to the floor. She scrambled to the far side of the tent, sat against a wooden pole, and wrapped her arms around her legs. Tears slowly coursed down her cheeks, and she brushed at them, sniffing. "I'm sorry, Rork. Sorry I didn't tell you I love you—loved you from the moment I saw you." She slipped one hand to her belly. "I'm sorry you'll never be able to hold our baby." Regret choked her, and her tears fell. She sagged down and curled up into the fetal position. "Please hear my heart, Rork. Know that I love you and always will, even after death."

The flap opened, and the woman crawled in with food on a wood trencher. She sat cross-legged with the trencher between her and Leila. "Eat."

Leila wet her lips and picked up a fire-roasted ear of corn. She ate with little finesse and helped herself to squash and meat. She reached for more meat.

The woman slapped her hand. "No, pig."

Leila grit her teeth. It seemed all her manners, carefully taught by her mother, had disappeared. Lord, have I become savage like this land I traverse? She wiped her hands on her trousers. "I'm sorry," she mumbled.

The woman handed her a bowl of water with herbs floating in it.

Heat invaded Leila's cheeks, and she washed her hands. "My apologies for my bad manners." She managed a smile. "What is your name?"

"Little Star."

"You speak English. What will happen to me?"

"Red Arrow needs woman."

Leila blinked. "H—he wants a concubine?"

Little Star picked up the trencher.

Leila grabbed her arm. "I-I'm married." One white lie didn't seem important, but something cautioned her not to divulge her pregnancy.

Little Star grimaced. "Not matter. If he come, Red Arrow kill him." She shrugged. "No more husband."

Leila gaped at her. There has to be a way out of this. Maybe Tom will find me before Red Arrow ravishes me. She clenched her hands. I'm to be a concubine—a whore. He will have to rape me because I'll never submit.

Night descended for the third day, increasing Leila's anxiety. Would Tom come soon? She had no idea how he would secure her freedom if he did. Leila tossed and turned on her pallet. *Perhaps he doesn't know what happened to me.* She pounded the bedding. "How can he not know? He's supposed to be this wondrous tracker."

Dawn finally broke, and Leila sat listlessly on the pallet. *Is today the day he rapes me? Death is preferable.*

Little Star peeked through the doorway and crooked her finger. "Come."

Leila crawled out and blinked against the intense light. Rising stiffly, she stretched, enjoying the sun on her face. She smiled at children laughing and playing between the tipis.

A group of women waited for her. "You bathe."

Leila almost laughed with relief.

The women led her silently to a copse of trees. A stream gurgled over the rocks. They stripped her clothes off, urged her into a deep pool, and washed her with a chunk of herb-scented soap.

She reveled in the cold water until an elder hustled her out, drying her with scraps of soft hide.

Stony faced, the elder worried her gums and mumbled something as she rubbed oils on Leila's body. Deep crevices on her face sagged in a perpetual expression of discontent. The elder peered over Leila, her small black eyes glittering with malice. She rattled off an angry tirade.

One of the young women giggled behind slim fingers. Leila glanced from one to the other. "What did she say?" Little Star arrived with a hide garment over her arm and handed it to the elder. "She say you white like chicken fat and don't know why Red Arrow want you."

The truth dawned on Leila, the moment she'd dreaded. She backed away, holding up her palms. "N-no."

Snarling, the elder grabbed Leila and issued brief instructions. The other women hastily pulled the buckskin dress over her head. Beads and feathers decorated the soft garment. Had circumstances been different, the dress would have delighted Leila. The women took her arms and led her back to the lodge.

Red Arrow stood in the center of a clearing between the tipis, hands behind his back, black eyes impassive.

Leila's heart pounded, and she hung back. The woman shoved her, and she fell to her knees at the warrior's feet. "I-I will not be your woman—your whore." She took his callused hand. "Please, I have a husband."

He shook her off. "You obey."

"I can't—won't."

Red Arrow looked at Hook Nose. The leader nodded at a group of warriors. They stepped forward and hauled Leila up, dragging her from the clearing.

She twisted around. "What are they going to do to me?" she cried.

Hook Nose rose from his mat with difficulty. He held his side, bandaged with leaves held in place with leather thongs.

"You are of no use to Red Arrow anymore."

Fighting to escape, she screamed at Hook Nose as he walked away, "What will happen to me?"

A warrior barked something at her. He brought up his arm and backhanded her.

Leila's head snapped to one side. Her senses swam, and she sagged. They jerked her up and dragged her from the lodge. "Wait! Wait! I'll do as he wishes—be his concubine!"

Red Arrow held up his hand, and the warriors released her. He ambled toward her and planted his fists on his hips.

Leila ran a tongue over her dry lips and stared up at him. The sun gleamed on his bronze, muscular torso. The finely chiseled planes of his face held no compassion. "Please, I will be your woman."

Red Arrow crossed his arms. "You trouble." He barked something at the warriors, and they grabbed her arms, dragging her to the tipi she'd occupied.

Lightheaded with relief, Leila crawled into the now familiar tipi and lay on the floor, drawing rapid breaths. Her fingers curled, digging into her palms.

CHAPTER THIRTY-SIX

orced to do labor-intensive tasks, Leila worked in
silence, planning an escape. She staggered under the
weight of a bison leg and tried to hang it on a hook to cut into
strips for drying. It slipped and fell to the floor.

The elder picked up a strap and flailed Leila's back, screaming, "Bad. Useless worm."

Leila ground her teeth and picked up the leg. "Those seem to
be the only words you know, you evil-tempered old hag." A foot
slammed into Leila's backside, sending her to the ground. She
cried out and fell hard. She rolled and clutched her stomach.

The elder jabbered insults in her tongue. She leaned down
and pulled Leila's rawhide dress up, exposing her stomach and
genitals.

Leila glared at her and jerked the dress down. "Stop that, you
horrible bitch."

Little Star stood over Leila. "You not call Red Arrow's
mother bad names." She pointed at Leila's stomach. "You have
child in belly."

Leila scrambled backwards, shaking her head. "Red Arrow's

mother? I-I didn't know." She wrapped her arms across her stomach. "And I'm n-not having a baby."

Little Star spun away and left the tipi. Moments later, Red Arrow and Hook Nose arrived and stared impassively at her.

Hook Nose folded his arms across his chest. "You dare to insult Red Arrow's mother, squaw."

Leila pouted. "She insults me all the time."

"You worthless." He conferred briefly with the warrior and turned back to Leila. "Red Arrow not want you."

Icy fear coursed through Leila's veins. "Why not?" she stared at her accuser, her arms stubbornly folded over her bosom.

"Child in belly."

She shook her head, pressing against a pole. "No, I have an infection of the bowels."

"We not need paleface sickness."

"Then let me go."

"You insult Red Arrow mother."

"I'm sorry. I didn't mean to, but she kicked me."

Red Arrow kicked Leila in her ribs—she cried out and rolled onto her side. He walked out with Hook Nose. Leila screwed her eyes shut and held her side. What now? She tried to draw a breath. Warriors yanked her to her feet and dragged her out.

With her head reeling from pain, she hung between them. They hauled her to a copse of trees beyond the tipi lodge. Two warriors held her down and tied her to a tree. "You learn now."

"Oh, God. No." She slithered down to the ground, her head hanging. They left—her hands tied in front of her. Her body roped to the tree, like one of their tethered horses.

She looked around. She couldn't breathe. It felt like she had mud stuck in her throat that prevented her from sucking air. Dead, I'm dead. I must stay awake. How long will they leave me here, and what do they want me to learn? Submit. They want me to submit. How do I escape? Oh God, where is Tom?

A hand came out of nowhere and covered her mouth.

"Shhh, be quiet." A man's voice broke off, and he slowly removed his hand.

She stared up at Tom with relief in her eyes.

"I've been hanging around for over a week. I'd have rescued you sooner, but because of the proximity of the tipi to the lodge, I could not." He began to untie her and cocked his head. He stopped." He re-tied the ropes and melted into the forest.

Crying out, Leila shook her head. *Where did he go?*

Red Arrow stepped into the clearing and stood over her, legs spread and arms folded, glaring. "You come now." He began untying her. "Where are you taking me?"

Leila's eyes dilated.

Tom appeared behind him. With a swift movement, he had the Indian in a headlock. His knife flashed, and blood spurted from Red Arrow's throat. He dragged the Indian into the undergrowth, ran to Leila, and freed her.

Leila lamented with relief from the horror of her experience. She stumbled after Tom.

He pushed her up onto a horse hidden in the bushes. "We need to move fast. It won't be long before they find that Indian."

She whispered, "Where are we going?"

"West. As planned."

Leila ground her teeth—her ribs hurt. And Tom silent as ever.

"When did you realize the Dog Soldiers had caught me?"

"Shhh, hush up."

They rode for what seemed like forever before Tom said, "I saw when they took you."

"Tom, thank God you came. Thank you. Thank you. I worried if you'd come or not."

She stared at him. "Why didn't you shoot them?" She winced and rubbed her ribs. "God, my ribs, they feel broken. It hurts to breathe."

He looked at her as she rode beside him. "Try to bear the

pain. I'll wrap you when we can stop. In answer to yer question, if they killed me instead, no one would know what had happened to you." He scowled at her. "Enough jabbering."

He tapped his horse, increasing the pace.

She resisted rubbing her painful ribs and urged her horse to move faster.

Eventually, Tom called a halt and slid off his horse. "Okay, let's wrap those ribs. Get down here."

She obeyed. "On yer horse, there's a shirt in that there saddlebag and pants for ye to ride with. Get them fer me. We got to get a move on. Let's speed this up."

"Here." With her arm close to her body, she held up the shirt by the collar.

"It's an extra of mine." He ripped it into strips.

"Wait. Stop. Why do I need this? It will be miserable and suffocating."

"Stop bitchin'. Lift ye dress got to wrap ya so ya can ride yer horse."

"I am not lifting my dress."

"Gads girl, how do ye expect me to fix ye?"

"I'll do it myself. Give me those strips."

"Suit yerself, but those Injuns are gonna catch up. Here you go."

"Turn your back."

She slipped on the pants. They were too large, but she made do with rope. Tom kept around to tie up any bandits he caught. She laid the strips on the ground and kneeled. "I think I have to take off my dress. Um, this will not work, will it, Tom?"

"Tell ye what, Leila, turn around, so ya back is facin' me. Come on, get up."

"Will it hurt?" She didn't bother keeping the distrust out of her voice as he wrapped the strips around her.

"Oh my God, this is better. I can breathe. Thank you."

"Get on your horse."

He ran to his horse and vaulted onto it. "Let's go, gal."

It seemed to take forever, but once the pain abated, relief. She glanced at Tom. "It worked. Thank you. Sorry I'm such a ninny."

He laughed. "Wouldn't expect less from you, gal."

"What's that supposed to mean? I don't find a compliment in there."

"Nope, ya won't."

CHAPTER THIRTY-SEVEN

*T*wo weeks later, they arrived at Fort Hall. Once more dressed in boy's clothes, Leila sat slumped in the saddle. The fort walls surrounded her, and she felt safe for the first time in weeks. Exhaustion overwhelmed her. In the long trek across the country, they barely stopped. They ate as they rode and snatched sleep at brief intervals. Tom seemed tireless.

He glanced at her. "We won't be here more than a few hours."

Leila shook her head. "I cannot go on."

"All right, we sleep and move out at first light." He swung off the horse and helped Leila dismount. "I must speak to the person in charge."

Leila rubbed her arms and sank to the hard ground.

Soon, he returned and pulled her up. "Come on. I have a room for ya and a hot bath."

"I am so grateful."

Tom grinned. "Yeah." Half carrying her, he took her to a low log building. "Yer quarters."

Leila stared at a tub of steaming water in the center of a tiny room. A dark blue dress lay on a narrow bed. She laughed and threw her arms around his neck and kissed his cheek. "Thank you, but why the dress?"

"I'm leaving ya here." His eyes crinkled. "I'm sure ye're lookin' forward to dressin' like a woman again."

She grinned. "I do, without the stays. No more instruments of torture."

He guffawed. "I'm sure. Never did cotton to why women like wearin' all that crap."

"We're slaves to fashion."

He lifted one eyebrow, his yellow eyes sparkling. "I didn't peg ya for the sort of gal to follow stupid fashions."

"I'll take that as a compliment. I used to be, but I'm not that girl anymore." She stared at her torn fingernails. "My life has changed."

"I'd say ya changed for the better, but didn't know ya back then, of course."

She smiled—one corner of her mouth turned up. "You would have liked me even less."

"For the record, I've grown quite fond o' ya. There's a platoon of soldiers here, and the commander said a group of travelers is moving out west in about three weeks. I've arranged for ya to travel with 'em."

She touched his rugged cheek. "I'd rather travel with you. I need to find Rork."

He stepped back. "He can't go further than the west, Leila. Ye'll probably find him in San Francisco." He walked to the door. "Besides, the commander asked me to help him track down the Dog Soldiers that took ya. They've been attacking and killing travelers for over a year."

Her heart fell. How do I survive in this wild country? "I don't feel safe without you."

"Seems the people ye'll be traveling with rode with a stage-coach attacked by them Dog Soldiers. One of the men saved their skins with an interestin' tactic." Tom chuckled and rubbed his cheek. "Instead of runnin' from the Indians, he rushed 'em and caused confusion, killin' a few." He touched his hat in a loose salute. "I'm sure ye'll be in good hands." Then he walked out.

Brief panic coursed through her, and Leila stared at the closed door. "Well, don't say goodbye, you damn ornery trapper," she bellowed. She clapped a hand to her mouth and giggled. "If Mother could hear me, she'd wash my mouth with soap."

She removed her filthy clothes and sighed, anticipating the delights of soaking in a hot bath.

Leila stretched, waking refreshed but aching all over. The smell of bacon tantalized her, and she smiled in anticipation of a hearty breakfast. Exhausted the night before that she'd gone to bed without dinner. She picked up the dress, and a blanket fell off the chair. Where did this come from? God, did Tom creep in while I slept and put the blanket in here? She held up the blanket and ran her hand over the woven cloth. Oh my, this is beautiful. It looks like it's from the Arapahos. She couldn't remember the last time she received a gift from anyone.

When she went back to dressing and completing her toilet, Leila examined her reflection in the cracked mirror. She turned one way and then the other looking thinner whichever way she turned. She smoothed her hand over the slight belly bump. He face had a golden-brown glow with a sprinkling of freckles. Mother would have a heart attack. She brushed her hair, smoothed the simple cotton dress, and walked out with the blanket draped over her arm, following the smell of food to another log building.

The door creaked open, and Leila adjusted her eyes to the dim interior. Light filtered through small, grimy windows. Five people sat at a trestle table in the far corner.

A rotund man with a bushy, red beard flipped pancakes on a hob. He turned as Leila approached. "Howdy, li'l lady. What can ol' Red give ya to eat?" He swept a fat, hairy arm over the hob. "Got bacon, eggs, cornbread, and these here pancakes."

"I'm starving."

His eyes swept her from head to toe. "Aye, ya could do wi' a bit o' fattenin', gal." He tossed a thick slice of buttered cornbread onto a tin plate and scooped up scrambled eggs, followed by thick slices of crisp bacon.

Leila's eyes widened as he added a huge pancake dripping with syrup.

"There ya're, honey. That should fill ya good." He pointed. "No cause to eat alone. Join them folk over there." He wiped the sweat from his face and turned back to cooking.

Leila picked up the plate and walked toward the group in the corner. *Maybe these are the people Tom arranged to travel with me.*

Light from a window fell on a man near the wall, catching gold highlights in his shoulder-length hair.

Leila caught her breath.

A hoarse cry crossed the divide between them. "Leila!" Cornelia and the others looked around—their jaws dropped.

"Rork." The plate slipped from her numb hands. Her senses swam, and her legs gave way. In an instant, Rork came to her, his strong arms surrounded her. They sagged to their knees.

She leaned against him, sobbing. "I thought I'd never find you."

"It's all right." He stroked wisps of hair from her face, her misting eyes set upon him.

Brushing away teardrops, he bent and kissed her cheeks. "Oh, my Leila, my Leila." He slipped his fingers into her hair, drawing her closer. He frowned and lifted the short hair. "You cut your hair."

Leila pushed him back and surged to her feet. "And that's important how?" She glared down at him, hands on her hips.

He jumped up and tried to take her in his arms. "It isn't important at all.

"Hair? All you can say is my hair is short?" She pummeled his chest with both fists. "What's important is that you just left, you damn coward."

He grabbed her wrists. "Leila, I had to make you see some sense. I couldn't be with you knowing you wanted Hank. You grieved for him incessantly."

At that moment, everything became too much for her—she wept, gasped for air, and doubled over, holding her ribs. Rork put his arms around her and stroked her hair. He lifted her chin, kissed every teardrop, and wiped away his own with his shirtsleeve.

She pulled free. "You're a snake." Her arm came up, and her fist connected with his jaw.

His head snapped to the side. He stepped back, rubbing his chin. "Damn, Leila. Where the hell did you learn to punch like that?"

"I've learned a lot of things in my quest to find you, you cowardly bastard." She lunged at him. Food scattered on the floor, rendering her footing treacherous. She squeaked as her feet slipped out from under her. Breath left her lungs in a whoosh as she landed on her back.

A slow smile spread on Rork's face, and he bent to pick her up. "Let's stop this nonsense."

"Smug swine. You started this—this *nonsense*. My ribs hurt and now look what you've done." She plucked bacon and egg from her hair. "I'm a damn mess, and I'm sick of being a mess." She scrambled up, slipping on the mangled remains of her breakfast. She talked to the cook, brushing off bits of food. "I'd like another plate of the same, please."

Red laughed. "For that bit o' entertainment, ya get a double portion." He filled a plate and handed it to her. "Ya pack a mean punch, gal."

"Thank you. My pleasure." Without a glance in Rork's direction, she walked to Cornelia and Michael. Slamming her plate down, she sat and spooned food into her mouth.

Her friends stared at her. A smile spread on Cornelia's face. "Hungry?"

"Famished," Leila said between mouthfuls. "Haven't had a decent meal for God knows how long."

Eyes twinkling, Cornelia leaned across the rough wooden table and whispered. "Joy to see you're safe. You seem a little, ah, savage."

Rork sat next to Leila. "I think that's a rather mild description. First, she attacks me and then she eats like a trapper. What happened to the genteel lady I'm betrothed to?"

Her voice had a fast, focused, hunter-on-the-move rhythm. "I seem to recall you being rather pleased that I'd changed." She pointed the knife at him. "And just to be clear, I don't recall our betrothal." Now she had a light, playful tone to her voice.

He arched his eyebrows. Rork rather enjoyed this. He raked his fingers through his hair. "Damn it, Leila. I asked you many times to marry me."

She stared at the plate, sucked in her bottom lip, and bit down, just enough to ease her frustration, but not so much to make it bleed. Her hand drifted to her belly. She rubbed her throbbing temples.

Rork caressed her back with soft strokes.

The barest hint of exasperation washed over Leila's features as she said. "Life crossing the plains of this country is risky, challenging, and downright dangerous. We rode bareback over the open prairie day and night under the threat of wild animals and renegades. We killed animals for food and slept on the ground. Tom's hearing and keen senses kept us safe. He knew how, when, and where to hide us in the rocks. The worst happened when the Dog Soldiers captured and held me for days, until Tom rescued me."

Cornelia's eyes widened. "What? How did that happen?"

"We were trying to hide from the Indians, but I couldn't keep up with Tom. I slipped and fell down the hill, and they found me."

"Were you mistreated?"

"Not until the mother of Red Arrow told him about my pregnancy. He kicked me. I didn't know what they would do with me. I served no purpose anymore, so warriors dragged me into the forest and tied me to a tree far from the tipis. Tom quietly sneaked up and after killing Red Arrow, we escaped. It still hurts to take a breath. I rather enjoy breathing."

Leila pushed away her half-full plate.

Rork dipped his chin in acknowledgment. "My God, Leila, we almost lost you. I too almost lost my life with my crazy attack on the Dog Soldiers when I took an arrow in my shoulder."

Leila turned to Rork, her eyes wide. "Oh, no. I heard you rushed the Indians instead of running, and shot Hook Nose in his side."

His lips slanted up at one corner. "There can't be any other Hook Nose? My God, he's still alive, and he's the same Indian that kicked you?"

"His mother kicked me, but Red Arrow broke my ribs."

Heat invaded his gaunt cheeks. "I'm sorry I left you, can you forgive me?"

"How do you feel about having a second pregnant woman on the trip?" Leila mumbled, praying her confession didn't drive him away. He'd never mentioned wanting children.

"What? A baby? How is that? You are pregnant with my baby?"

Leila scowled. "Who the hell do you think the father is, if not you?"

"I'll be damned." He dropped his jaw, a bemused expression on his face.

Mouth trembling, she stared at him. "You'll be damned good, or damned bad?"

Laughing, he drew her close and held her against his heart. "Good—all good." He held her at arm's length, his eyes sweeping over her. "You're so thin it's hard to tell you're pregnant."

"I wouldn't cast stones, Mr. Millburn. You are just as scrawny."

"Well," Cornelia said, rising briskly, "we have a wedding to plan."

Within two days, Cornelia had arranged for a pastor to marry them. She altered one of her dresses to fit Leila and pilfered lace from other garments to enhance it.

Standing in front of a full-length mirror, Leila stared at her reflection. There were no hoop petticoats. The creamy white-colored dress with its high neck and full sleeves fell from her shoulders to the floor and curved at the waist in layers of lace. Wildflowers woven into her hair with ribbons gave her the air of a princess.

"Oh," Leila gasped. She ran her fingers down the bodice and held the lace in her hand. "It's so beautiful. The flowers—where did you find them? In the meadow? My goodness." Her eyes misted. "Thank you."

Cornelia hugged her. "Every woman deserves an extraordinary wedding day. Come on, let's get you wed."

Alone with Rork, he cupped her face and kissed her. "Mine at last. I love you, Mrs. Millburn." He kissed her forehead. "You have grown up, my ingénue."

Leila put her palm on his cheek.

He drew her into his arms, capturing her mouth in a searing kiss.

She melted into him.

He ran his hand over the slight bulge of her belly.

She placed her hand in his. It was warm and comfortable. And safe.

It felt like they had known each other forever. A fire raged in his heart. Her deep blue eyes held him captive.

EPILOGUE

*R*ork paced and listened to Leila's cries. "To hell with this." He marched into the bedchamber. The midwife had her hands between Leila's thighs. "Push!" She glanced up and glared at Rork. "Get out, Mr. Millburn."

"Not on your life. I'm staying with my wife."

"Make yourself useful and apply wet cloths to her face."

Relieved he didn't have to layout the midwife—he moved to Leila's side and took a wet cloth from a bowl of water. He gently swabbed her flushed face. She cried out, arching as a contraction tore through her.

"One last push, dear." The midwife smiled. "There we go." She held up a baby—a slap resounded, followed by a wail. "You have a fine boy." She cradled the baby in her capable hands and beckoned her assistant. "Wash the babe and wrap him in swaddling clothes."

Leila laughed and stretched out her arms. "Give him to me first."

"Wait until he's bathed and wrapped."

"Give the baby to my wife," Rork said through clenched teeth.

The midwife scowled but laid the bloodied infant on Leila's chest. Throat clogged with emotion, Rork stared at the tiny being. Tentatively, he touched the baby's hand, and fingers curled around his huge forefinger. "He's beautiful." He leaned down and kissed Leila and his son. "Your joy is my joy. Thank you."

The baby emitted a howl. "Oh, my, he's strong." She looked up at Rork, her eyes glowing. "Just like his papa."

Cornelia burst into the room, carrying an infant. "What is it?"

"A boy," Rork beamed.

The midwife took the baby from Leila. "Y'all need to get out."

Leila gasped as another contraction gripped her. "What now?"

Cornelia chuckled. "It's just the afterbirth, Leila. Then it's all over. Michael and I will see you later."

Leila gripped Rork's hand, pushing and grimacing. She fell back with a sigh. "Thank God that's over." She smiled.

Rork slipped his arm behind her and held her close, kissing her softly. He looked down at her. "Leila?" Her eyes were closed, and her breathing shallow. "Leila!"

The midwife laughed. "Relax, young man. She's fallen asleep. But I need to stitch her where she tore." The midwife took a water bowl and washed Leila, who woke and groaned.

"Will it cause her pain?"

"She won't feel much." Working quickly, the woman soon sewed the tear. She washed Leila, put her on clean bedding, and gave her a fresh nightgown.

Rork walked to the window and stared across the rooftops of San Francisco. Whispers of snow drifted on the wind and settled on the buildings. Baby's soft snuffling noises and Leila's even breathing filled his heart. He sighed.

"Rork, lie with me, please."

"With pleasure." The bed dipped. He gathered her into his arms.

Leila pressed a palm to his cheek. "Maybe we should leave for Tis-sa-ack before winter sets in."

"We'll wait until spring when the blooms are radiant. Painting in freezing weather is not appealing. Even better, let's go home—to New York?"

Leila sat up and leaned back. "What?" she inhaled. "Why?"

"For our children. New York has the best schools and unique opportunities."

Leila beamed. "I love the idea. When?"

"Soon as I can get some sketching and small paintings done at Tis-sa-ack. I need them to do large important paintings."

"I'm so thrilled. I have missed the city and our family, my Aunts and cousins. My goodness, it can't be soon enough."

"Don't you think we should name our son?" Rork laughed. "But he has to be his own person, no naming after any relatives."

Leila's gaze remained on her baby. "I've been thinking, do you like the name Liam?"

"What does it mean? Have you heard that name before?"

"The Indians know about names and have told me stories. It means warrior and protector."

"Liam is a perfect name for our son. Rest now, my darling."

Rork held his son, and with an arm around Leila's waist, he gazed at the panorama before them. Leila smiled and leaned against him. "Tis-sa-ack takes my breath away." Leila glanced up at Rork, her belly fluttering as she studied his handsome face.

Cornelia put an arm around Michael's waist. "Shall I take Olivia?" He held their baby girl against his chest. "No. She's had her feed, and my princess is fast asleep."

"We should get down to the village and find Galen Clark."

Cornelia looked at Rork. "Are you sure he has accommodations for us?"

"Well, when I had lunch with him last month in San Francisco, he said he'd hold rooms in the small hotel he runs." Rork mounted his horse in one fluid movement with Liam in his arm. "Best we get going."

Leila studied dark clouds billowing over the imposing cliffs of the valley. Flashes of lightning burst from a cloud's belly. "We should hurry. I think a storm is coming."

The first fat drops of rain fell as they rode into a small village. Rork hailed a passerby. "Excuse me. We're looking for Galen Clark's house."

The man pointed. "That be his place over yonder."

"Thank you." They rode to a modest log establishment. Rork dismounted and walked to the open front door. "Hello, anyone here?"

A door opened in the entrance hall, and a thickset man walked out. "Ah, Mr. Millburn, welcome to my humble hotel." He looked at the baby in Rork's arms, and his gray eyebrows beetled up. "I see you have a new addition."

Rork grinned. "Yes. I'd introduce Liam, but he's fast asleep."

Galen Clark peered past Rork. "Well, don't leave your party out there. It'll be pelting down any moment." He shook each person's hand. "This must be the most guests I've had at one time." He smoothed his full gray beard, his eyes twinkling as he perused them. "I can see you've been busy populating our beautiful country." He turned and strolled down a wide passage. "I'll soon have you settled. We serve dinner at six-sharp. Plain fare, I'm afraid." He opened three doors in succession. "There you go. I'll get my servant to light fires in your rooms. Tis-sa-ack gets real chilly come night, especially when it storms."

. . .

Leila hurried down the road, sidestepping puddles from the spring rains. She carried a picnic basket in one hand and Liam in the other. Today, the first cloudless day in two weeks—the mountains sporting wildflowers, announcing their presence with sweet fragrances and sparkles in the sunlight. Almost midday, she climbed into a borrowed buggy and lay Liam on the seat. Thoughts of having a picnic lunch with Rork at Pohono Falls excited her. His mood would be one of ecstasy after painting all morning.

"Well, well, hasn't life just gone your way—as usual?"

Heart lodged in her throat, Leila spun on the seat and stared into Sissy's sneering face. She wore a daring low-cut, red dress, but a scuffed hem betrayed the quality. "Sissy," she said breathlessly. "I thought you were in the City."

Sissy twirled one red ringlet around her fingers, exposing nails in sore need of a manicure. "It didn't suit me. The fashionable set isn't interested in me without Hank around." Her painted lips curled into a sneer. "You know how that feels." She flicked a speck of dust off the lace falls on her sleeve. "You were always the little shadow in Hank's life."

Liam wailed.

Leila picked him up and rocked him gently. "Hush, baby."

"Whose brat is that?" Sissy threw back her head, hooting with laughter before bringing her mirth under control. "Hank dies, and you scurry off to the first man who'll have you and spread your legs." She snapped her fingers. "A virgin, indeed, what a lie."

Leila's eyes narrowed. "Watch your mouth."

Sissy snorted. "And what can you possibly do if I don't?"

"Don't test me."

Moving closer, Sissy jabbed Liam, causing him to howl. "So, whose bastard is this?"

Tight-lipped, Leila soothed Liam and set him down again. She alighted from the buggy and faced Sissy.

"You overstepped the mark when you poked my son."

Her arm came up in a blur, and she punched Sissy on the chin, sending her to the ground. Leila stood over her nemesis, shaking her aching hand. "I've wanted to do that for a very long time."

"Bitch." Sitting up, Sissy scratched through her reticule.

Leila stared down the barrel of a pistol and backed away. "You already have one murder on your conscience. Put the gun away, Sissy. You don't want to do this."

Scrambling to her feet while keeping the gun on Leila, Sissy snarled, "Oh yes, I do. You've waited all these years to punch me. Well, I've waited all these years to kill you."

Leila held up her hands as she moved away from the buggy, praying Liam wouldn't start crying. "Think before you act, Sissy. This time you have witnesses who will not concern themselves with your welfare. Why ruin your life?"

"You ruined my life the moment you married Hank. You stole him from me."

"What?"

"You heard me."

"I had no idea you loved him."

A menacing laugh bubbled up from Sissy's throat. "He took my virginity and swore he'd marry me." She waved the gun. "Problem is, my father did not have the thousands that your doting papa parted with." She shrugged, her mouth twisting down. "Hank chose you. Then I discovered my pregnancy."

Regret and compassion welled up from deep within Leila. "I'm so sorry, Sissy. I had no idea."

"You ruined my life." Sniffing, Sissy brushed at tears, leaving a smear of dust on her cheek.

"What happened to your baby?" Leila slowly moved away

from the buggy, hoping to get near Sissy before she discharged the weapon.

"Why do you care?" Sissy glared and jerked the pistol up, aiming at Leila's head. "Stay where you are."

"Of course, I care. I've known you since we were children. We may not like each other, but I still care that Hank ill-used you."

"My father sent my baby to a family in France. I haven't seen her since I birthed her."

"Oh, Sissy. I'm so sorry. Did Hank know?"

"Of course, but he didn't want children—ever."

From the corner of her eye, Leila saw Rork close in. With a snarl, he ripped the pistol from Sissy's hand and wrapped his arm around her, pinning her arms to her sides. "This time, you'll not escape justice."

Sissy screamed and struggled to escape. "Leave me alone, you son of a bitch."

"Rork, no. Let her go!" Leila cried.

He stared at her. "Why? The bitch held a cocked gun at your head!"

"I'll explain later." Leila walked to him and tried to pull his arm off Sissy.

"No, my love. This time Sissy gets her comeuppance."

"Hey. What ya doin' with my woman?" a man yelled.

Rork spun, still clutching Sissy. "Your woman is a murderer. Now back off." Rork leveled the pistol at a burly, bearded digger.

"Randy, help me!" Sissy screamed.

The digger's lowbrow furrowed, his beady eyes shifting from Rork to Sissy. "What's this fella talkin' 'bout, gal?"

"She murdered her lover a year ago and has just attempted to kill my wife."

"Rork, release her." Leila glared at him, her hands on her hips.

She walked to Sissy. "I know you think I'm to blame but had I known you loved Hank, and that you carried his child, I would never have married him." She placed a hand on Sissy's shoulder. "I am so sorry for all you've suffered." Leila glanced at Rork. "Please let her go."

"You are much too soft." He released Sissy, but he took her arm and forced her to face him. "I want you gone. If I ever see you again, I will press charges of murder and attempted murder. Understand?"

Sissy nodded, wiggled out of his grip and walked to the digger. "Come on. Let's get out of this place."

Rork pulled Leila to his side and held her tight, his voice cracking. "My God, I thought, I can't lose her again. Are you all right?"

"I'm fine." Leila leaned her head on his broad chest. "What are you doing here? I had a picnic lunch to share with you at Pohono Falls." She looked up at him through her lashes.

He grinned. "I heard the commotion on my way back to the lodge."

Leila stroked Rork's face. "My hero, my love, let's go back to the falls and have our picnic."

Rork helped her into the buggy, tied his horse to the rear of the vehicle, and fetched his bag of art materials he'd thrown down. He joined her, took the reins, and glanced at Liam, fast asleep against her. "Tell me what happened."

After she related the tale, Rork said, "I knew of Hank's infidelity, but I had no idea how far he took it." Leila stared ahead to the falls in the distance. "It hurts to see her brought so low."

At the falls, Rork jumped down and put out his arms for Liam. Leila paused and stepped down from the buggy. Rork laid the sleeping baby on the buggy seat, gathered Leila to him, and softly kissed her eyelids, her face, and her mouth. She moved her hands tenderly up his back. They melted into each other. Her hands slid down, and as if on cue, Rork did the same. She clasped Rork's hands and looked into his eyes. He stared back, trying to read what Leila wanted him to know. She smiled and kissed his cheek. Rork ran his fingers through her silky hair. Nothing mattered anymore except her and him and their son.

The End

I hope you enjoyed *The Memorable Mrs. Dempsey.*

Reviews are important for authors. Would you mind leaving a review on Amazon? Thank you.

Look for *The Unforgettable Miss Baldwin,* my other American historical romance on Amazon.

ABOUT THE AUTHOR

Gail Ingis

Author Gail Ingis enjoys writing, painting, and piano among other creative arts. Before beginning her career as a romance writer, she worked as a professional interior designer, architectural consultant, educator, and professional artist.

She is a member of ASID (American Society of Interior Designers). Her degrees include a BFA from the New York School of Interior Design, and master's studies in Architecture and Design Criticism at the New School. She founded the *Interior Design Institute* (IDI) in 1981 and later merged the school with Berkeley College. Besides her design work, she taught watercolor and oil painting, interior design, and history of architecture and design at IDI and several universities in the tri-state area.

Tennis is an integral part of her life. She is a retired certified instructor with membership in the United States Professional Tennis Association (USPTA).

Gail adores her children, twelve grandchildren and two granddaughters-in-law. You can find her historical romance books, *The Memorable Mrs. Dempsey* (formerly Indigo Sky) and *The Unforgettable Miss Baldwin,* on Amazon. Look there for her forthcoming memoir, *A Girl Grows in Brooklyn.*

Currently, she serves as a trustee at The Lockwood-Mathews Mansion Museum, Norwalk, CT. She is a juror and curator for the Lockwood art exhibitions. She finds time to play tennis, travel, ballroom dance and occasionally watch football and soccer with her hubby of almost thirty years.

You can follow Gail on Twitter @gailingisauthor, Facebook, BookBub, Amazon, and her blog, where she has written over 500 articles about food, family, fashion, and more.

Check out her website: gailingis.com.

facebook.com/gail.ingis
twitter.com/gailingisauthor
bookbub.com/authors/gail-ingis